THE
HOAX

PAUL CLAYTON

First Edition published 2021 by

2QT Limited (Publishing)

Settle, North Yorkshire BD24 9RH United Kingdom

Cover Design by Charlotte Mouncey with images
from iStockphoto.com and Unsplash.com

Printed by Amazon Inc

A CIP catalogue record for this book is available from the British Library

ISBN - 978-1-914083-05-1

Author/Publisher disclaimer: This is a work of fiction and any resemblance to
any person living or dead is purely coincidental. The place names mentioned are
real but have no connection with the events in this book

Paul Clayton is best known to television audiences for five series of the award-winning sitcom *Peep Show*. Other appearances include *Him and Her, Hollyoaks, Coronation Street, Doctor Who, The Crown, Shakespeare and Hathaway* and *This Time with Alan Partridge*. This is his second novel.

He is a regular columnist in *The Stage* and patron of the children's literacy charity Grimm and Co.

For Richard
and
Les Quizerables

Chapter One

There was no way of telling the time, no clock on the wall, and they'd taken her watch and phone. Truth be told, it was the narrowest bed she had ever seen. Lying on it, she could touch both sides of the room with her hands. Cool, smooth walls. Unadorned. She could see the stained grey ceiling where a murky glass sphere held a single bulb. In one corner of the room stood a small metal cupboard bolted to the wall beneath a tiny window. Too high to see out of. Hard for her to tell if it was day or night. Something about the room seemed eerily familiar.

This isn't the place I should be. These are not my clothes. Hell, this is not my life. Why did I let them bring me here?

Her fault. Standing naked, being searched, handing over her clothes, her bag and some paltry possessions in exchange for a grey tracksuit, a pack of basic underwear, socks and trainers.

At what point had this room become hers? Was it yesterday, when she learned the truth? Or did her journey begin a long time ago?

She pulled the sheet towards her chin. A faint stench of unwashed clothes filled the air. This was, after all, a bed in which murderers had lain awake. A bed where killers had rejoiced in their deed. A bed where she had time to reflect upon what she had done.

Dispossessed of her clothes, stripped of her rights, stranded in this concrete box, the principle of innocent until proven guilty had never been so meaningless. They had taken away her world beyond these walls. A tiny darkening window, no clock, no watch, no phone. No friends, no family, no one. And she knew she could be here for a long time.

Possibly forever?

Chapter Two

One Year Earlier

Frankie Baxter loved her kids. Jonny, Shannon and little Henry were her pride and joy. She adored them a little less than normal by the Friday of half-term week.

Having run out of the money she kept in a beer glass in the kitchen cupboard for outings and treats, Friday loomed long and large in front of her. She never failed to try and do something special on each day of half term. Taking the week off work to be with her kids was one such example. It cost her wages but saved on childcare. Yet by the time she had woken early on what was the last day of the week, she had run out of ideas about keeping them busy.

The grocery cupboard was bare too, and the lunch she'd prepared of tinned soup and crusty toast hadn't gone down well.

'What d'ya mean no yogurts?' said Jonny, prone on the sofa in front of *Bargain Hunt*.

'I mean no yogurts.' Frankie moved through to the living room of the flat and switched off the TV. 'I haven't had a chance to get down to the supermarket this week.'

She cast a glance at her eldest son. Lanky like his dad, her first husband, Frankie often found it hard to see any of herself in him. 'Do you have no homework you need to do for school on Monday? You could get that done this afternoon so the weekend's clear.'

'Done it.'

Jonny reached onto the floor, picked up the remote between his feet and lifted it back to the sofa in a rare show of athleticism, before turning the telly back on.

Frankie picked up the soup plate from the coffee table in front of him and took it back into the kitchen. 'Anybody like to do the washing up today?'

'How much?' said Shannon.

Frankie looked at her daughter. How did a fifteen year old understand the need for money so well? 'A walk in the park and a game of crazy golf?'

'You serious?' Shannon laughed.

'Yes I am, Miss. I took time off for your holidays so we could do things as a family. You've barely moved your arse from that sofa for the entire week.'

'I'm on holiday.' Shannon reached for her headphones.

Frankie reached over and whipped them out of her hand. 'Oh no, you're not. We are having a family walk with ice cream at the café and crazy golf. And if you don't like it, you can kiss goodbye to any thought of clothes shopping next week for that party you're dying to go to.'

'It'll be fun, Shan,' said Jonny, ever the diplomat. 'And think how much easier things are when Mum is happy.'

'For all of us,' Frankie interjected. She was sure she had a tenner in her purse. If not, she hoped the crazy golf shack took cards.

'Yeah!' yelled Henry. He rushed up and gave Frankie a hug. She loved it that Henry still liked to cuddle her, even though there was so much more of her to cuddle these days. She knew Henry's cuddles almost always meant that he wanted something. 'Can we take Dimwit too?' he asked. 'Please, Mum. Can we?'

Hearing his name, Dimwit stirred in his basket in the corner of the kitchen. One day the smelliest, ugliest and stupidest dog imaginable had turned up on their doorstep. Frankie had made the mistake of allowing the kids to feed it. Unsurprisingly, it had never left. Six years on and the dog ate its way through a healthy portion of her housekeeping money every week; an appropriate introduction for it would be as a food-processing machine that occasionally walked. Frankie had no idea as to Dimwit's breed and she couldn't care less.

'Let's get coats and do this.' She dried her hands and emptied the sink.

'Mum!' yelled Shannon in horror. 'Mum, you can't go out like that.'

Frankie glanced at her clothes. 'Like what?'

'You've got pyjama bottoms on.'

Frankie spent as much time in pyjamas and track suits as she could – sweatshirts, tops and pants, anything a size too big. She didn't have a problem with being a bit on the large side but didn't want to emphasise it by wearing anything fitted. 'They'll be fine,' she said. 'Big coat, big boots. No one in the park will be looking at me.'

'Change them, Mum. Per-lease,' implored Henry.

'You do know that people talk about you when you take us to school.' Shannon bounced off the sofa and stood facing her mum.

'What if they do?' The last thing Frankie cared about was

11

what other people thought. After all, she kept herself to herself and her family.

'Trisha's mum says you look a mess,' Shannon continued.

Frankie pursed her lips. As far as Tricia's mum's clothes were concerned, Frankie just hoped she'd kept the receipts. But she could certainly do without a needless row with her daughter, especially with the weekend to go and then back to school. 'Okay. I'll pop upstairs and put on some trackies then, Miss Fashion Pants.' She headed for the hall.

Shannon flopped back onto the sofa with Jonny. Battle won.

Frankie stopped in the doorway and turned back to her three children. 'You do know that Trisha's mum looks like a man in drag, right?'

Even Jonny couldn't resist laughing at that one.

***

The February afternoon threatened to darken as the small, bedraggled group plus dog approached the park. This was not looking good, and already a fine mizzle was soaking into Frankie's large woollen jumper and sweatshirt.

Sloping down from the main road, Kelsey Park divided itself into two routes: Dogs and No Dogs. Dimwit knew the way and pulled Henry to the right-hand path around the lake. This was the way to the crazy golf course. Frankie followed them down the path.

'It won't be open, Mum,' insisted Jonny.

It looked like he was right. 'Let's check. If not, we can always go to the café.'

'It's a shit caff, that one,' said Shannon. 'Like totally crap.'

'It's cheap, love. That's the main thing.' Frankie smiled at her daughter, desperately hoping she might understand how things were for once. 'It means we can all have something in there. Tea, cake, pop.'

'Pop!' spluttered Shannon. 'What you on, Mum?'

'I'm on the edge of my patience, that's what I'm on, love. Now, are you coming or not?'

Jonny stepped up to join his sister. 'Mum, what if Shan and I go for a walk round the lake, up the No Dog path and meet you and Henry back at the café? How would that suit?'

Despite his general lethargy, Jonny's ability to be the peacemaker always impressed Frankie. The elder brother stepping in. How could she say no? 'Okay. Back at the café in half an hour. We all agreed?'

Jonny gave a quick wink. Shannon set off with no acknowledgement, and Henry grabbed Dimwit's lead and headed off down the dog path.

'See you at the café,' called Frankie to their disappearing backs.

A little further into the park along the dog path was a clearing amid the leafless trees. Separated from the lake by a rack of weeds were some twenty benches, each with a memorial plaque. Frankie loved sitting here. Whenever she strolled in the park, she'd find five minutes' peace and contentment on one of the seats. She loved the stories that the inscriptions told. One bench was dedicated to Ivy Tillson and gave the date of her death. Then there were the words, *Margaret, daughter,* and a date three years later. Frankie could see Margaret staring out of a lonely kitchen window after Ivy had gone and letting go to be with her mother.

She couldn't imagine Shannon troubling herself with grief.

Tough, independent Shannon, very much her father's daughter, Frankie rarely found love in her eyes. Her mother had always said, 'When you find love in their eyes, keep them safe in your arms forever and they'll do the same for you.' Frankie couldn't see her name on a bench with Shannon's.

A few birds skimmed the lake as the afternoon darkened. Frankie stood up, pulled her hood around her and started towards the café. The lake stretched away down the centre of the park and she assumed Jonny and Shannon were walking round it. Henry had long since run off with Dimwit, who was no doubt getting filthy chasing sticks through the undergrowth. In front of her stood the children's playground, which all her children now considered themselves much too old for. Once the steel tube of a slide that coiled its way down from a yellow trapezoid climbing frame had been the main pleasure for Henry. Now it was of no interest at all.

The café was a low hut with a corrugated iron roof, magnolia paint peeling from the outside walls. As she pushed open the doors, Frankie was grateful for the warm fug of steam from the counter.

There was no sign of the kids. She bought herself a tea and settled in the seat by the window from where she could see the lake. The whole park was a place of memories. It was around this lake that she had pushed little Henry in his pram, Jonny and Shannon in tow; hot, sunny Sunday afternoons when she thought they would be a family. Henry's father hadn't been there to help her push in the maternity ward – he'd barely been there at the conception. She didn't mind. Somewhere inside her was enough unconditional love for the three of them. She was the eye of their storm, quiet and still. She knew she was the one who would walk with them through life, her only reward being that of keeping them safe.

As she took a sip of her tea, she saw Jonny and Shannon running towards the café. The doors burst open. Frankie gave Jonny the last of her change to buy drinks and they joined her at the table with their Coke. 'Good walk?' she enquired.

'Boring,' said Shannon, without looking up.

Jonny took a large swig of his drink. 'Yeah. Tried to kill a duck for tea but no luck.'

'I don't think we're that desperate yet. There's lasagne in the freezer.' Frankie smiled at her eldest boy who could be remarkably understanding at the strangest of moments.

'Look.' Shannon's voice told Frankie something was wrong.

Through the window, she saw Dimwit running across the grass, turning round and round on himself. Jonny was out of his seat and through the café doors. Frankie followed him with Shannon lumbering behind.

'What's he doing?' asked Shannon.

'He's chasing his lead,' replied Jonny. 'Why's he got his lead on?'

Frankie stopped, out of breath. Looking at the dog, she immediately knew what was wrong. 'Where's Henry?'

Chapter Three

PC Oliver Ashley made his way up the path outside the building in search of Flat 23C. The small block stood on the corner of a major road opposite the railway station. A visit to this area on the edge of the council estate usually meant trouble, but on this occasion there had been a call to the station and his sergeant had dispatched him to take the relevant details.

Flat 23C had a frosted-glass panel at eye level in the front door. Lights were on in the hall and he stood for a moment looking through the glass. Everything seemed quiet and still. Pressing on the doorbell, he heard no sound; assuming it broken, he rapped on the door. A shadow appeared in the hallway and the door was flung open.

The woman facing him was small, about five three, thought Oliver. Flame-coloured hair, which didn't seem particularly natural, and a shape that could be described as dumpy. She wore some patterned pyjama bottoms and a sweatshirt top, and from the redness of her eyes she seemed to have been crying.

'Mrs Baxter? Mrs Frankie Baxter?'

'Yes, that's me, officer. You want to come in?'

Oliver stepped inside. At the far end of the hallway, he could see the face of a teenager with floppy blond hair peering around a door. 'In here, please, where our Jonny is.'

Tucking his cap under his right arm, Oliver reached into his top pocket and pulled out his notebook. It made him feel a little more in charge. He followed the teenager into the room.

The place was a tip. The furniture seemed too big for the room; two armchairs and a sofa were fighting for space and faced a television which, at a conservative estimate, must have had a fifty-inch screen. Clothes lay scattered around, and mugs and drink cans covered a cheap coffee table in the centre of the room.

The boy Oliver had seen looking down the hall was sitting on one end of the sofa. In the armchair opposite him, engrossed in her phone, was a younger girl with cropped hair. Both of them looked up as he walked in. The woman followed him and gestured for him to sit. He perched on the other end of the sofa.

'Mrs Baxter, you rang the station. Your son has gone missing?'

At first Frankie could hardly speak but then the words started coming and wouldn't stop. 'He wouldn't do this. He's never done this before.'

Several times Oliver had to ask her to slow down while he made notes. Most of what she told him she'd reported on the phone. He knew his colleagues at the station would be going through the details, but this was his chance to double-check the information face to face. 'And you've rung his phone?'

The teenage boy, who Oliver learned was called Jonny, told him they'd rung the number and left several messages. 'He's always running out of battery. It's an old phone. His battery's shit. He's probably just gone off with some mates.'

'Jonny! We've rung his mates, officer, the ones we have numbers for. No one has seen him, not since Dimwit came running back without him.'

PC Ashley made a note. 'And is this Dimwit a mate of his?'

The girl in the armchair laughed. 'It's a dog. Dimwit.'

Oliver made a note, keeping his head down to hide his blushes.

'Shannon! Show some respect. The policeman is trying his best to help,' Frankie snapped. 'I'm sorry, officer. She's upset. We're all upset. I just keep thinking the worst. He could be lying hurt somewhere.'

'Mum, it's much more likely he's been abducted.' Shannon realised it was the wrong thing to say as soon as the words left her mouth.

Frankie turned white and fell into a chair.

Chapter Four

Henry was cold. Cold and wet; cold and wet and miserable, and ready to go home. But this was a challenge, something he knew he had to do. One night, that would be enough. The rules on Facebook said forty-eight hours. You had to stay away from home without telling anyone where you were for forty-eight hours. It was the Blue Whale Challenge, and Angus McKinnon had challenged Henry. Angus McKinnon was not a person you could let down. Henry knew life would be easier if he were in Angus McKinnon's favour.

Having managed to lose his mum, Shannon and Jonny while they were out on the walk, Henry had made his way straight into town. He filled the afternoon by wandering in and out of shops. As evening approached, he'd tried to sneak into the cinema. On previous visits with friends, someone had always managed to get in without a ticket but today that hadn't worked and Henry was stopped at the bottom of the stairs. He had patted his pockets, pretending to look for his ticket.

A skinny man with a *Get Your Cinema Here* T-shirt and a bad comb-over had pulled him to one side. 'Go back to the desk, to the person who sold you the ticket. They'll be able to look up the transaction and give you a replacement.'

Henry knew the man was trying to be helpful, but it was

no good. He couldn't go back to the desk because he hadn't bought a ticket.

He'd pushed his way through the cinema doors and gone back onto the street. A cold wind was now pushing across the roundabout and down the high street. Henry shivered. He had an extra jumper under his parka, but that was his only preparation for sleeping rough. He'd pushed a cereal bar found at the back of a kitchen cupboard into his pocket, but he'd eaten it half way through the afternoon and now lack of food was becoming a problem. He hadn't charged his phone before leaving home and, as he pushed at the screen, it gave up and turned off. Not that he would have messaged anyone because the challenge had to be done alone, but his phone was a comforter like a rosary. He felt better when it was in his hand and he could touch it.

Now the shops were closing and places to find warmth were becoming fewer. Henry thought of the shelter at the end of the lake in the park. Sometimes, when they were out walking Dimwit, he'd seen people curled up on the benches wrapped in newspaper or worn-out sleeping bags. Mum said they were homeless people. On one occasion, she'd given a pound coin to an old woman who was half-lying on a bench. Henry had asked why, and Mum had said, 'Because sometimes, my love, you just feel you have to help.'

He walked down the high street and turned into Park Road. The main gates to the park were closed with a large chain and padlock. The lights of the park-keeper's cottage gave it the look of a fairy-tale dwelling, like something from a story with a happy ending.

Henry turned and walked along the posh side of the park.

He no longer knew where he was. This was somewhere he rarely ventured. It was very cold now and he started to shiver. Through the tall green spiked railings, the bushes and trees were almost silhouettes, the blackest of greens. A path stretched away into wooded gloom.

Following the side of the park involved scrambling over some low walls that belonged to two blocks of flats. He pushed his way through a hedge and crossed the end of a private garden, looking for a gap in the railings or perhaps a tree he might climb and drop from to enter the park. The drizzling rain from earlier had melted the leaves underfoot to slush and it was hard to walk without slipping. He held onto the railings.

He emerged from the private garden into the darkness of a road. The glow of the streetlamps helped him find his way and he walked a little quicker. Then, a little further along the side of the park, he came to a gate in the railings. He pulled at it. It wouldn't budge. Henry tugged in frustration at it with both hands, but it wouldn't open. Then he saw there was a lock on the gate. Henry wondered where he might get a key from. If he could get into the park he would feel safe and the oncoming night would not seem such a threat. And there would be a good chance he could stay dry.

He looked at the apartment blocks behind him. Lights in windows, curtained and cosy. People appearing at them, peering out into the drizzling night. Opposite him stood a tower named Parkside. Large letters in white across a glossy black porch. Henry counted eight floors of steel-and-glass balconies. Perhaps he could climb onto one of the lower floors and stay out of the rain that way.

He turned back to take one last look into the locked park.

A wind had risen and the trees swayed, filling the air with a whisper. Leaves scurried along the path and the wind brought goosebumps to his arms. He knew he had to find somewhere else for the night.

Heading back to the road, he dashed across where the lighting was at its poorest. Suddenly, car headlamps swarmed over him. Henry hesitated, unsure whether to run forward or to retrace his steps. He could hear the car braking and, just as he thought he was clear, he felt something hit the side of his hip. Henry jerked away in some degree of pain and tumbled to the pavement.

The car engine noise fell silent and the door of the car opened. 'Hello.'

Henry twisted his neck to look back.

A figure stood silhouetted by the headlamps. 'Hello there? Are you okay?' The figure moved forward and offered Henry a hand.

He lifted himself to his feet with help. He wanted to cry but no, that would not do. He shouldn't be here. For some reason he felt lost and alone, and he shouldn't be on this side of the park.

'I didn't see you. You ran into the light. Are you all right?'

Henry's hip felt bruised but one or two uncertain steps told him he could walk. He nodded in reply, unsure what he should say.

'What were you doing? You do know this is a private road, don't you? That's why I didn't expect to see anyone.' The figure came into the light and Henry saw her for the first time.

The woman had glossy tomato-coloured hair sticking out from beneath a woollen bobble hat. Large thick spectacles covered a lot of her face, which seemed tight and mottled, and a bright-red-lipsticked gash of a mouth smiled at him. She held a green-and-yellow chequered coat close around her.

Henry hid his smile. He could see blue slippers on her feet. Each slipper seemed to be a cat of some kind. Henry thought of Mr Twisty the Clown, or a woman in an old sitcom about a holiday camp who made his mother laugh. Perhaps she was a witch.

'Are you wanting to get into the park, my love?' Her words pushed a cloud of steam out into the night. Henry could smell her breath; it reminded him of when Frankie had been to the pub.

He waited and said nothing. The Blue Whale challenge was secret, after all. And who was this clownish woman with the terrible slippers?

'The gate's locked. It's a private gate, for residents use only. You shouldn't be in there at night,' she continued. 'I know people do go in for all sorts of things. Men, mainly. The people from the council don't like it.'

'Yes,' mumbled Henry. 'Sorry. I wanted to sort of sleep there. It's a dare I'm doing.'

'Is it?' The woman took a step towards him. 'How exciting. Then we ought to see what we can do to help.' She bent down and breathed into his face. 'Would you like me to help you?'

Henry nodded.

'Where were you thinking of hiding in the park for the night?'

Henry liked it when she said hiding. Suddenly he knew she understood, she was on his side. He told her of his plan – the shelter with the benches overlooking the lake, how he planned to set an alarm for early in the morning on his phone so he wouldn't get caught by the park keepers, although he didn't tell her about his phone battery dying.

'No sleeping bag or anything, I see,' she said. 'You have to prepare if you're going to sleep in the park overnight.'

Henry giggled. 'I didn't think.'

'Will you let me help you?'

Henry looked at her again. He nodded. The woman laughed. Henry thought it sounded like a pig snorting.

'It's the least I can do. And I won't tell anyone about you running out into the road like that and causing the accident.' She smiled at him again and held out a hand to lead him to the railings. She didn't seem like a proper grown up. Something about her told him she understood, that she got it. He nodded.

'Wait here and give me five minutes. I can get you a sleeping bag and some things for the night.'

Henry rattled the gate.

'And don't worry about that. I have a key.'

Henry settled down by the gate as the clownish woman waddled away into the darkness.

'Please come back,' whispered Henry to himself. 'Please come back.'

Chapter Five

'It's a ten-year-old kid, Sarge. Ran off while he was out with his mum and the dog this afternoon.' PC Ashley was filling in his report at the station and doing his best to convince Sergeant Chescoe that they should do something.

'I've got everything here in the report book. I'm not sure what we can do now.' Chescoe paused and saw the disappointment in Oliver's face. That was the trouble with these new coppers. Too bloody eager.

'Why not show willing and go grab somebody who's free? At least, you could walk around the park. It's all locked up by now, so there'll be nowt to see. As long as it looks like we've done summat, then we're in the clear. If the little bastard's still missing in the morning, we can ramp it up.'

Chescoe continued to enter the details of the constable's report into his computer. If he ever left the force, the sergeant's looks would get him work in any Christmas grotto. His demeanour would not.

'Most of these buggers come to nothing. He'll have pissed off with some mates, phone out of battery, and never given a thought about his mother worrying her bloody tits off at home.'

Oliver found himself torn between thinking that the desk

sergeant was probably right and the desire to be part of things, which had made him a constable in the first place.

'I think I might do that, Sarge.' Chescoe didn't look up from the computer so Oliver pushed his way through the swing doors into the canteen to see who might be free. Early evening on a Friday, most available constables were either out on a call or hadn't yet logged on. But in the far corner, sitting with a cup of some sort of herbal infusion and swiping on her phone, was WPC Graham.

Oliver sighed. Pamela Graham was the last person anyone wanted to spend an evening out on the beat with. Earnest, over attentive and with a sense of humour as prickly as a porcupine, she was hard work through and through. Yet she got results. Many of her junior male colleagues envied her conviction rate. She had a habit of seeming to be in the right place at the right time, and whatever she did always turned up trumps. It wouldn't do any harm to ask if she would take a quick turn around the park with him.

Once she'd heard his story, Pamela picked up her drink and grabbed a plastic cup from the counter to decant it into. 'Liquorice root,' she said to Oliver, pouring an unhealthy look-ing dark concoction into the cup, though he'd not asked for an explanation. 'Boosts energy and focus and encourages good bowel movement.'

'Right. Just what I need.' Oliver pulled his cap on and made to walk out of the room.

Pamela followed close behind and seemed anxious to give him more information about the benefits of the drink. 'It contains adaptogens, you see, Ollie.'

He winced at the diminutive of his name. 'Great. I'm more

of a Pepsi Max and a Mars Bar man myself, Pam,' he replied. 'But thanks.'

After a twenty-five minute walk, they had covered the perimeter of the no-dog side of the park. It was hard to see into it; other than a little floodlighting on the lake, the undergrowth, trees and bushes were in darkness. There was no sign of movement and it looked like the wrong environment in which to spot a stray ten year old.

They crossed the top of the park, past the park-keeper's cottage, and followed the railings to an area where the houses were much bigger. They were large 1930s' half-timbered residences, the sort with four cars parked outside them. These didn't belong to people who worked around here; these were the houses of people who worked in the city's banks and boardrooms.

'Do you think he has gone missing?' said Pamela. 'Or is it another kid off with his mates?'

'The mum seemed very upset, and the sister and brother said it wasn't like him. Well, the brother did – the sister didn't seem to care. I asked all the usual stuff about whether there'd been a row or any trouble, but no. They were all out together taking the dog for a walk, then the dog came running back with nobody on the other end of the lead.'

'If he was just messing about, why would he let go of the dog? Anything could have happened to the poor thing. Some people just don't deserve to have animals.'

For the briefest moment, Oliver wondered what pet Pamela Graham had. The only thing he could think of was stick insects. 'That's what worries me. The dog. Evidently the lad's very fond of it.'

By now they had followed the road onto Lakeside Drive, a misnomer as the lake was out of sight, separated by undergrowth, trees and the tall green railings. Ahead of them, a woman stepped out of the shadows. She crossed the road holding her coat around her.

'Excuse me,' said Oliver. The woman stopped and they caught up with her. 'Sorry, madam, but have you just come out of the park?' To his right there was a gate in the railings.

The woman smiled at them. 'No, officer, I haven't. I've lost my cat. Normally he's back home by now. I came down to see if he was around.'

'You wouldn't have a key to that gate by any chance?'

She looked at the gate and turned back to him. 'I'm sorry, I don't. I think you have to pay for a key. It's for residents of the flats and houses on Parkside. Not the sort of place I could afford.'

'You haven't seen any young children around here, have you?' Pamela asked. 'We're looking for a ten-year-old boy who's gone missing. There's a chance he might be in the park.'

'If he's in there, dear,' replied the woman, 'he's in there till morning. They lock the gates at half past five during the winter, and I think most people would find it hard to climb over those railings.'

'Yes, they're a bit spiky and unpleasant,' Pamela said.

Oliver glanced at her. He wondered if she was describing herself.

'I think they're Victorian, actually,' said the woman. 'They didn't get taken away in the war to make Spitfires. The park originally belonged to Lord Cator, you see. A private park. Amazing what some people can get away with, isn't it, officer?'

She smiled at Oliver then pulled her coat more tightly around her. 'If I can be of no more help, I'd like to get back inside.' With that, she walked across the street and disappeared into the darkness between two of the blocks of flats.

Oliver watched her go for a moment, then continued his journey around the park.

'Shouldn't you have asked her name and address?' Pamela asked a little breathlessly as she caught up with him.

'Yes, I should.' Oliver knew she thought he was in the wrong, but three-quarters of the way around the park the warmth of the station canteen had started to appear very attractive. 'She hadn't seen anything. Some old dear looking for a cat. She looked a bit Scooby Doo for my taste. Awful choice in footwear.'

Pamela looked puzzled. 'I liked them. Cats with whiskers. Nice.'

So that was her pet, thought Oliver. Another bloody woman with a cat.

Chapter Six

After the young policeman left, Frankie knew that she had to do something. She pulled on a coat and trainers.

'Where you off to, Mum?' asked Jonny.

'I'm going out to look for Henry. I can't just sit here.'

'Come with you, shall I?'

Frankie smiled at her son and then looked over at his sister lying on the sofa. Settled in front of the television, she showed no inclination to move. 'No, it's all right. You stay here with Shannon. I'm just going to walk round the park and into town, see if I can learn anything. See if anyone knows where he is. You stay here. That'll be a help.'

Frankie retraced their afternoon walk to the park. The gates they'd gone through now had a huge chain and padlock wound around the centre. She made her way as near to the fence as she could up to the park-keeper's cottage at the top end of the lake. It was too dark to see anything.

Once or twice her heart pushed her to call out. 'Henry. Henry. Please, Henry.'

She cut across the supermarket car park and walked up the high street as far as the cinema. Shops were closing; only a few stayed open late. They seemed unwelcoming, with bars on the doors or locks operated from inside.

She pushed her way into a newsagent. Swiping through pictures on her phone, she found a photograph of Henry wearing a pair of red swimming trunks taken at Center Parcs She thrust her telephone at the newsagent.

'No, love. He's not been in here. We discourage kids after about seven o'clock.'

Frankie's heart fell.

After two hours futile wandering and enquiring in a few more shops, she returned home. Jonny was waiting in the kitchen and put the kettle on as soon she walked through the door. Shannon hadn't moved from the sofa and was still glued to the television.

Jonny gave her an enormous hug and she nestled her head against his chest, the benefit of having a tall son on the verge of manhood. 'No luck,' she muttered, trying to hold back tears.

'He'll be back. You know Henry. He'll be back.'

She thought Jonny sounded uncertain.

They passed the rest of the evening in the lounge, Shannon engaged with the television, Jonny casting sideways looks to check on his mum, and Frankie biting her nails and swiping her telephone in desperation for ideas. 'He hasn't got a Facebook account or anything like that has he?' she asked.

Shannon shrugged.

A little after one in the morning, the kids went to bed. Frankie washed up the cups on the coffee table and left a light on in the kitchen. It was tempting to leave the door unlocked, but she realised how foolish that would be.

She crept upstairs and into the bedroom she shared with Shannon. Three kids and a single mum in a two-bedroom flat was not an ideal combination. Her daughter was asleep and the room was in darkness.

Frankie pulled a chair over to the window and looked out. The last southbound train was pulling out of the station and a couple of stragglers were scurrying across the road. She sat there as one hour morphed into two, and two hours trickled into three. Every moment, she hoped the shadowy form of Henry would turn the corner and walk along the road.

Henry was her special one. She'd suffered Jonny and Shannon's father for almost five years of marriage; things hadn't been easy and her answer had been to run away. That's what marrying young did for you. Henry was unplanned, the result of a cheeky encounter on a girls' night out. She liked to pretend that she never knew who the father was. What she *did* know was that, from the moment she'd felt Henry inside her, she wanted him. It was her job to protect him, to look after him and keep him safe. She would love him now and always – for as long as always lasted.

Her eyes had closed by the time the first crack of dawn appeared across the sky. She awoke, back and neck stiff from the hours spent in the chair. Creeping out of the room, she went to the bathroom and splashed water on her face. As quietly as she could, she made her way into the kitchen and put the kettle on. When it had boiled, she sat at the kitchen table warming her hands on a large mug of tea. The thought of another day without Henry haunted her and a tear ran down her cheek. She wiped it away.

She wasn't sure how long she'd been sitting there when there was a knock on the door.

Chapter Seven

It had all seemed like such a magnificent idea, such a straight-forward thing to do. But from the moment he'd let go of Dimwit's lead in the park and urged the dog to run back in the direction of his mum, Henry's feelings of doubt had grown. He could make it work; he could do this. Forty-eight hours wasn't long. But as he scurried away behind the trees, his ten-year old's sense of bravado weakened. After a miserable afternoon and evening, bumping into the woman's car by the park had turned out to be nothing short of a miracle.

At first he'd thought she might be a witch or a clown of some sort. He'd seen clowns in horror movies. Red hair, blue shoes, green-and-yellow coat and thick comedy glasses – it all added up. That would have been just his luck. But she'd turned out to be an angel.

The best thing was that she hadn't told him off and sent him home. She'd disappeared into the darkness and for a few moments Henry thought that she'd gone for good. Five minutes later, she'd returned with a large holdall and a key in her hand.

She opened the gate and let them both into the park. 'Now, let's find you somewhere safe and as dry as possible and hidden away for the night. Then we can sort things out in the morning.'

Henry smiled at her.

'After all,' she went on, 'if it's a dare, you have to do it. I used to get dared to do things at school. "We dare you to write on the blackboard, Cora."' She smiled at him again. 'And do you know what? I did. I always did my dares, even when I made them up myself. So, we'd better make sure that you can do yours …' She paused.

Henry realised why and held out his hand. 'I'm Henry. Henry Baxter. And thank you for helping me.'

'I'm Cora, Henry Baxter, and it's my pleasure. After all, we have a secret to keep, don't we, Henry Baxter?' And with that she'd disappeared off into the bushes. Henry had limped after her to keep up.

She'd done what she had promised. In the middle of the undergrowth, about a hundred and fifty yards away, was an enormous tree. Henry was sure it was an oak tree. Robin Hood had an oak tree as his home – he'd read all about Robin Hood at school.

Cora opened the holdall and pulled out a bright-blue sleeping mat. 'It's a yoga mat, Henry, but it's soft and it will help you sleep.'

Henry hadn't thought about where he would sleep that night; he'd certainly never imagined that it would be on a comfortable blue yoga mat. Cora laid a shiny dark-green sleeping bag on top of it. What a wonderful bag – it had a hood like the one Bear Grylls slept in on the telly. This was getting better and better by the minute.

Cora placed a small bottle of water and a torch beside the sleeping bag. 'Now, I think you're old enough to sort yourself out, Henry. The park's locked and you're well hidden, away from prying eyes. You should be able to sleep and …' She stopped. 'If you need the bathroom, use those bushes over there.'

'Thank you,' he said. 'Thank you. This is going to help so much.'

'I'll come and get you in the morning, as soon the sun starts to come up. We'll pack away this bag and then I'm going to walk you home. Agreed?' Cora looked rather stern, but Henry could see a twinkle in her eyes.

'Yes, that would be great. Thank you, Cora. 'It was the first time he had spoken her name out loud, and it sounded mystical. He didn't want to tell her that the full dare was for two days. It didn't matter. As long as he spent one night out on his own, it would impress Angus McKinnon and the people who had dared him, particularly as he'd managed to sleep inside a park after they'd locked it to the public. He squatted down and clambered into the sleeping bag.

'I'll see you in the morning then,' said Cora.

***

Now she stood behind him as he waited for the door to open. He bit back a tear as Frankie appeared in the doorway. Looking at her, he knew she had missed him; he knew he had done wrong and caused her pain. That was something Henry never wished to do because he had the best mum in the world.

She stepped forward and pulled him into the tightest of hugs and he knew he never wanted to be away from her again. Stepping back, he turned and put his hand out. 'Mum, this is Cora. She helped me and she brought me home this morning, so don't shout at her. She's a very nice lady.'

Frankie smiled at him and looked at Cora. 'I'm not really sure what to say, but thank you. Thank you. I've been so worried.'

'Don't worry, my dear. Take him inside. I'm sure you want to check him over. Quite a big adventure for such a little chap.'

Henry released himself from his mother's arms and turned to face Cora. 'Thank you for helping me.' And with that, he slipped past his mother and into the flat, doing his best to hide the soreness of his hip.

'Goodbye, Henry,' Cora called after him. 'I'm sure we'll meet again.'

But Henry didn't hear her. Jonny was busy ruffling his hair and firing questions at him, and all the commotion had even managed to waken Shannon.

Chapter Eight

Cora watched Henry disappear into the house. 'Don't be too hard on him,' she said. 'I think he was doing it to impress somebody. No harm done in the end, though.'

The boy's mother glared at her. She folded her arms and squared off in the doorway. 'No harm done? I've been to the police. I've been up all night, and he turns up this morning with you in tow, and you say don't do anything about it?'

Cora took a card out of her bag and offered it to the woman. 'Sorry, but I don't know your name. It didn't seem right to question Henry or be over-inquisitive or frightening.'

The woman unfolded her arms and took the card. 'I'm Frankie. Frankie Baxter.'

'I'm Cora Walsh. That's my number. If you or the police need to talk to me, then give me a call. I only did what I thought was best. And if it's any consolation, I didn't get much sleep either.'

Cora walked down the path, crossed the road and headed past the station. She was glad Henry was home and hoped that his mother would understand why she'd helped him on his night-time escapade. How wonderful to be a child so loved that your absence robbed your mother of sleep for a night. To be a child who could cause worry, who gave his mother such an immense sense of relief as soon as he was back in her arms.

A child who was wanted and loved.

On her way home, Cora picked up some shopping in the supermarket. It wasn't busy so early in the morning, which she liked. She put the key in the door of her flat and pushed it open with her shoulder, both arms laden with bags. She put the shopping in the kitchen. Taking off her coat, she unpacked it and set about making herself a cup of tea.

She took the tea to a table by the window and flipped open the laptop that lay there. As she waited for it to boot up, she gazed out of the window at the park below.

She'd lied to Frankie: she hadn't lost any sleep over the boy in the park. Cora had slept, woken up when her alarm sounded and dressed to go down and find Henry in the park.

She took a sip of tea and smiled to herself. Opening a new document on her screen, she typed two words at the top as a title: *Frankie Baxter*.

***

Frankie couldn't stay angry with Henry for long. She made him a cup of hot chocolate and let him have banana milk on his cornflakes as a treat. There wasn't any money for such extravagances, but his safe return called for it.

She sat at the breakfast table as he wolfed down his breakfast. Her head was full of questions but she didn't let any of them escape. 'Wait until he's ready,' she told herself.

After dispatching Henry upstairs to have a shower and dress in clean clothes, Frankie picked up the phone. She called the police station using the number PC Ashley had left her. It wasn't the constable who answered but a young female who seemed less than interested.

'I want to speak to somebody about my son who was reported missing last night,' Frankie said.

A quick burst of something classical and she heard a different voice. 'Front desk. Sergeant Chescoe here. Is that Mrs Baxter?'

Frankie took a deep breath. 'Yes it is, sergeant. I'm calling to say that my son turned up this morning. He slept rough last night. Some kind person brought him back home. He's fine.'

There was a harrumph at the other end of the phone. 'No missing boy, then? Well, that all's good, isn't it? Lucky kid.'

'Yes, he's very lucky. Please thank the constable who came round last night. I think he said he was going to search the park.' She thought about adding, 'But he didn't, otherwise he might have found my son.'

'Thanks once again,' she said aloud and ended the call.

Things were looking a little more like a normal Saturday morning. Shannon was in front of the television, Jonny getting ready to leave for his Saturday job, and Henry was washed, fed and back home. Frankie sat at the kitchen table and put together a shopping list for later in the day. As she wrote *banana milk*, *burgers, pizza*, her attention wandered to the card lying on the table.

There was the name *Cora Walsh* and a telephone number. No address, nothing else, just a number. Almost inviting her to call.

Chapter Nine

From the window of her flat, Cora could see the café on the other side of the lake in the park. Although it was early in the year, there were a few tables and chairs outside to catch the late February sunshine. Cora picked up the pair of binoculars she kept on the window ledge and focused them. No sign yet.

It had thrilled her to get the phone call that morning. Although she'd left the card, she hadn't been sure Frankie Baxter would actually call. In fact, Cora had started to work on new ways of getting back in contact with Frankie. Something casual – a chance meeting in the street, perhaps? She had ways of getting in touch with people.

She wondered if Frankie wanted to forget her youngest son disappearing off into the night and being returned by a perfect stranger. Cora believed a stranger was a friend you hadn't met yet. But it seemed the allure of the telephone number and the name on the plain card with no other information had worked its spell; this morning, Frankie had called and arranged to meet for a cup of coffee in the park.

Cora surveyed the tables outside the café once more. There were now three people in view: a couple at the table nearest the lake, and a single person sitting in the shelter of the café wall. Judging by the mismatch of colours, that was Frankie Baxter.

***

'Did the police give you any hassle for wasting their time?' Cora asked.

Frankie gratefully sipped the latte that Cora had bought. The park café might be a bit of a dump, but the cost of two lattes was a meal for her family. 'No, they were quite happy about it. The desk sergeant I spoke to was a bit old school, but they seemed pleased it was another case they could tick a box next to.'

'Well, that's a relief,' said Cora. There was a silence. 'And how is the wonder boy?'

Thinking of Henry always made Frankie smile. 'He's doing fine, though he's got a massive bruise on his hip.'

'I think he might have been trying to climb the park railings when I found him. Bit of a fall. Has he said any more about it?'

'No, and I haven't pushed him. I can't help wondering if it was something I did. You do, don't you, with your children? If anything is wrong, the first person you blame is yourself.'

Cora tried to nod, as if in agreement. 'I don't have children. Difficult for me to say.' She sipped her coffee. 'Though I'm sure you didn't do anything wrong.' How much should she say? Just enough to make her knowledge powerful, but not enough to upset Frankie. 'From the little he said, I think it was some sort of dare. To spend a night or two out on his own.'

Frankie held the latte in both hands. 'It's just so hard. I worry all the time. I don't want to interfere, not be a nosy mum, but these days you don't know what's happening. As far as I know, he doesn't have any social media or anything like that, but I haven't checked his phone. It's a pretty basic thing, he bought it second hand. Jonny showed him how to set it up. Jonny's sensible and I've asked him if Henry has a Twitter or SnapBot account or whatever. Jonny says he's pretty sure he hasn't, but he hasn't checked. I was tempted to ask if he would, but getting one of my kids to spy on another – it's not the way you do things, is it?' She stopped to take a breath.

'I think parenting must be very difficult to get right.' Cora stirred her coffee and offered Frankie a biscuit.

'I shouldn't. It'll make me fat. But you know what? At the moment, I feel so down and guilty, I could eat the plate.' Frankie laughed.

Cora joined in. 'Go on. Eat the lot of them.' She pushed the plate a little closer and Frankie bit into a biscuit. 'I'm around, you know.'

Frankie paused mid-cookie. 'Around?'

'Yes. You know, if you need somebody. I mean, I'm sure you have loads of friends, but does it ever do any harm to have another?' Cora took a big gulp of her coffee and placed the mug on the table. 'I like having friends. They're important to me.'

Frankie looked at her. 'Yes. That would be nice.'

They walked back into town together. Frankie had parked at the supermarket in order to do a big family shop. She told Cora about where she worked at the call centre on the industrial estate down by the railway.

'It sounds important,' said Cora.

'Not at all. They ring up, they ask questions. We put the questions into a computer and the computer tells us whatever is wrong with their washing machine or their tumble dryer or their dishwasher. And if they're not happy with what the computer tells us to tell them, we tell them to fuck off.' She saw Cora's look of alarm. 'We don't really,' she laughed. 'But that's what we want to do. We tell them to go online and log a complaint. It's a chronic boring job, all day on the phone, never talking to anybody who hasn't got a problem.'

'Then why do you do it?' Cora asked.

'Because it lets me work the hours I want so I can take the kids to school in the mornings. I can take off half term or take time off if one of them is ill. I lose money, of course. Most days I have a manny.'

'A what?' Cora seemed to be finding it hard to keep up.

'A manny. It's a male nanny. They're all the rage. This one's not qualified. He's an out-of-work actor. He put an ad in the newsagents and he's cheap.'

'Sorry, I know it's none of my business, but should you be leaving Henry with somebody like that? Does he know what he's doing?'

'He's really nice. He keeps them all entertained and Henry adores him. They play games together, which I suppose he loves, being an actor. He's been on the telly – six lines in an episode of *Holby*. Jonny looks up to him and Shannon pretends not to notice he's there. He does it for the money. Out-of-work actors do anything for cash.'

By the time they arrived at the supermarket, Frankie was ready to say goodbye but Cora grabbed a basket. 'I'll wander around with you, if don't mind. I've got a few bits and bobs to get.'

Frankie ploughed her way up and down the aisles, filling the trolley with as many things in packets as she could find that were easy to cook and cheap, with a bit of fresh stuff as treats for the weekend. Anything on a BOGOF – Buy One Get One Free – went into the trolley; she'd work out what to do with it later. She noticed Cora's basket remained largely empty: tea bags, moisturising cream, a tub of luxury rum-and-raisin ice cream and a hunk of cheese from the deli counter.

As they walked along the wine aisle, Cora took two bottles of Prosecco from the shelf. She put one in her basket and placed the other in Frankie's trolley.

'Hey, what you doing? I can't afford that.' Frankie reached down and grabbed the bottle.

Cora stopped her. 'No. It's a little treat from me. You deserve it. You're wonderful with those kids. Go home, pour yourself a glass and disappear into the bathroom for an hour. That's what I do.'

Frankie laughed. 'Thank you.' Still smiling they headed towards the tills. Having paid their bills, Frankie pushed the trolley towards the exit.

'You will be in touch again, won't you?' Cora asked.

'Yes, I will. Yes, soon.'

'I've got your number now.' Cora smiled.

Frankie started to walk out of the shop. They had reached the top of the ramp to the car park where they would part ways when the air was rent with a tearing, metallic sound. Shopper's heads turned to see what was going on.

Frankie saw the cause straight away. 'Oh God,' she said. 'No. Please. No.'

Chapter Ten

Susan Steadman's aim was to get around the supermarket as quickly as possible. This wasn't her shop of choice; if it were down to her, she'd be up the road in Waitrose. But since her husband Damien had lost a well-paid job in media management, she'd had to make cutbacks.

The first time she'd come into this particular supermarket, she'd worn a scarf and a high-collared coat just in case any of her neighbours saw her. She'd picked up a few items and immediately removed all the packaging when she'd returned home. As time went on, she had returned.

The main thing was that everything was cheaper. Damien panicked every time she arrived home with the shopping. 'How much have you spent?' he would yell at her across the kitchen island. 'You've got to cut back, Susan. Cut right down. It's what I'm doing in every department. I've reduced the golf club membership to weekends only. Who knows where all this will end?'

It usually ended in another of their violent rows. The result was that, often with sunglasses covering a bruised eye, Susan made much more regular visits here and bought all her fresh produce. She didn't dare tell Damien she was visiting a bargain supermarket but after she'd spent hours converting ingredients into a vegetable parmigiana or a cauliflower and tofu korma, no one was any the wiser where they had come from. Damien just shovelled it down, belched and retired to the sofa.

She didn't like to spend long in the supermarket. The worst thing was being spotted by a member of the book club. That would not do. Richenda Michaelson-Smythe ran the book club like a minor branch of the Waffen SS.

Susan always shopped from a list and she worked fast. Making her way past two women who were gossiping at the end of an aisle – something about bottles of Prosecco – she paid for her goods and wheeled her trolley into the car park. The back window of her car was open a tiny crack so that Mercedes, her beloved russet-coloured cockapoo, didn't suffer while Susan braved the crowds.

Groceries packed into the boot, she pushed the trolley to one side. There were people who came to collect them who needed the work. She climbed into the driving seat. She hated this car; they'd had a nice Lexus, which had been a dream drive, but this second-hand Audi was another of Damien's economies.

'I got a wonderful deal on the Lexus. This is a splendid car,' he told her over a home-made lasagne one night, served with a cheap bottle of wine that Susan had decanted. 'It'll do all the shopping runs you need, and my airport trips, and it does mean we've got nine grand in the bank from the part exchange.'

Cheap doesn't necessarily mean good, thought Susan. She threw her bag onto the passenger seat. Mercedes stuck his head through the gap between the seats, anxious for a little affection. Susan was not in the mood. 'Down please, Mercedes. Not now.'

She pressed the ignition button, pushed her foot to the pedal and engaged gear. Mercedes shot forward through the gap between the seats. The car seemed to be moving backwards. At speed.

Before Susan had time to process the fact that reverse wasn't the direction she wanted, there was a huge crashing noise. She panicked and, instead of moving her foot to the brake, she caught the edge of the accelerator. The sound of metallic scraping increased as the car made a desperate attempt to pick up speed, crushing the car behind it into a brick wall.

Susan knew that this wasn't her day.

Chapter Eleven

'Oh, God,' said Frankie. 'No. Please. No.'

Cora watched as she let go of her trolley and started to run across the car park. Cora wasn't sure what to do with her own small basket. Dumping it into the top of Frankie's trolley, she pushed it to one side of the shop entrance and followed as fast as she could.

An enormous silver car had reversed and smashed another car into the wall. This was the source of Frankie's distress. 'Stop it! Stop it now!'

The car that had caused the damage had come to a halt. The driver's door on the far side opened.

Frankie stood stock still in amazement, looking at her car that had been shunted into the wall. 'My car. That's my fucking car!'

Cora put the language down to how distressed Frankie was. The driver of the other car got out and stood looking at the scene, then she calmly walked to the passenger door. She was a tall woman, thin and elegant in a grey-velour tracksuit, with a silk scarf tied around her neck and blonde hair pulled into a chignon. Cora thought she had the look of a haughty breeding mare.

'Mercedes. I must get Mercedes out of the car. Mercedes,

my baby,' the woman cried.

Both Cora and Frankie turned their heads on hearing the word 'baby'.

'Baby? Where?' Frankie asked.

'My baby. My darling,' screamed the woman, yanking open the passenger door. A large bundle of russet fluff bounded out. The woman grabbed it and held it close. 'Mercedes. My baby. You poor baby.'

Cora couldn't believe what she was seeing and Frankie's jaw had fallen almost to the floor. 'Your baby? That's your fucking baby? What about my car?'

'It might have hurt him.' The woman glared at Frankie as she lavished her care and attention on the cockapoo. 'Baby, baby, baby.' She bent down to let the dog nuzzle her face.

'I don't care about your fucking dog,' said Frankie. 'That's my fuckshit car you've smashed into a pissing wall, you stupid fuckhead of a dozy bitch.'

Cora was impressed by Frankie's command of the advanced Anglo-Saxon insult, and she wondered how the woman would deal with the screaming harpy that was now Frankie Baxter. Thirty minutes' conversation in the café had given Cora no idea of the possibilities of Frankie's rage and she found it exciting to behold.

A youthful man in a dark-green polyester jacket, and with the beginnings of a moustache arrived more than a little breathless. 'Now ladies, please.'

'Who the fuck are you?' barked Frankie, advancing on the new arrival.

'I'm Warren Hedgeman …' He fought to summon the courage to continue. 'I'm the duty manager.'

Sensing an ally, the tall woman turned her smile on him. 'I'm so very sorry. There seems to have been a minor accident.'

'A minor accident? Too fucking right, love.' Frankie was turning a shade of puce and Cora began to worry for her health.

'Frankie,' she said, 'why don't we get the shopping and step back into the store with this gentleman to sort things out? Insurance details and the like?'

'What an excellent idea,' said Warren, relief pouring off his forehead in the form of sweat. 'After all, the last thing we want is a fight in the car park.'

At which point, Frankie punched the other woman in the face.

Chapter Twelve

PC Ashley sat at the kitchen table and sipped his tea. 'She's not going to press charges.'

Frankie had been pleased when she'd opened the door and seen his familiar face but she hadn't, as yet, been able to offer a suitable explanation for what had happened. Why had she hit the woman? 'Let me tell you, constable,' her inner voice shrieked, 'it was the cockapoo, that wiry bundle of bum fluff excuse for a dog.' But she kept her silence.

It wasn't the first time. At junior school, she'd once punched a girl called Christine Evans in the face. She couldn't tell anybody why, not the teacher who'd asked her at length during detention nor the headmistress, Miss Nelson, who interrogated her in her office.

'I don't know, miss. I just had to,' was all Frankie could manage.

At secondary school, she'd been in a gang, not one of the wallflower crowd who'd hung around as part of a gang for their own safety, but an instigator. They broke the rules on school uniform, hiking their skirts above the regulation length, wearing their ties in hot and ingenious ways around the body, and typically sticking two fingers up at the world. There had been some shoplifting – sweets and cigarettes mainly – and a few instances of minor crime, if stealing a neighbour's bicycle to ride down to the cinema and then dumping it in the canal could be called a minor crime.

Shouldn't motherhood have knocked away these urges? Frankie knew that if it came to it, she would always defend her children as fiercely as she could, though there was little chance of Shannon ever being involved in any altercation as she hardly left the sofa. But she hadn't been fighting for her children, she'd been fighting for a battered, well past its best, maroon Fiat 500 that had been turned into an ashtray in front of her eyes in the supermarket car park.

'As I said, Mrs Steadman is not going to press charges,' said PC Ashley. 'But she doesn't want any contact with you. She has admitted fault in as much as something distracted her. She's given me her details so that you can get in touch with her insurance company. I understand they took your car to a garage. Yes?'

Frankie nodded. Her exact memory of what had happened after launching the punch at the stupid woman in the tracksuit was hard to recall. Cora seemed to have taken charge and spoken to the necessary people. There had been a quick visit to the police station and she'd had the pleasure of meeting Sergeant Chescoe face to face. She'd recognised him instantly from his voice as the person she'd spoken to on the night Henry had disappeared.

'Ah, Mrs Baxter. In the soup again, then?' he said with a chuckle. Neither Frankie nor the constable got the joke and an awkward silence ensued. Chescoe frowned at her; he wasn't fond of people who didn't get his sense of humour.

Frankie had returned home to find that Cora had taken

charge. Luke, the manny, had been sent home and tea rustled up for the kids. Evidently Cora had told them that 'Mummy was doing something with the car'.

Frankie could well imagine their reactions to the word 'Mummy'. Shannon was no doubt punching Cora's lights out within minutes of her saying it. Even affection-craving Henry never resorted to 'Mummy'. Yet they didn't seem to mind Cora being in the house. Everything seemed relaxed as she joined them at the kitchen table for the remains of the meal.

'I didn't know what a nugget was,' said Cora. 'But Henry's been such a great help.'

Henry beamed at Cora and Frankie felt herself relaxing. She'd found a new friend, someone she could rely on. Since the years in her teenage gang she'd preferred her independence, but sometimes it was good to have someone around whom you could trust. Someone to get you out of a mess.

Now, the following afternoon, PC 'You Can Call Me Oliver' Ashley finished his cup of tea and picked up his cap off the table. He poked his head into the other room to say goodbye to Henry and headed for the door.

'Thanks, constable,' said Frankie. 'Thanks for letting me know what's going on.'

'You shouldn't have any more problems. But stay away from Mrs Steadman and contact her insurers. And you might want to say thank you to Miss Walsh ... or is it Mrs Walsh? Warren from the supermarket said she was very impressive. Evidently not someone who takes no for an answer.'

Chapter Thirteen

The little girl didn't have any friends. Certainly no friends were allowed into her home to play. She played in the garden of the tiny house on her own, inventing her own worlds. At school, the children sat side by side in the classroom, except for her. She sat at the front of the class by the door on her own in a pair of desks of which she was the only occupant. It had not happened deliberately; where possible the teacher had sat the pupils alphabetically, and that was how it fell.

The other children didn't know how to deal with her. By now they knew she would not come to their birthday parties. On the occasions when they arrived at school with a satchel full of envelopes to hand out, there wouldn't be one for the little girl who sat by the door.

She no longer expected to receive invitations. She didn't have a birthday. She couldn't invite them in return. Her mother and father had always told her that they didn't celebrate birthdays. Her father thought that birthdays with pink cakes and party games were a waste of time. Her father had wanted a little boy.

One evening, after they had finished their meal, she had gone into the kitchen to wash up the dishes as normal. Looking over her shoulder, she saw her father holding her mother's hand and giving her a small, prettily wrapped box. She turned away in case they caught her watching but later she noticed that her mother was wearing a new silver locket. A birthday present.

Her parents bought her things – she was not without toys – but there was no celebration of her particular day. At Christmas she got presents like every other child. Yet she noticed that all the packages they gave her had no name on the label. They rarely used her name or any Christmas greetings. It was at Christmas that she began to acquire her dolls.

A visit to the dentist meant walking up the hill past the toyshop. One window was often filled with items designed to attract adolescent girls. Sometimes her mother stopped for a moment to light a cigarette or to attend to her makeup in the glass, and Little Girl would peer into the window and point at the dolls with their exotic names. Barbie, Sindy, Petal, My Little Angel. By now, although she was starting to reach the age when most children would be putting dolls away, she had collected over thirty of them in many shapes and sizes. They were her friends. They were the people to whom she told her secrets. They were the people with whom she shared her grief and her excitement.

Katie-Jane's birthday party was to be a lavish affair. Held in the gardens of Katie-Jane's parents' house, it would have clowns, face painting, makeovers, and a disco. It was taking place on a Saturday afternoon. Katie-Jane had handed invitations out to all the class in blue and pink envelopes, according to gender. She placed an envelope on Little Girl's desk as she passed. 'It would be lovely if you could come.'

'Thank you,' said Little Girl. She knew she would not be allowed to attend, but at least she could take the invitation home.

'No, no, no!' screamed her mother. 'I thought you understood. We don't have birthdays in this house.'

Little Girl looked up at her, summoning up the courage to make the request a second time.

'And Miss Fletcher was told that you were not to receive invitations to people's parties. It was silly of Katie-Jane to give you this. It'll only cause trouble. You're not going.'

At three o'clock on Saturday afternoon, the appointed time for the birthday party to begin, Little Girl sat in the kitchen. She arranged twenty of her dolls around a makeshift table, an upturned cardboard box that she had pulled from the rubbish in the pantry. She made sure that all the dolls looked neat. She pulled their arms forward so they could balance on the box, ready for the birthday feast she imagined would be placed on her party table.

Her father was out and her mother was snoozing in front of something on the television in the front room. Happy that all the dolls looked comfortable and the party was ready to begin, Little Girl went into the kitchen. She pulled out the small stool that her mother used to reach the upper shelves and, from the cupboard at the far end where all the baking ingredients were kept, she found what she wanted.

She climbed down and replaced the stool. She sprayed the liquid over the dolls' table and along the carpet into the hall. Now the party could begin. She lifted her hand and clicked on the blowtorch. The blue flame oozed out of it. She leant forward until the box was alight and then she sat back on her heels and waited until the dolls were aflame. The fire spread.

Little Girl walked out of the house and down to the end of the garden. She sat on a low wall to watch the house burn.

Chapter Fourteen

After the car park incident, Cora started calling Frankie every other day to check on how she was doing, friendly calls where she let Frankie do most of the talking. She resisted the temptation to offer another invitation for coffee or lunch. She knew that Frankie's working hours prevented her from spending much time with friends, and she didn't want to be a distraction. And Cora had other things she could do to fill her days. She often spent time sitting by her window, making notes on her laptop and watching the world.

She had rung Frankie on Thursday night for a quick chat to see how things were going, so she was a little surprised to see Frankie's name appear on her phone in the middle of Friday morning. 'Hello, you,' she said. 'Everything all right?'

There was a pause.

'Could we meet up? Something's come up and I would love your …' Cora could hear how difficult Frankie was finding it to ask for help.

'Are you working this afternoon?'

'No,' said Frankie. 'I finish at lunchtime.'

'Then meet me at Deli Do. Half-past one. Yes?'

There was another pause.

Deli Do was the town's latest upmarket coffee shop; no

change out of a fiver for a turmeric latte. Not, Cora deduced, the sort of place where Frankie would be wanting to spend her hard-earned money. 'My treat. Latte and a sandwich?'

Cora heard Frankie's sigh down the line. 'See you there.'

Being new, Deli Do was packed with people trying it out for lunch. There was an inviting smell of baking. Cora was glad she'd found a table pushed right back against the wall in the furthest corner from the door. She suspected that whatever it was Frankie had to share, she wouldn't want to do so while brushing shoulders with other people.

The waitress brought the two lattes. Cora was just starting hers and gazing into space when the door opened and Frankie came in. She was wearing blue harem pants with what looked like white horses on them, and an immense plum-coloured sweatshirt under an orange padded gilet. Not so much an outfit as a cry for help, thought Cora. Then, as she approached, Cora saw how apprehension was gripping her.

Cora stood up to do the half-kiss, half-peck on each cheek that she was accustomed to giving, but it seemed to make Frankie even more uneasy. They sat and Cora took a big sip of her coffee. Frankie looked at her cup but didn't drink.

'Right. What's wrong?' asked Cora, placing her coffee back down on the table.

Getting three children off to school never ceased to be a challenge that Frankie failed. This morning had been pandemonium and, as a result, Henry had been late for school. Shannon had not been on time, either – not that it would have worried her – and Frankie had rolled into work ten minutes late. As they were leaving the flat, the postman was delivering mail. Frankie had grabbed the letter he proffered and pushed it into her bag without further thought.

Given the morning had proved so chaotic, Frankie had gone into the kitchen at work to make herself a cup of tea at the first opportunity and taken the letter out of her bag.

Cheryl, who sat three booths down from Frankie and took remarkably few breaks, sauntered into the kitchen.

'Bastards,' muttered Frankie under her breath, but Cheryl caught the word.

'Who?' She flicked on the kettle and leaned against the sink.

'Fucking insurance.' She told Cheryl what had happened.

'That's all right. Insurance should pay up. That's what they do.'

'That's just it,' said Frankie. 'I'm not insured. Only third party. And this bloody woman's insurance company say my car is a write-off and they've offered me what they see as the replacement value.'

'That's all right then,' said Cheryl. She turned back to her tea making.

'Oh yes, that's fine. What car I can get with £300?' Frankie picked up her tea and went back to her kiosk before Cheryl had any further chance to share her wisdom,

The company banned personal calls at work, but in this instance Frankie took the risk. After a few minutes on hold, during which Frankie kept an anxious eye out for the supervisor, they put her through to someone whom she suspected was sitting in a room not unlike the one she worked in herself.

'I think there's a mistake with the valuation,' she began after they had taken her details. 'It's her fault without a doubt. She's liable for replacing the car and £300 isn't going to do that.'

'I'm afraid Sunquest insurance's policy is to assess the current value and roadworthiness of the vehicle and make an offer based on those factors. That value has been calculated on the Fiat, and the offer is £300. We can have that paid into a bank account, or we'll send a cheque if you'd like to give us the details and confirmation you are the person who suffered the loss.'

Frankie took a deep breath, trying to use the technique they had taught her to deal with difficult customers. It didn't work.

'I'd like to give you what for,' she said. 'It's a fucking racket. You know that car's worth more than three hundred quid. There's no chance of me replacing it for that, not even with an old pile of shit. I've got two kids and a school run to do and you don't give a fuck.'

'Here at Sunquest Insurance, we do take abuse against our staff very seriously. If you continue to use language of that sort, it will force me to terminate the call.'

'I'm sorry,' replied Frankie. 'Why don't you take the opportunity to do that? Terminate the call. And while you're at it, why don't you shove your handset so far up your arse that you couldn't shit it out if you tried?'

With that, Frankie ended the call and breathed deeply.

'I take it they won't be paying up, then,' said Cora.

Chapter Fifteen

Sue Steadman lived in Larchwood, the most luxurious block of flats overlooking the park, in an elegant three-bedroom apartment on the third floor. Sue had never liked houses. Here she had balconies; a rear-facing one where she could grow her herbs, and a glorious front balcony laden with artificial grass and plants for presenting herself to the world. A picture of refined sophistication. Sue didn't have green fingers and, quite frankly, she didn't need them. Just as she didn't need children. Little bundles of soiled pants running around her home. Her maternal instincts had never flourished and she was perfectly happy to keep it that way.

What motherly love she had she lavished on Mercedes, and the dog was glad to receive it. He was her baby; he was her darling. She had long since ceased to be the foremost object of affection in Damien's eyes, but Mercedes loved her unquestioningly and she adored him back.

That's why the episode in the supermarket car park had upset her so much. It was an accident, that was all, an accident – and accidents happen. The dumpy woman had made such a fuss. If it hadn't been for the delightful man from the supermarket and that peculiar red-haired woman who'd helped sort it all out, heaven knows what would have happened.

The sudden recollection made Sue sit down in the kitchen. Having achieved a remarkably low score on Pop Master with Ken Bruce, which she listened to most mornings, she now got the Colombian Arabica roast ready to make a pot of coffee. She would take the coffee and sit in the lounge to catch up with the *Daily Telegraph* on her iPad. Sue liked to keep abreast of current events.

As she put everything on her tray, the doorbell rang – not the entry phone where visitors to the block buzzed in but the bell for the door to her flat. That meant that whoever it was had already got into the block. It was probably Leslie, the caretaker and groundsman, but there was a slight unease in Sue's gut as she walked down the corridor to open the door.

She had long wanted to drill a spyhole, but Damien had been against it. 'We've got the video system,' he'd said. 'What do we need a hole in the front door for? And don't forget it can be used both ways. People can put their eyes to the door and have a look down the hallway.'

Sue thought he was being unreasonable as usual. Other people installed little brass covers over their peepholes which pushed to one side. Given that Damian organised most of the practical things in the household, it had never got done.

Sue opened the door a little. 'Oh. It's you. Should I ask you in?' As the visitor stood and stared at her, Sue adjusted the necklace around her neck and ran the beads through her fingers. 'Is there something you wanted?'

'I want to make things fair, about you and your insurance company not compensating for the car you wrecked.'

Sue didn't like the visitor's tone. And this was nothing to do with her. 'I've said all this before. I gave all my details to be circulated to the relevant parties. My insurance company will have decided what's best, and they're the people dealing with it. I'm sorry, but you've had a wasted journey.'

She moved to close the door but found the visitor's left foot pushing against it. 'That's not helping. Would you kindly remove your foot?'

Sue pushed the door open again and stepped forward with the intention of making the visitor take a step back. As she put her foot on the threshold, a pair of hands reached out and grabbed her wrists. Hands squeezed and fingers dug into her inner arms.

Sue gasped. 'I'm sorry. That's hurting. That's really hurting.'

The visitor pulled Sue forward by the forearms across the carpeted hallway.

'What are you doing?' screeched Sue, struggling to keep both her dignity and her hold on the door frame. She felt herself being dragged along the white railings which bordered the staircase.

The block had a large central glass atrium. A sudden vision filled Sue's eyes as to what was going on, and her breathing became ragged and harsh. 'What are you doing? Please. Please.' A paralysing alarm spread through her body like icy liquid metal.

'Help?' Her throat closed and tightened as she tried to call again. 'Help, please help somebody!' she shouted but she knew she was unheard. The people in the other flats on the top floor worked during the day. She was often the only resident at home, and she knew there was no one who could come to her aid.

Sue could hear only one sound, that of her own throbbing

pulse. As they reached the top of the staircase, the pressure on her forearms increased and she was yanked savagely forward and spun round at the top of the stairs.

She looked into her visitor's eyes, pleading, one last faint cry leaving her mouth as her forearms were pushed and she plunged backwards down the stairs, a crashing, head-splitting, bone-breaking fall.

Her visitor walked down the staircase and, reaching the second-floor landing, stepped over Sue Steadman.

Sue felt a pair of hands lock across her forehead and what seemed like a knee or an arm in the small of her back. The hands twisted, and there was blackness.

Chapter Sixteen

Frankie liked the growing closeness with Cora. As a young-ster, one thing she'd always been short of was friends. When she was at school, her mother had never wanted her to bring people home and it became hard to keep in with the other pupils in her class. She'd never found it easy to make friends yet, ever since the morning when Cora had turned up on her doorstep with Henry, something had been different. It just worked. Cora made it so easy.

Frankie stood in the kitchen with Henry by her side. He was balanced on a small stool doing the last of the washing up. She ruffled his hair. 'All done, my love. Thank you. You can watch telly with the others now.' Saturday morning always meant telly for the kids whilst Frankie did some tidying up around them. Then it would be a supermarket run.

But now she had no car. That meant a fair walk there and carrying heavy bags back. Maybe she could persuade Jonny to help. Henry would jump at the chance, but he couldn't carry much. And it would be pointless even asking Shannon.

She was just counting up the cost of getting a taxi back from the supermarket with the boys when her phone buzzed.

'Morning.' The cheery voice on the other end of the phone sounded familiar.

'Hello. How are you?'

Cora laughed, sharp and loud. 'I was ringing to find out how *you* were. Forgive me if it seems like prying, but I think this is another Saturday without the car to go shopping. Am I right?'

'Too right.' Frankie turned away from the kids. 'I was just working out the logistics and who could carry what.'

'That's why I rang. I think I can help you, my dear. I'm popping round in half an hour. Okay?' And before Frankie could reply, Cora rang off.

Frankie stood by the sink gazing out of the window. 'What do I know?' she thought. Cora had walked into her life and now she was becoming part of family shopping outings. She understood their problems. She was a brilliant listener. Whenever they met for coffee, it was Frankie who did most of the talking. Cora nodded and listened, made the occasional remark, and she always paid for the coffee and wouldn't have it any other way.

The way she'd stood up for Frankie in the supermarket car park and dealt with everything had been remarkable. Just being there, listening to Frankie having a good moan when the insurance company sent their letters had helped. It was as if Cora had landed from another planet or come from some parallel world.

Frankie had never counted herself as a lucky person. She didn't win raffles or competitions and, although she bought a lucky dip every week on the lottery, the most she'd ever won was £30. Yet here was Cora giving her time and friendship. Perhaps being lucky sometimes came in other forms.

***

'You mean it's ours?' asked Henry, as the five of them stood on the pavement looking at the car. A blue Hyundai i10, no Aston Martin but certainly the smartest car Frankie had ever seen.

Her amazement at its arrival with Cora at the wheel had almost matched that of the kids. They'd all piled out of the flat, Shannon still in pyjamas. There was an embarrassing blue bow attached to the bonnet.

'You can't give us a car, Cora.' Frankie knew this was ridiculous; it would cross a boundary of friendship. And yet she wanted it so much. To her, at this moment, it was the most beautiful car in the world.

'Why not? I don't use it and it's been sitting in a garage for over a year. The marvellous thing is, I can stop paying rent on the garage – and you'll have a car to do your shopping.'

'To go to the seaside!' yelled Henry. 'Seaside, seaside, seaside,' he chanted.

Frankie looked at the car and then at Cora, who was standing next to three beaming faces. Even Shannon had turned her normal grimace into something approaching a smile. Jonny was encouraging Henry to bounce around and shout even louder.

Cora reached into the front passenger seat and retrieved her bag. 'Now, I've got the paperwork here but I've changed it all online and put it in your name. It was a little presumptuous of me, I know, but once I got the idea I just couldn't stop. How about we make an enormous pot of tea and sort everything out?' She threw her arms wide. 'Then who wants to go for a drive?'

'To the supermarket,' said Frankie.

'And then the seaside!' shouted Henry.

Jonny laughed at his brother and soon they all joined in.

They were all still laughing when the police car pulled in next to them.

Chapter Seventeen

Little Girl liked the children's home. It looked like a doll's house she'd once seen in the window of the toyshop, with a tall pointed roof with green paintwork, a huge front door in the middle and windows, tall and rectangular, on either side.

The children's home was crowded. Little Girl didn't have her own room; she shared with four other girls and she found it difficult to talk to them. What she liked was that they didn't seem to mind. There were other children who kept themselves to themselves. The only thing she hated was the locking of the bedroom door at night. If she needed to go to the toilet, they used a chamber pot or what her grandma had called a 'gazunder' because, she would say through her laughter, 'it goes under the bed, dear'.

Every morning they woke early and dressed, all of them virtually identical in pale-green dresses with a belt, cheap white plimsolls, white socks and dark green cardigans if the weather was cold. The staff who looked after them were not hurtful, but not caring either. After breakfast it was lessons, and after lessons it was lunch, and after lunch it was lessons, and after lessons it was dinner, and after dinner there was a little time when they were allowed to watch television. They were not to change the channel and had to watch whatever the member of staff who was in charge that evening wanted to watch.

Little Girl became enthralled with the lives of the people on television. The programme she liked most was about a Yorkshire village where the family had been farmers but now were involved all kinds of things like plane crashes and post-office robberies. The programme was what she felt real life must be like, not her own life but that of other people. People who talked to each other, which was what she learnt to do.

Little Girl's best friend was a few months older than her and was called Lottie.

Lottie and Little Girl talked because it was a way of misbehaving in class. The more the teacher tried to shut them up, the more they snatched hidden, illicit conversations. Lottie said she was in the home because her mother hadn't been able to keep her. That was how Lottie had put it, but Little Girl could tell there was another reason, something Lottie never spoke of. Yet Lottie had something that made Little Girl very envious – she had a birthday. And she'd had a birthday party with cake and friends in her home.

Little Girl told Lottie how she'd never had a birthday, how she didn't have a birthday date, and her parents had never held a party for her. Eventually Little Girl told Lottie about the dolls' birthday party and how, in a moment, she had decided it was all wrong and fetched the torch to burn the dolls and the box. She remembered how her father had returned home and stood next to her in the back garden of the house, horror-struck at the blaze. The acrid smell of melting plastic limbs and synthetic hair filled the air as the sound of her singing grew louder and louder. 'Happy birthday to me, happy birthday to me.'

It was the first time she'd spoken of such things. As she told

Lottie, she knew that she would probably never return home. Then one day Lottie told her why she was in the home.

Chapter Eighteen

Frankie couldn't remember ever having cause to go past the front desk of the police station. Other than an unsuccessful attempt to get a ticket from a cocky parking warden revoked, she'd never been into the building, even when Jonny was in his most troublesome teenage years.

Now she found herself sitting in a room familiar to her from the last half-hour of *Midsomer Murders*, the one where the prime suspect 'fessed up to everything. Except she wasn't a suspect, or at least that's what they had said.

PC Ashley had got out of the police car accompanied by a WPC called Barbara Something. Frankie sent the kids indoors and waited with Cora to see what the constable wanted. He was as charming as on his previous visits and said they were investigating an incident involving someone called Susan Steadman.

Frankie glanced at Cora. That was the woman in the supermarket car park with the mad Audi and the wire-wool dog.

'Yes,' replied PC Ashley. 'That's correct. There's been an unfortunate turn of events, I'm afraid, and we'd like to ask you some questions.'

Cora asked what he meant by 'an unfortunate turn of events'.

He looked a little uncomfortable. 'I'm not at liberty to say, but I need Mrs Baxter to come down to the station and answer some questions.'

Frankie's gut did a little flip. You'd only go down to the station if you were a suspect, and if you were a suspect you'd need a lawyer, and if you needed a lawyer it was already serious. WPC Barbara Something assured her that at this stage it was just some questions, but they did need to do it at the station.

'I'll come with you,' Cora said.

'Thank you, Cora,' said Frankie. 'Though I'm sure it's not necessary.'

Now, here in the interview room waiting for someone to show up, Frankie was calmed by the knowledge that Cora was sitting by the front desk. The door opened and WPC Barbara Something, her uniform blouse revealing a bosom of intimidating proportions, stepped into the room. The man who followed her had hair best described as sparse, and a day or two's stubble. He was shorter than PC Barbara Something and together they had the appearance of the little wooden couple who might pop out of the doors of a weather house.

They sat on the opposite side of the table. WPC Barbara placed a laptop in front of her, which she opened and turned on.

'I'm Detective Sergeant Webb,' said the man. 'I understand that it's been explained to you that, at this point, you are just helping us with our enquiries.'

Frankie wasn't sure she liked the sound of the words 'at this point'.

'You are not under any suspicion and this is an informal interview which we will not be recording.' Webb had a marked South London twang. It sounded as if he were trying to be cheerful and yet was not quite achieving it.

'So, what is it that you want to know?' asked Frankie. The sick feeling in the pit of her stomach hadn't disappeared, but they were all treating her perfectly pleasantly. It couldn't be anything serious – but if it wasn't, why insist that she come into the police station?

The detective opened the folder of papers on the table in front of him. He kept his head down while reading from it. 'Let me take you back to Friday the 15th of March. An altercation occurred in the car park of Marshalls' supermarket.'

Frankie wasn't sure she wanted to listen any more. 'I'm not sure what an altercation is, but if you mean did some posh woman decide to drive her bloody car backwards and turn my car into a sheet of tin metal pushed against the supermarket wall, then yes.'

Webb looked up at her. 'And afterwards you became quite vociferous?'

'It upset me.' This couldn't be the root of the problem, Frankie thought. You weren't brought into the police station because you'd had a shouting match with a few four-letter words, were you?

The detective looked down at his notes again. WPC Barbara Something was staring at her.

'Is that it? Is that why I'm here?' Frankie asked.

The detective took a photograph out of the folder and laid it in front of her. 'The woman you had the altercation with was a Mrs Susan Steadman. Yesterday afternoon she was found at the bottom of a flight of stairs at Larchwood, the block of flats where she lived.'

Frankie looked at the photograph. She couldn't tell if it was the same person. The woman in the picture was wearing a similar sort of leisure suit, but the head was at a very funny angle. 'That's awful. Obviously. But why am I here? Just because the poor woman fell, it doesn't mean …'

'We have reason to believe she didn't fall.' Webb nodded at the policewoman.

WPC Barbara spun the laptop around to face Frankie. The screen showed the front of a block of flats, which Frankie recognised as one of the posh ones on the other side of the park. A camera angled down one side of the driveway. The WPC pressed a button and the screen blinked into life. A car moved past the end of the drive, then another, and then after about twenty seconds a figure came into the picture and walked towards the front of the block. As the figure filled the front of the screen, it was easy to see a plum-coloured sweatshirt, blue pants and an orange padded gilet.

The figure looked extraordinarily like Frankie Baxter.

Chapter Nineteen

Cora glanced at the clock above the counter. She'd been sitting there for more than ninety minutes. Comfort wasn't the foremost priority of the police station lobby, and there was an unusual smell of detergent and despair. The one bench with its stiff wooden seat was making her back ache and, as she suffered, she started to worry. What was keeping Frankie in there for so long? What did the police want to know?

Cora wracked her brains. Nothing that Frankie had done in the supermarket car park was illegal. A silly car crash and an argument which had become somewhat heated, that was all. She was about to ask the desk sergeant what was happening when the door to his left opened and Frankie walked out. She looked a little the worse for wear. Cora could see that she had been crying.

A short, paltry excuse for a man in a dreadful suit lingered behind her in the doorway. 'If we need to speak to you again, Mrs Baxter, we'll be in touch. In the meantime, please don't do anything silly.' He closed the door.

Cora knew this was the moment to give her new friend the biggest and warmest of hugs that she could manage. She enveloped Frankie in her arms, trying her hardest to relax.

'Can we get out of here?' said Frankie.

Cora held open one of the double doors of the police station and they stepped out onto the High Road. 'I could call an Uber if you want,' she said. 'Nice cup of tea at home?'

'Let's walk. I've got something to tell you.'

They linked arms and set off towards the park in a companionable silence. Cora bided her time, waiting for Frankie to tell her what had happened. A little way into the park, they reached a bench. The metal plaque told them it was 'Dedicated to Ivan Russell'.

Frankie sat down and Cora joined her. For a moment they stared at the swans on the lake. A slight breeze rustled the leaves and the air was warmer than forecast. A beam of sunlight caught Cora's face and she unbuttoned the top of her coat.

Frankie took a deep breath. 'I did something very silly.'

Cora waited. She knew all about silence; there had been so much of it in her life.

'Please don't tell the kids.' Frankie turned to her 'Do you remember the day I met you in the café? The day that I'd had the letter from the insurance company?'

Cora smiled. 'Yes. Two lattes and a lot of calming down.'

'After I left, I didn't go straight home. I was still angry. I knew the insurance company had made the decision, but I couldn't believe that woman, Mrs Steadman, would want to let them get away with it. I thought she might feel guilty about what she'd done.'

'You didn't see her?' Cora's expression tightened.

'I went round there. I had the address from the police incident form. She wasn't having any of it. "If that's what the insurance company decided, then that's what they are paying.

77

That's what I have insurance for, my dear," she said. Stuck-up bitch.'

Cora looked puzzled. 'But why did the police want to question you?'

'They found her later that afternoon. Someone had pushed her down the stairs. The CCTV on the block of flats caught me walking up the drive and I'm pretty sure they think I had something to do with it.'

Cora looked out across the lake. Two swans were fighting over a piece of bread, elegant and violent in their struggle. 'And did you?' she asked.

Chapter Twenty

Even as a tiny child, Lottie knew that her parents loved her. She saw how much her mum and dad wanted her. They'd always wished for a baby daughter but, as they told her, 'God never allowed us to have a child of our own. God told us we must look after someone else's little girl.' So that is what they had done.

Joan and Harry Morgan were a normal couple in everything except their childlessness: a modest house, a respectable job for Harry and a busy social life for Joan. Yet no matter how much they tried to fill the house with the joyous sound of children, they were unsuccessful. Then Lottie came along – or Charlotte, as they preferred to call her. They became her parents when she was six months old. Now their domestic life was complete and their hearts fulfilled.

Joan was forty-three when the little bundle of joy arrived, and she wasted no time in ensuring Charlotte had everything she could desire. Harry tried to be strict but Joan constantly undermined him; he resigned himself to the fact that Charlotte was Joan's darling.

Lottie was extremely quick to learn she could get whatever she wanted. As a baby, that meant ferocious yelling or squealing, and as a small child she mastered outbursts of ever-increasing originality. She knew how to stamp; she knew how to flail her arms. She learned how to punch her mother's thighs at the perfect level to turn irritation into injury and leave Joan with little bruises.

Joan never said anything to Harry. She knew Charlotte didn't mean it. 'Charlotte's had a tough start in life,' she thought. 'It's my job, through God, to help Charlotte in every way.'

Lottie had a room at the top of the house, a picture-perfect palace of a bedroom for a precocious little princess. Dolls, books, toys, and most of all, cuddly animals. Lottie loved every kind of animal. She had a moose in a Mountie uniform, which Harry had brought all the way back from a business trip to Canada. She had a large duck with orange feet and white staring eyes, which had once held an oversized Easter egg. She had a purple dragon and a spotted green furry snake. She had several penguins and, most importantly, she had an enormous floppy-eared cuddly black-and-brown dog called Harrison.

Lottie knew full well that one day she would have a real dog and she would call him Harrison too. Every birthday and every Christmas she asked the same question: 'Can I have a puppy, Daddy?'

Harry would tell her that she wasn't old enough.

'Can I have a puppy, Mummy?'

Joan told her she would have to grow up a little more to be able to look after a puppy.

'I want a puppy, Mummy. Want a puppy, Mummy. I want one, Mummy.'

Lottie knew that if she asked enough times, Joan would say yes. Joan knew she couldn't do anything without Harry's approval. Harry was adamant they were not having a dog.

'I want a puppy, Mummy. Want a puppy, Mummy. Want a puppy.' The words echoed and rolled around in Joan's head, pushing a migraine behind her eyes as her daughter's words smacked into her face. She grabbed the side of the kitchen table to steady herself for a moment then, taking a deep breath, she reached out and took Charlotte's hand and led her up the stairs to her bedroom.

She opened the door and yanked Charlotte into the room. 'You have lots of animals, my little darling. Now play with them,' she shrieked at Lottie, who jerked back onto the bed in surprise.

Joan walked out of the bedroom. Then, doing something she had never done before, she locked the bedroom door. She could hear the cries and wails of her daughter but the further down the stairs she went, the quieter they became. Sitting in the living room with the lights out and the curtains drawn, she was able to find a kind of peace.

As the years went on, although Harry didn't know it, the locked bedroom became an answer to more and more of Charlotte's incessant requests. Lottie knew Harry was strict and there was no point in complaining to him. She learnt how to judge her yelling and stamping, how to fine tune her tantrums so that her mother almost always reached for her. Then she escaped. But, when it became too much, Joan would grab her by the wrist, drag her up the stairs, throw her into the bedroom and lock the door.

If Joan then had to work in the kitchen, the room below her daughter's bedroom where she could still hear the noise, she turned up the radio. How well *Steve Wright in the Afternoon* covered the anguished yells.

Things became less troublesome when Lottie went to school. She was liked by her school friends because she seemed to have everything. That gave Joan a new justification for giving Charlotte what she demanded. 'She needs it for school, darling,' she would tell Harry, and Harry would make certain that Joan had the money. Things improved so much that, on Lottie's tenth birthday, Harry relented and they bought her a puppy.

Lottie raced home from school every evening to be with the puppy. Harry had bought it from somebody he'd met in the pub, a Labrador-setter cross. It was as much of a match for the colours of Charlotte's toy dog Harrison as he could find. Yet Lottie called the puppy Brandy, because Harry liked drinking brandy and she liked the colour of it in the decanter on the sideboard.

Lottie loved the puppy with all her heart. At home she spent all the hours she could with him. Then one night Lottie came home from school to find an empty house, except for Brandy. She didn't know where her mother was and she felt alone and lost. She sat in her bedroom and hugged her puppy.

It was three hours before Harry came home. He sat on her bed and held her hand. 'They had to take Mummy into the hospital this afternoon.'

After this, things changed. Harry wasn't good at cooking and cleaning; Harry was good at spreadsheets and telling people what to do. Harry's sister, Muriel, moved into the house to look after Lottie. Muriel didn't have any children of her own. She was a thin, pinched woman with a beak of a nose, several moles and ill-permed hair. She lived in a strange mix of flared skirts and T-shirts and spent most of the day in plimsolls, which made her look like an ageing cheerleader. Muriel smoked, something Harry would never allow in the house, so she sat in the back garden to light a cigarette. Sometimes, to Lottie's amazement, Muriel sat in the front garden at the top of the path where all the neighbours could see her smoking. Muriel's cooking consisted of cans and packets. Lottie didn't like it, but she knew that Mummy was very poorly and she didn't want to complain.

Every evening after work, Harry went to the hospital and stayed with Joan for several hours before getting home for a plate of something out of a can that Muriel put on the kitchen table. Lottie saw how her father looked: his skin was grey, his eyes had lost their shine and he seldom spoke. He looked like a silhouette, as if he had walked out of the wedding photograph on the windowsill and left only blackness. He was so worried that he didn't see Lottie sneak Brandy into her bedroom each evening and let him sleep on the bed.

A few weeks later, Brandy became ill. The dog curled up in a corner of Lottie's bedroom and started to shiver. He whimpered and, no matter how she tried, she couldn't encourage him out into the garden. He'd grown bigger now and the ten year old girl could hardly lift him. She carried and half-dragged him into the open air each day when she returned from school in the hope that he would recover. Lovingly, she filled his water bowl and stroked him and gave him all the love she had inside her. She didn't tell Harry.

One night a few days later, after a silent evening meal, Muriel went down the road to the pub. 'Just to get out of your hair for a while, Harry.'

Harry sat facing his daughter. 'You know Mummy is very ill in hospital, Charlotte,' he began. Lottie nodded. 'Tomorrow the surgeons are going to operate on Mummy. The very top doctors.'

'What's operate, Daddy?' said Lottie.

Harry thought for a moment. 'It's where the doctors open up your insides with very special knives. They look at whatever is wrong and they make it better. Then they sew you up again and help you get better. Then Mummy can come home to us.'

Lottie went to bed and dreamed of men opening Mummy up with their knives to make her better.

Harry came back to the house after a long day at the hospital. He pushed open the door; everything was quiet. He walked through into the kitchen. There was no sign of Muriel or Lottie. A pan was simmering away on the stove and there was a scribbled note on the kitchen table. *Had to go out. Sorry. Stew in the pan. Back tomorrow if I can.*

Harry lifted the pan lid. The stew had started to scorch the sides. He turned off the hob and removed the pan. As he did, he looked out of the kitchen window. He could see Lottie in the garden, kneeling down, bending over something.

As he was putting plates on the table and getting the cutlery for dinner, he noticed something was missing: there was an empty space next to the bread bin. His heart jumped and he dropped the plate he was carrying, which smashed onto the floor.

He pushed open the back door and stopped at the top of the steps down to the garden. Lottie was kneeling in the middle of the lawn, a white bathroom towel in front of her. Next to it was the missing knife block from the kitchen, and on it was Brandy.

The dog lay sliced open and pinned to the towel by three kitchen knives and a cake fork.

'I'm making him better, Daddy.'

Chapter Twenty-One

'I can see the sea,' yelled Henry, bouncing up and down on the back seat of the car and creating considerable discomfort for Jonny on one side and Shannon on the other. She'd been trying to sleep so as not to have to engage with anyone.

In the passenger seat, Cora turned her head and smiled at him. 'Do you like the sea, Henry? Are you going to go for a swim?'

'He's going to go for a paddle and he's going to be careful. Aren't you Henry?' Frankie's hands gripped the steering wheel and she focused on the thickening traffic as they drove into Brighton.

The seaside trip was Cora's suggestion. After Frankie's renewed protestations of innocence regarding Susan Steadman, Cora had walked back with her to the flat. As soon as they stepped in through the door, the kids wanted to know why the police had taken their mum away. Even Shannon seemed interested, while Jonny asked rather probing questions. 'Did they interrogate you Mum? Was it recorded? What were they asking you about?'

Henry was much more concerned with his mother's welfare. 'Are you okay, Mum? They didn't hurt you, did they?'

Frankie pulled him to her. 'No, they didn't. And it's all a bit of a mistake. Something unfortunate happened and I was on a closed-circuit television camera near to where it took place. It's all a misunderstanding.' Henry tightened his hold round her waist and she kissed the top of his head.

'You sure?' said Jonny. 'They shouldn't be giving you any grief, Mum.'

'Grief?' laughed Frankie. 'Oh, my darling, you sound like you're on some dreadful TV cop show.' Jonny looked a little crestfallen. 'They didn't give me any grief – and if they had, I would have called you to sort it,' Frankie told him.

Although Jonny was fighting a daily battle with teenage traumas in many areas – acne, facial hair, wet dreams – he saw himself as the man of the house. 'Good. They'd better not.'

Cora decided it was time to take charge in a more practical way. 'Should I make us all a cup of tea?'

They sat in the living room with tea and the last of a packet of shortcake biscuits, which were rather past their best. Without giving any specific details, Frankie told them more about her visit to the police station, but their focus was on Cora's gift of the car.

'When can we go out in it, Mum?' asked Henry. 'To the supermarket?'

Cora looked at Frankie and both of them laughed. 'I'm not sure that's the best place to go at the moment,' said Cora. 'But I always think a good way to test out a new car is a trip to the seaside.' Henry gasped in delight. 'What about tomorrow?' she continued.

Frankie looked rather alarmed. 'Tomorrow?'

'Oh please, Mum!' shouted Jonny and Henry. Only Shannon seemed less than thrilled at the prospect of another family outing in which she'd be forced to participate.

Frankie nodded.

'Okay. That's decided then,' said Cora. 'You've got the car and it's got a full tank of petrol. We leave here at nine in the morning, and we're all off to Brighton.'

They all cheered. Shannon put her hands over her ears.

***

Frankie managed to find a parking space in a multi-storey just a few blocks back from the seafront, although she was rather nervous to see that it was going to cost more than ten pounds to park for the day. She unlocked the boot and took out their backpacks and the small picnic hamper that Cora had brought that morning. It was full of sandwiches and squash and, rather to the children's alarm, fruit.

Although the calendar said it was the first official day of summertime, it wasn't very sunny. Clouds skimmed across the sky, a rough woollen blanket of mottled grey, and allowed the sun to make only an occasional appearance. It wasn't cold though and, as they turned the corner onto Marine Parade to look at the beach, they saw they weren't the only people who'd had this idea on a Sunday.

'Let's walk further along towards the West Pier,' said Cora. 'There'll be fewer people there and we can have a bit of a picnic. And those who want to can go into the sea.'

They found a spot past the looming skeleton of the burnt-out pier away from other beachgoers. Cora opened the hamper and pulled out two travel rugs. She laid them on the sand and sat down. Frankie had a supermarket carrier bag with her, in which she had a couple of towels. She stretched out, using the towels as a pillow. 'This is very nice, Cora. Thank you.'

'Can I go for a walk, Mum?' Jonny asked. 'Check out the slots.'

'Yes, that's fine,' said Frankie without looking up at him. 'Don't be too long. About half an hour, then we'll have lunch. You want to take your sister?'

From the expression on his face, it was the last thing Jonny wanted to do. Shannon grunted a reply that could have meant anything, but she followed him up the beach towards the road.

Frankie was thrilled that both of them had come along and she didn't expect either of them to stay with her for the day. She just prayed they wouldn't get into any trouble.

Henry was already pulling off tracksuit bottoms under which he wore a pair of bright-yellow swimming trunks. He jumped up and down. 'Can I go in the sea, Mum? Can I go in the sea?'

'It'll be cold. Stay where we can see you, okay?' said Frankie, sitting up for a moment. Henry nodded vigorously. 'And no swimming. Just paddling, and stay near the shore.'

Henry charged off down the beach and crashed into the sea before returning to the edge as he discovered how cold it was. Frankie lay with her head on the towels and Cora sat cross-legged on the picnic rug, sorting out sandwiches and drinks.

'Do you think the police will want to speak to me again?' Frankie asked without looking up.

Cora arranged the sandwiches, which were on little plates wrapped in clingfilm. It looked like a doll's tea party. 'Why would they? You told them it wasn't you. And you said they have video footage of you leaving.'

'Yes, they do, not long after. And not running or anything. I had nothing to run from.'

'Stop worrying about it. Enjoy the day. Relax. No point in worrying about things you have no control over, is there?' Cora reached into the hamper and took out a book. She found her page and started to read.

Frankie closed her eyes. Sometimes the worst of things brought the best of things. They spent so much time squeezed into the tiny flat and it was hard at times, yet there were so many brilliant evenings full of laughter and surprises and a never-ending discovery of just how wonderful her children could be. And here she stood, accused of a crime she hadn't committed and yet enjoying a surprising new friendship and a day at the seaside with her family. She couldn't remember how long it was since they'd all done something together.

Wandering in a netherworld between thought and sleep, she lay until something woke her. She sat up. Cora was engrossed in her book. 'Did you hear that?' Frankie asked.

Cora looked puzzled. 'Hear what?'

On the breeze, they both heard the cry for help.

***

Henry loved the sea and each year it was a highlight of his holidays. He knew Mum didn't have the cash to take them away, but they did go on days out. She had a special membership of something she called the National Trussed, which sounded odd, but the ticket she had got them into lots of old castles and grand houses. They were all right, but they weren't as much fun as the seaside. Every year they had at least one day out somewhere on the coast – Eastbourne, Hastings or even Margate. Now they were having a trip in a new car to Brighton. To Henry, it was all just seaside and fantastic.

With an older sister and brother, Henry was used to amusing himself so it didn't worry him as he ran down to the sea alone. The touch of the wet sand thrilled him. As he jumped the first two slight waves and landed with a splash, the cold bit into his feet. He dashed back to the beach for a little more warmth. He knew this was how it worked.

Next time, he ran in up to his knees and ran back out again. Even though he was alone, he squealed at the icy water. His third run into the sea lifted the water past his waist. Pulling in his tummy, he struggled to hold his breath to battle the chill. He closed his eyes and lost his balance, slipping backwards and plunging under the water.

Spluttering up for air, he stuck out his tongue at the taste of the sea. With his shoulders submerged, the cold was less of a problem. 'It's nice once you're in,' he'd often heard people say, but it was never the case.

He waded out a little more until the water came up to his chest. At school he was learning to swim and he could manage six strokes breaststroke or eight strokes doggy paddle. In the swimming pool, where you could see your feet touch the bottom of the pool, it felt safe; here, the darkness of the water made things a little more unnerving. Although he could feel the sand and the odd rock beneath his feet, he couldn't see where he was standing. Exciting, and yet worrying.

He launched forward and managed five breaststrokes before turning to shore. He splashed with his feet, feeling for the sandy floor of the sea. It was no longer there. He moved his arms as if he were climbing rocks, but there was only water around him.

With what breath remained, he called out to the distant figures on the shore but the water stole away the words, washing them out to sea. He slipped under the surface and his brain clicked into full panic. He clawed through the thin liquid, but his limbs seemed to slow down as if the sea were sticky treacle.

Pushing up his chin and angling it to the sky, he knew there was no longer anything under his feet. Nothing to stand on, nothing to grip, and no way of moving through the vastness of the water. He started to splash with his feet, as if they were on some imaginary bicycle, but the sea held him and started to pull him down.

***

Cora was clear about what she'd heard. She threw the book to one side and stood up. Frankie was next to her. 'It's Henry,' she said. 'Where is he?'

They scanned the water for any sign of him. Frankie cried out and pointed a little further along the coast then started to run down to the water's edge, lumbering across the sands. Cora followed and, being quicker, arrived first at the water's edge. They could see the flailing arms of the small boy a hundred or so yards out into the sea and hear his cries.

As Cora saw his head dip under the water, Frankie turned to her. 'I can't swim!' she yelled. 'I can't go into the water.'

Cora pulled off the somewhat inappropriate coat she'd been wearing, kicked away her boots and stepped out of a skirt which was far too smart for a day at the seaside. She ran into the sea. Frankie wanted to call out to her that she was still wearing her glasses and hat, but no words would come.

The seabed dipped and Cora thought that she would have to walk for quite a while until she could swim towards Henry.

He was simply a little out of his depth, but she could see he was panicking.

His flailing arms and frenzied cries came to her as she splashed through water that was now up to her waist. She called to him, 'Breathe deeply and calm down, Henry. Tread water.'

At that moment, Henry's head sank below the waves again. Cora could hear Frankie's cries from the shore. Three more strides and she would have the child.

Henry sprayed out another mouthful of sour water. His legs were beginning to tire and he started to feel that he was losing the battle. Water was wrapping itself around him and it felt heavy, thick and sticky. Cora was close to him, but how long could he hang on for? Push down, one leg to leg, one leg to leg, like riding his bicycle but with no pedals to push against.

Suddenly he felt himself being grabbed and he relaxed. The current turned him to face out to sea. Cora was behind him; he couldn't see her face but he felt her seize his shoulders. Then abruptly a hand landed hard on the back of his head and thrust him under the surface of the water. He had no time to close his mouth and he swallowed large mouthfuls of salty sea.

Just as instantly he saw the sky and he spluttered, trying to make words. 'What … ?' But before he could say any more, the hand forced him under the water again. This time, it was as if he were being held there. He sensed his body going limp. Then, all of a sudden, hands were under his arms pulling him backwards and lifting his head above the surface.

He felt a burning in his chest and his eyes stung. Second by second, sleep was coming over him.

Cora reached the shore pulling Henry behind her. She dragged him onto the wet sand and dropped him at Frankie's feet then stood looking down at the motionless boy.

Frankie bent down and turned his head towards her, slapping his cheeks. 'Henry, Henry, don't. Please don't.'

Cora saw people racing down the beach. Shannon and Jonny were among them; keeping pace with them was a young man in a T-shirt and shorts with the word 'lifeguard' across his chest. He knelt down next to Henry. Asking Frankie to step aside, he fixed his mouth onto Henry's and started to breathe into the boy. Then he raised his head, placed his hands on Henry's tiny chest and began to pump.

Time stood still for those watching. A brackish breeze nudged the matted carpet of cloud across the sky; the day was no longer warm. Jonny and Shannon held their breath, Cora panted from her exertions in the sea, and Frankie rocked on her knees by the side of her boy as tears rolled down her face.

The young man grabbed Henry's cheeks one more time, pushing his small boyish lips into a goldfish pout and covering them with his own to breathe deeply into his chest. Seagulls called above, a lamenting cry as they circled the group on the beach.

Suddenly Henry fought back against the breathing lips. As the lifeguard turned his head to one side, the little boy spewed water onto the beach before a fit of coughing shook his tiny body. Frankie fell across him with a sob so hard it split her soul.

Someone had called an ambulance and two paramedics clutching Medi-bags reached the group. 'Who's this, then?' The first paramedic had a squat rugby-player build and a generous smile hiding behind a ginger beard. He lifted Henry's head and cradled it.

'His name is Henry.' Frankie stammered out the words. 'He's ten.'

'Okay, Henry who is ten,' The smiling paramedic lifted him a little higher and sat him up. 'I think we'd better get you looked at. How do you fancy a ride in an ambulance?'

Henry nodded. The paramedics helped him stand up and covered him with a blanket.

'Are you his mum?' asked the second paramedic, a slim blonde girl with a crew cut and a nose ring.

'Yes,' said Frankie, getting to her feet.

'You'd better come with us, my love. I'm sure he's going to be fine.'

The small procession, led by the ginger paramedic and Henry, walked to the promenade where the ambulance stood. Cora stayed behind to collect the picnic things and her damp clothes from the seashore. By the time she caught up with the group on the promenade, the ambulance doors were closing. Jonny and Shannon stood on the pavement looking lost.

'Let's go back to the car. I need to get some dry clothes.' Cora shepherded them across the road. 'Then we'll go to the hospital.'

Inside the ambulance, Henry lay back on the bed. Frankie held his hand, and the paramedic girl placed an oxygen mask over his face. It hurt to breathe and his chest was sore. Whenever he closed his eyes, he saw the water swirling around his head and, for a moment just before he fell into a deep slumber, he felt the hands once more forcing him under the water.

Chapter Twenty-Two

It was late that night when Cora got back to her flat. Pushing the door closed behind her, she threw her keys onto the table. She paused in the darkness. This was when she felt most alone. Or was it lonely? She knew you could feel lonely with people around. You could be alone and feel good. Perhaps you were at your best when you felt most alone.

She didn't turn on any lights and wandered into the open-plan kitchen to pour herself a glass of wine from a half-open bottle of red that stood on the side. Taking the glass to the table by the window, she switched on a low lamp and booted up her laptop.

They had kept Henry in the hospital for about three hours. Cora had walked back to the car park with Jonny and Shannon; passing a large branch of Primark, she'd picked up a purple tracksuit for less than twelve pounds. The new tracksuit and her outlandish coat gave her the look of some mystical character from an unpublished Roald Dahl story. She also purchased a pair of red imitation Converse trainers because no one had been able to find her boots on the beach.

As they sat in the hospital waiting room, Shannon had turned to her. 'He will be all right, won't he, Cora?'

'The doctor didn't give us much information. Let's hope so.'

A hospital waiting area was an unusual place to be on a Sunday afternoon. A silent television played in one corner. Cora thought all hospitals smelled green: minty, antiseptic, Eau de Nil.

The whole experience seemed to have exhausted Jonny, who stretched out his long legs over two chairs and quickly fell asleep. Perhaps this was what encouraged Shannon to speak to her, thought Cora. Perhaps she didn't like talking when other people were around. Perhaps she liked being alone, too.

They left the hospital just after four o'clock. Henry was given pride of place in the front seat on the journey home and Cora squashed into the rear next to Shannon, with a sleepy Jonny in the far corner. The car fluctuated from being full of excited chatter to an expressive silence. In one of the silent moments, Shannon took Cora's hand and gripped it.

They pulled into a drive-through McDonald's once they had left the motorway and Frankie splashed out on meals for all of them. It was impossible for everybody to eat in the car, so they sat at a picnic table in the car park. It was while they were halfway through the meal that Cora remembered the bags of sandwiches in the boot.

'Oh,' said Frankie. 'They were so nicely wrapped up. I'll put them in the fridge when we get home and the kids can have them for lunch tomorrow, if that's all right.'

Cora was past caring.

They found a parking space not too far from the flat. Frankie unloaded all the bags from the boot and gave them to the kids to carry. Cora pulled on her coat and took her bag. 'I'm not going to come in, Frankie. Not tonight. I think everybody is terribly tired.'

'Okay,' said Frankie. She locked the car with a click of the key fob, took a step towards the flat and then turned back. 'Cora, I haven't forgotten. But when I say thank you, I want it to sort of mean something. You know?'

Cora looked down at the pavement, as if embarrassed for herself and even more for Frankie's failure to string words together. 'It's fine,' she said.

'He wouldn't be back with us if it wasn't for you. I couldn't get into the water. I couldn't … And you … It was amazing, Cora.' The tears flooded down Frankie's face.

'Stop it. You'll start me next.' Cora pulled her coat around her. 'I'll ring you tomorrow. Meet for a cappuccino?'

***

The laptop booted up, and the light from the screen illuminated Cora's face. Several quick keystrokes brought up the white page headed with the words *Frankie Baxte*r. Across the page below Frankie's name, equally spaced, Cora typed:

Jonny,
Shannon,
Henry.

She stared at the names on the page and then, pressing the spacebar, she started to type.

Chapter Twenty-Three

The day trip to the seaside changed everything. Although nobody spoke about it afterwards, it brought them all closer, and Frankie and the kids started to treat Cora as a member of the family.

Cora and Frankie never spoke about the day at Brighton. Their chats at Deli Do over a cappuccino covered all manner of things: Frankie's work; how she was finding the new car; whether the police had been back in touch about Sue Steadman's unsolved death, but never Brighton.

Frankie remembered how useless she'd felt standing on the beach, unable to run into the water. Once, she leant across the table and placed a hand on Cora's. 'Thank you.' Cora didn't reply. Frankie thought she had the look of a naughty child who found praise as uncomfortable as remonstration.

As the weeks progressed, Cora joined them for family meals at the weekend and tried to help out in the kitchen. Her culinary skills were primitive in the extreme, so Frankie would sit her at the kitchen table with Henry to chop vegetables or some other basic act of preparation. Henry and Cora never said much to each other yet they looked to have a bond of some kind. It was Henry who had brought Cora into their lives. Now he owed his life to her.

Henry knew Cora had pulled him out of the water. He knew he would probably have drowned without her help, yet he couldn't help thinking about the moments when he felt himself being pushed under the water. It troubled him. Perhaps she'd been getting her hands into the correct position to drag him to the shore – but his doubt lingered, just as the thought prevailed that the accident on the night they'd met had been her fault.

Perhaps it hadn't been him running across the road that had been the problem. He recalled how she'd staggered as she got out of the car, how she had smiled at him in the dim glow of the streetlamps. She had a strange smile, as though her skin were too tight for her face and the smile hurt her. Then he remembered all the good she had brought into their lives, the treats, the outings, and the way she'd become such a wonderful friend to them all. He pushed his darker thoughts to the farthest corner of the dustiest unused cupboard in his mind and closed the door.

Cora liked the time she spent with the family. She was like a familiar sort of mad auntie dropping in with treats, who made things better and who required no explanation. It made her feel good. It made her feel loved and needed. But Cora wanted more.

One day, Cora offered to do some child-sitting after school in the summer term. 'You can pick up a few more hours at work. I can collect them after school and bring them home. And if you're worried about my cooking skills not being up to it, I can always order in fish and chips or a Deliveroo.'

Cora knew Frankie didn't have the cash for treats. Frankie shopped well but simply on the trip that Cora often helped her make in the car on Saturdays. She came back with a few bags of shopping that had to provide meals for the week for all of them.

'And another thing …' Cora went on. 'It would save you some money. You wouldn't need that manny boy, would you?'

It made perfect sense. Frankie's last two hours at work just about covered three hours payment for Luke to look after the kids. If she didn't have to pay that, she could either work less or have more money in her pocket. Both options would help. 'I'm not sure. To be fair, I think Luke needs the work, and he's done me so many favours. It seems unfair to dump him.'

Luke Buchanan was eighteen months out of drama school. A Lancashire boy by birth, he'd come down to the Smoke from the outskirts of Manchester to follow his dreams. A place at a top drama school had kept him busy for three years and given him every degree of hope. The next eighteen months had proved tougher than he could have ever imagined. Not that he wasn't equipped for theatre or film. Six-foot, handsome, great cheekbones and an earthy Northern loutish quality that Jonny admired, Shannon was a tiny bit in love with and Henry found funny.

On two evenings each week, Luke, having worked his way through a day of unemployment, collected Henry from school. He was capable in the kitchen and could rustle up anything with chips and ice cream without help. Frankie saw his meals as an occasional diversion from her efforts to give her kids a healthy cuisine.

She liked the evenings when she arrived home from work two or three hours later than usual and found the four of them in front of the television playing some computer game. She didn't have to worry about her own supper. For a woman who fought her waistline, any evening when she could forego a meal was a bonus. She paid Luke in cash, an agreement that seemed to serve them both well.

As spring turned into summer, Luke, Shannon and Henry often turned the walk home into a trip through the park. Jonny would join them when he came out of school and they all helped Luke fulfil his passion of making films. His acting career in the past eighteen months had consisted of an episode of *Holby City*, a minor part in a fringe play in Kilburn about a serial killer, and providing the voice of a split condom for a radio ad. But Luke was mad about films. He had a digital video camera and had already made several online music promos which had scored thousands of hits on his YouTube channel.

He loved to make pastiches of his favourite films with the kids. Henry and his bike had featured in a low-budget remake of *ET*, which had involved Shannon in a leading role under a white sheet with slits for eyes. Jonny had used a sunhat and picnic rugs to create an *homage* to the spaghetti westerns of Clint Eastwood. He'd no idea what he was doing but was enamoured enough of Luke to do it.

Once the shoot was over, Luke used his idle hours to edit, add music, filters and the rest. The results were fantastic. The kids had teatime premieres and waited for Frankie to get home from work to show her what they'd been up to.

One day Luke and all three kids were in the park. Luke had his camera, and they were messing around shooting close-ups of ducks while trying to think what their next project should be. It was Henry who first spotted Cora and her remarkable coat walking along the side of the lake towards them. 'Look, it's Cora,' he shouted.

Luke swung the camera around and focused on the woman swishing towards him. The weather was warm for the green-and-yellow coat but, with her glossy red hair and outlandish outfit, she cut a splendid figure. Luke panned along the edge of the lake to follow her.

Cora walked up to the group. 'Hello, you lot.' She ruffled Henry's hair, something that she'd often seen Frankie do and had adopted as a sign of her own affection. 'How is everyone?'

'We're doing a film, Cora. Producing a film all of our own.' Henry bounced up and down with excitement. 'Luke's shooting it and directing it, and then he makes it look like a proper Netflix film.'

Luke smiled slightly. Cora held out her hand. 'May I see?' A moment of hesitation from Luke told Cora all she needed to know. 'Have you been filming me?'

'Only as you were walking along the lake towards us. Nothing special.'

'May I see it?' Cora's hand remained outstretched and Luke put the camera into it. He pressed the button to play the footage he'd shot. Cora saw herself walking along the side of the lake, first in the distance and then a sudden vicious zoom brought her features into full-frame focus on the screen. She held out the camera to him but kept hold of it. 'Delete it.'

'Sorry?'

'Delete it. I didn't give you permission to film me. Delete it.' She uttered the words in a tone that made Jonny, Shannon and Henry realise it would be wrong to say anything.

Luke had met her once before when she'd arrived at the

flat one evening to take everyone to the cinema. She'd been perfectly pleasant, if a little dismissive of him. Now he saw someone else: a steely-eyed, grim-faced witch of a woman. He reached out and pushed a button on the back of the camera. The frozen shot of Cora's face disappeared. 'All gone,' he said.

'We didn't mean anything wrong,' said Henry. 'And it would have been cool for you to be in our film.'

Cora released her grip on the camera and rounded on Henry, a smile cracking her face from ear to ear. 'That would have been nice, but your film will be much better without me. I don't look good in photographs. I always think it's better for people to remember things in their minds. We don't need all these selfies and these TikTok videos. Now would anybody like an ice cream?' She glanced back at Luke. 'Perhaps you too, Luke?'

Cora, Henry and Shannon headed towards the kiosk, which was doing a roaring trade. Luke stood holding the camera next to Jonny. 'There you go. She's quite a madam.'

'Yes,' said Jonny. 'Perhaps she's a vampire? They don't show up in photographs.' And giving a leering cackle, he ran off to join the others.

Chapter Twenty-Four

Once they had shared their stories, Lottie and Little Girl became closer. The staff at the home thought neither of them were brilliant talkers, but they spent a lot of time huddled together whenever they could. They saw no reason to explain what they had done. In their minds, burning the dolls' tea party and operating on Brandy were both reasonable acts. They didn't see themselves as bad people; it was others who felt this was a reason to keep them away from the world.

Neither of them had many visitors. At the beginning, Little Girl's father came to see her. There was a particular room for visits at the front of the house with an enormous bay window with two armchairs where visitors could sit. In the middle of the room, screwed to the floor, was a metal chair. This was where Little Girl sat. She was unrestrained, but on either side of the metal chair two steel poles rose from the floor around which they could attach a restraining belt if necessary.

It was sunny on the day Little Girl's father first came to see her. Rays of light slid through the window showing the dirt and dust on the glass and rendering her father little more than a silhouette as he sat in one of the big armchairs. He asked her if she was all right and she said yes. They didn't talk about happiness and they didn't talk about coming home. There was a great deal of silence between them. Then her father left and he never came back.

Harry came to see Lottie six weeks after she first arrived. He told her how Joan had died after the operation. Lottie didn't cry. She knew that operations went wrong; her operation on Brandy had gone wrong, too. That's why she was sitting with Harry in the bay window. She didn't like it here. 'When can I come home, Daddy?' she asked.

Harry looked at her. The words seemed painful to find. 'You're not coming home, Charlotte. I can't take care of you on my own, not now. Not after everything that has happened. You'll stay here for a while and they'll look after you. One day there may be another mummy and daddy who will want you.'

Lottie's body shook with sobs. Violent convulsions of sorrow and longing ripped her heart, more than she would ever have dreamed possible. She thought of the room full of cuddly animals. She thought of her many lovely things back in their house. She remembered how Joan had loved her and how, to begin with at any rate, she had been Joan's little princess. Was that never to be again?

Harry used the crying as an excuse to leave the room. A care worker came in, unfastened the restraining belt from around Lottie and led her back to her room.

'Do you think they will ever allow us out of here?' asked Little Girl as they sat in the garden under an old bent ash tree that had become their talking place.

'Yes, I do,' answered Lottie. 'They will give me a new mummy married to a new daddy.'

Little Girl knew that Lottie meant it, and somewhere inside she died a little.

Chapter Twenty-Five

Luke Buchanan lived in a shared house made up of bedsits that wouldn't have disgraced a seventies' student sitcom. He might have to spend most of his acting career unemployed but one thing he valued above everything was his independence.

He loved living alone. The tall Edwardian house, which he presently called home, consisted of nine separate little hovels. Luke's was first floor at the back, overlooking a junk-filled yard. The lettings agent had described it to him as a period studio apartment, which in reality meant a room with a large single bed in one corner. A dining table sat under the window and a screened-off kitchen comprised an old gas cooker, a tiny refrigerator and a ramshackle gas boiler fastened to the wall to provide boiling water. It all added to the glamour of having his own place.

Luke had acquired two comfortable chairs, one from a tip and one from IKEA, though it was hard to tell which was which. His pride and joy was a shelving unit he'd built into an alcove corner by the bed. It accommodated all his books and had a pull-down work surface for his computer. It was here he spent most of his time assembling his film pastiches.

He'd spent the previous day putting together the footage he'd shot in the park, a motley assemblage of ducks, people at leisure, Henry, Jonny and Shannon. Clever editing had turned it into an almost Hitchcockian thriller.

He'd used the shots of Cora. He still hadn't figured out the woman's reaction to being filmed; the look in her eyes as she'd ordered him to delete the footage made it clear that she had some sort of problem. But whatever it was, Luke didn't take it as sufficient reason to lose good shots of her sashaying along the side of the lake in that stupid coat. Now, with all the footage transposed into black and white and a stock track of some Rachmaninov, it was a classy piece about a serial duck killer. He'd been proud of holding out the camera and pressing the save button on the footage before he had showed her a black screen. She wasn't as clever as she thought.

He finished editing the film late in the evening. As invariably happened when he'd created a masterpiece, he found himself on a high, one that was impossible to contain within four poorly decorated walls.

The good thing about the cashless society, thought Luke, was that you never checked your wallet because it was always empty. But cards could buy you an evening of pleasure and that was what he needed.

A quick splash and change of T-shirt and, as most other people were thinking of heading to bed, he hopped onto a night bus into the centre of town. He was intent on finding some female company though he expected he'd end up settling for a few drinks.

It was one of those rare nights when he was lucky and found both. He knew a club in the centre of town which guaranteed he'd bump into other out-of-work actors. Halfway through his second pint, he found himself sitting next to Polly. Vivacious, blonde and with a cut-glass accent that Luke found highly arousing, she too had found herself thrown into the world of unemployment after drama school.

Polly made it obvious from the start that he was 'her sort of thing'. The night pulsed on and the two of them found themselves back at Polly's flat in the centre of the city overlooking the river. Luke gaped in amazement that anyone five months out of drama school could be living here.

'It's my parents' gaff. They're away, ya? So, it's all mine at the mo. I'm just so lucky I don't have to live in some dump in the suburbs, ya?' Luke knew he wouldn't be taking her home.

He woke just before midday. The other side of the bed was empty but he could hear sounds from the kitchen where last night they had enjoyed an extra couple of glasses of wine before indulging in their horizontal couplings. He found his pants and pulled them on.

'Morning,' Polly greeted him.

'Morning.' He walked over to grab her around the waist.

She turned, pecked him on the cheek and moved away. 'No time for that. I've got an audition. My agent rang this morning. I was leaving you a cup of coffee and a note.'

'Right.'

As an out-of-work actor, Luke found it impossible not to feel jealous when anyone else got a sniff of a role. It made no difference to him that Polly was female, blonde and five foot six; he knew he could have played the role she was going up for this afternoon better than her.

She headed out and he took his time wandering round the flat with its river views. He finished his coffee and found the rest of his clothes. He thought he'd wait until getting home before showering, but one look at the power-shower monster lurking in the bathroom and he changed his mind. Hot-water heaven, and he luxuriated in it for quite a while.

His cards were maxed out after his night on the town, so walking home was his only option. Five-and-a-half miles would up his step count for the day, and he wouldn't feel guilty spending most of the evening lying on the bed. He hadn't had a lot of sleep; it had been a magical night for which he was now suffering.

He put his key in the door of the house and pushed open the front door. The guy who lived in the studio apartment at the front and acted as liaison with their landlord was in the hall picking up some post. 'Hi, man. You look rough. Good night?'

Luke smiled. 'Yeah. Wonderful night. Nothing for me, then?'

The guy shook his head. 'No. Circulars and a couple of things for Maanuv upstairs. Nothing for us.'

Luke squeezed past him and made his way upstairs. He let himself into his room and flopped on the bed. There was a knock on the door. The guy from downstairs stood there.

'Sorry, meant to tell you. The landlord sent somebody round this morning to deal with your faulty boiler. It needed checking. He let himself in, so I just wanted to let you know.'

Luke looked puzzled. 'Not sure I have a faulty boiler.' He walked into the kitchen cubbyhole and turned on the tap. The flame lit on the boiler and hot water gushed into the sink. 'Seems to be working fine.'

'He's obviously done the job, then.'

Luke didn't think any more about it; domestic management wasn't something he'd ever been interested in.

He grabbed his laptop and settled back on the bed to find

something to stream. A documentary about a one-legged American baseball player who may have killed two of his wives came up as recommended and he clicked on the screen. As John Humboldt the Third started to tell his story, Luke's eyes started to close. His antics of the previous night were beginning to catch up with him and it wasn't long before he closed the laptop lid, turned over and headed for sleep.

He might have thought otherwise about domestic management if he'd known he wasn't going to wake up.

Chapter Twenty-Six

Frankie had never thought of herself as a bad person or a good person. She considered herself to be someone who got on with life. Sometimes she did things that she regretted afterwards, something she'd become more aware of as her family increased.

With the children dependent on her, she tried to manage her reactions but she found it hard. Her response in the supermarket car park was one occasion when, as Jonny would put it, 'You just lost it, Mum.' She worked incredibly hard not to lose it and yet sometimes everything seemed to conspire against her.

They all had a glorious summer. Having Cora around helped in so many ways and made things easier and more enjoyable. They had days out, and Shannon and Jonny seemed much keener to join in than they'd ever done when Frankie had suggested an outing. Frankie liked to think of them as a little group: the four of them and Auntie Cora, as Henry had started to call her on occasion.

School had started nearly a week ago, but getting back into the routine of making sure everybody was ready to leave at the right time was not yet the finely tuned machine it should be. Wednesday felt like the toughest day of the week, stranded as it was between two weekends. This particular Wednesday morning, nobody seemed able to do anything right.

Frankie laid the breakfast things on the table. She'd got up early to give herself some peace in the bathroom and put on a simple outfit, smarter than usual. This afternoon she was meeting with Mr Breen, the call supervisor. There was a vacancy for deputy supervisor and Frankie knew she had an excellent chance of getting the job. Same hours or less, more money, increased responsibility and a greater sense of achievement.

That was important to Frankie. Too many times in life she'd been told she would amount to nothing; too many times she'd felt pushed aside. She'd made an outstanding job of being a mum, she knew that, and yet the three people who'd seen her do it were the last people to realise it. Shannon was unlikely to come out with positive feedback on Frankie's parenting skills – or feedback on anything else, come to that.

Frankie was aware that Mr Breen liked her. In the kitchen on a coffee break, he often stayed a little longer than necessary and made conversation. Twice he'd asked her out. She'd said she was sorry, but she had to get back to the kids. If getting the supervisor's job meant being asked out a third time, then Frankie had decided she'd say yes.

'Henry, Shannon,' she called out down the hall. 'It's half past seven. Get yourselves up. You're going to be late.'

She filled the teapot, put out orange-juice glasses, cereal bowls, crunchy-nut cornflakes for Henry. A slice of toast for Shannon, which would almost certainly remain uneaten. Table laid. One of the things Frankie did every day was try to instil order, keep a nice kitchen like her mother had done.

There was a commotion outside the bathroom. Frankie went to see what the trouble was. Henry was battering on the door.

'Shannon ran in, Mum, and it's my turn and she'll be ages now and I'll be late.'

Frankie sighed. 'Wouldn't have happened if you'd got up earlier.' Henry's face fell. 'Come and have your cereal and then we'll knock on the door and get her out of there.'

Henry dashed into the kitchen in his pyjamas. Frankie stood savouring her cup of tea for a second while he wolfed down his breakfast. He darted back down to the bathroom door and banged on it. 'You gotta get out, Shannon. Mum says you got to get out.' He banged on the door again.

The door opposite flew open. Jonny, all bed hair and sleep face, stuck his head out. 'What's wrong? What's everybody shouting about?'

'Shannon's got the bathroom and it wasn't her turn.'

The bathroom door opened. Shannon emerged, body and hair swathed in towels. She pushed past Henry and went back into the room she shared with her mother without a word.

'There you go,' said Frankie. 'Your turn.'

Henry dived into the bathroom. Jonny disappeared back into the bedroom and Shannon closed the door to Frankie's room. A moment of peace. Frankie sipped her tea.

Five minutes later, the compact kitchen resembled a game of Twister, everybody reaching for cereal or toast, struggling to pack schoolbags and finish dressing. Frankie stood by the door, car keys in hand, repeating, 'Somebody is going to be late.'

Henry flew back into the kitchen, bag hanging from his shoulder, and bumped straight into Shannon, who hopped out of his way as she was finishing a glass of cranberry juice. There was an outbreak of moans, hoots and mirth as the cranberry juice poured down the front of Henry's white school shirt.

Shannon giggled. 'Oops.'

Henry looked on the brink of tears. 'Mum!'

'Fasten your blazer, nobody will see it.'

'I'm reading in assembly,' wailed Henry. 'I have to take my blazer off. I'm doing the New Testiments.'

Shannon stood at the door and laughed. 'You? Reading?'

Henry managed to get out the words 'clumsy bitch' under his breath before thumping her in the breast. Shannon screamed, mainly for effect. Frankie pushed her way across the kitchen to separate them. 'Henry Baxter, you do not hit your sister and you do not use language like that, whether you're covered in cranberry juice or not.'

At this point Jonny emerged from the bedroom fully dressed, hair immaculately dishevelled. As soon as he saw Henry, he couldn't resist a smirk. 'Been paintballing?'

Henry lashed out at Jonny, who shielded himself from his brother's blow as Frankie caught the back of Henry's blazer and dragged him through the kitchen. She hauled him out of the front door and stepped straight into Cora. Henry glanced up at Cora, shame faced. Shannon piled into them in her attempt not to miss a lift to school and Jonny sauntered out of the flat, locking the door as he left.

'Everybody off to school?' asked Cora.

Frankie gritted her teeth. This was the last thing she needed.

Jonny headed off down the path but Henry couldn't resist getting Cora on his side. He flung open his blazer to reveal the stain on his shirt. 'Look, Cora. Shannon threw juice all over me. This is my shirt for this week. Mum doesn't have any clean ones and I've got to read the New Testiments in assembly and everybody will laugh.'

'That's not good, is it? What can I do to help?'

Frankie pushed Henry towards the car. 'Nothing, thanks, Cora. He'll deal with it. We all have to learn that sometimes life throws cranberry juice at you.'

Henry and Shannon clambered into the back of the car, Henry resolving to punch his sister again at the first opportunity.

'I could walk him to school if you want, Frankie. We could stop at that bargain shop on the high street. I could pick up a clean white shirt for him for a couple of pounds and he wouldn't be too late. Shall I take him?'

'No, thanks.' Frankie got into the driver's seat and pulled the car door closed. Cora was still speaking, so she wound down the window. She turned on the ignition.

'It wouldn't take a moment and it would make him feel better if he's got something important to do. And I'd pay for the shirt. I'm more than happy to.'

Cora's words made no sense in Frankie's head. It was the last thing she needed on a morning such as this. She thrust the car into gear and leant out of the window toward Cora. 'Learn when not to interfere. Yes? So, for now, fuck off.'

She pushed her foot to the floor and the car sped away.

***

The interview with Mr Breen did not go well. After pushing Henry and Shannon out of the car at their respective schools, Frankie screeched into the car park twenty minutes late for her shift. She clocked on and raced to her booth, dumped her bag on the desk, put on her headset and booted up her computer. Mr Breen came over.

When Frankie had first met him she'd been sure he was gay

with his glowing cheeks, swept-back blond hair and highly coordinated sense of fashion. According to several of the girls who worked alongside her, he most certainly wasn't.

The Techno Factory was a contact centre that provided technical support and guidance to customers who had bought technology from independent websites. That was the official description; in truth, it was an office of thirty staff, mostly female, who knew little about technology. They sat at computer screens and answered calls from the public. They were guided through the solutions with on-screen prompts. If those didn't solve the problem, the staff generally resorted to that most cunning piece of technological support advice: 'Have you tried turning it off and turning it back on again?'

Frankie liked working there. The room always hummed with conversation but you didn't have to talk to people. In fact, personal chat was against phone-room regulations. Mr Breen wandered round the booths once or twice an hour. Often he plugged his headset into someone's computer to listen in on their call and check they were providing advice according to the Techno Factory's code of conduct. He could have logged on and listened to calls from his office at one end of the floor, where he sat watching the staff through an enormous glass wall, but these personal checks gave Mr Breen an excuse for increasing his physical proximity to the girls who worked for him. On more than one occasion, a casual brushing of his crotch against a shoulder had led to the back row of the Odeon cinema, two margaritas and a bed for the night. Most of the staff avoided him.

'Morning, Frankie. Cutting it a bit fine.'

'Yes, Terry. Sorry, one of those mornings. Bit of a problem getting the kids off to school.'

'Don't let it turn into a regular thing.' He stooped down nearer to her ear. 'And don't forget we've got an interview scheduled at 11.30.'

'How could I?' smiled Frankie.

'Looking forward to it.' Mr Breen moved down the line and plugged his headset into Monica Savage's computer. His face collapsed into a grimace of alarm.

***

Cora paid for her coffee in Deli Do and strolled down the high street and into the park. A Wednesday morning in school term and there were few people around. Just how Cora liked it.

She set off down the No Dogs side of the lake. She preferred it there, with its manicured lawns and tidy flower beds running down to the water's edge. The memorial benches on this side of the lake seemed more tranquil.

She sat on the third bench she came to. There was a powerful smell of mown grass mixed with the aroma of lakeside flowers. Two swans glided over in the hope of breadcrumbs but soon left her alone.

She hadn't meant to offend Frankie or to interfere. She'd made a kind offer. Most mothers would have jumped at it. But not Frankie. Cora wanted to help – that was what being a friend meant, didn't it?

Cora had few friends. She didn't seem to have the knack of turning casual acquaintance into friendship. She'd had a wonderful summer – the trip to the seaside, expeditions into the country and on several occasions she'd dog-sat for Dimwit while Frankie had taken the children to the cinema for an afternoon.

This morning she'd been passing, hoping she could offer to do the same. Some days Dimwit was left in the house and even Cora, as a non-dog lover, knew that was wrong. On other days Frankie's ageing neighbour, Mr Jenkinson, looked after the dog for a few hours in return for an occasional basket of shopping.

What had upset Cora was the anger with which Frankie had shouted at her from the car. They were friends; you should be kind to your friends. That's what everybody said. You had to be kind. All the newscasts, even weather forecasts, now ended with a plastic smile and the words 'Be safe and be kind'. That's all Cora was trying to do, be kind.

In many ways being kind was the last thing she wanted to do. Being kind for no reason and no payment made no sense to her. Yet she tried.

Perhaps now it was time to stop trying.

***

Terry Breen clicked his mouse and closed down his computer screen. 'Thanks, Frankie – sorry, *Mrs Baxter*. That's all the information I need. One final question. What makes you think you're suited to being deputy supervisor?' He grinned at her and an oleaginous expression crossed his face.

Frankie wondered what his aftershave was. She thought it might be Market Day, smelling as it did of citrus and decaying cabbage. She grinned back. This needed to go smoothly. She'd dealt with all his questions and he seemed happy.

'I think I'm well trained. I think I understand what we do here and I have a great record for my call delivery. I'm popular enough with the girls, but I'm not one of the gang so much that I couldn't tell people when they need to pull their socks up.' She'd rehearsed the answer in her head the previous night but somehow, as it spilled out into the air, it didn't sound quite as good as it had done.

'I think you're right. I suppose the last question is, what do you like to drink on a night out and what do you like for breakfast?' Breen gurgled like a radiator trying to get to full heat.

Frankie waited a moment then looked him straight in the face. 'I don't get chance for a night out and, as far as breakfast goes, I have three kids to get ready for school. I tend to put my social life last.'

'Be good if I had a chance to find out. Particularly if I'm going to propose you for deputy supervisor. I think we should get a little closer, see how things go. I've always liked the fuller figure.' With horror, Frankie watched him wink his right eye.

'Sorry?'

'You know what I mean.'

'You can't say that to me. This is a job interview. If I have a word with HR, you're finished.'

'They won't do anything.' He adjusted the angle of his computer monitor and gazed back at her, eyes wide, innocent. 'It's awfully hard for me to recommend you for the position if I don't really know you, isn't it?'

Frankie took a deep breath. 'Well, if getting to know me means having a drink and sharing your fucking Weetabix, it's not gonna happen.'

'Mind your language, Mrs Baxter. This is a formal interview.' Breen stood up. 'I think I've got everything I need for now. Thank you for your time.' He crossed to the door.

Frankie stood and watched him. 'So that's it, is it? I don't stand a chance of getting a job I'm dead right for unless I let you get into my knickers?'

'I couldn't possibly say. The key thing is that, as far as the record goes, I've done nothing wrong. Everything's been between you and me.' He held open the door.

'Done nothing wrong? Well, let's make them see it from another angle, shall we?' With that Frankie reached across his desk, pulled the computer keyboard towards her and hurled it straight out of the open door.

Mr Breen gulped air like an overexcited carp. Frankie moved round to the computer monitor. Picking it up in both hands, she heaved it at the glass that separated Mr Breen's office from the call-centre contact room. Thirty operators turned mid-call as the monitor smashed through the glass and onto the floor. It was quickly followed by several filing baskets, two large leather-bound directories, an iPad and a whiteboard.

Mr Breen backed out of the room. 'Somebody call security. She's gone bonkers.'

Silence froze the air. Eventually it was broken by the voice of Monica Savage. 'Oh, bloody hell, Terry. You didn't ask her out, did you?'

Chapter Twenty-Seven

Little Girl and Lottie continued to delight in each other's company. When one was feeling down, the other would cheer her up. After lots of smiles and gentle pleading with the staff, they now shared a room in the attic at the children's home. They spent as much time in it as they could.

The local authority provided a teacher for the younger children in the home during the day, whereas most of the older children went out to a local school and returned to the home in the evenings. Little Girl and Lottie knew that next year school awaited them.

'Next year, Charlotte, you'll be at a proper school. They won't allow you to behave like this. Now stop talking and finish your work,' said Miss Threapleton towards the end of a morning lesson where her patience was wearing thin.

Lottie picked up her pen and started to doodle. She knew there was nothing much Miss Threapleton could do other than send her to her room, and often that was preferable to being in the lesson. She smirked at Little Girl and they both put their heads down, pens in hands racing across the pages of their textbooks.

The classroom door opened and Mr Dale stepped inside. Whenever Mr Dale came into a room, everybody looked up.

He was the senior superintendent of the home and, as such, responsible for all their care. It was Mr Dale who handed out various punishments or authorised treats.

He was the Mr Bumble of his day and not unlike the Dickensian creation in manner and appearance. A cheery face with a deep, receding hairline, a swarthy complexion and a badly shaved upper lip made him frightening for the younger children and a figure of fun for the teenagers. He had picked up the nickname Dirty Dale. Lottie and Little Girl knew that wasn't down to his olive complexion.

Miss Threapleton turned to him from the blackboard. 'May I help you, Mr Dale?'

'Yes, you may, Miss Threapleton. I require a conversation with Charlotte. Would you join me in my office?'

Lottie glanced at Little Girl. What could she have done? She wasn't in trouble again, was she? She piled her notebooks into her school bag and edged her way between the desks to the front of the classroom. She walked past Mr Dale and into the corridor as he held the door open for her. He led the way down to his office.

Ashmere Court consisted of two large Edwardian houses knocked into one with an unsympathetic two-storey red-brick extension set to one side. Mr Dale's office occupied the front drawing room of one house. It was a cavernous affair with an odd smell; it reminded Lottie of the beer bottles that Harry had drunk from at meals. A vast desk sat in the centre of a bay window and bookcases filled two of the walls.

In front of the desk were two comfortable chairs in which a man and a woman were sitting. Mr Dale put his hand on Lottie's shoulder, led her around the desk and took his seat facing the couple. 'This is Charlotte,' he said. 'Charlotte, this is Mr and Mrs Cooper.'

The couple smiled. Lottie kept her face still, reserving judgement. Mr Cooper was sporting a red tracksuit top and had a cruel nose and greying hair. He made Lottie think of a vulture, an unfortunate analogy since Mrs Cooper resembled a plump little hen. A hen about to lay eggs. She had a bright little blotchy face, straggly blonde hair and looked like one of those toys that refused to fall down if it was pushed over.

'Say hello, Charlotte,' said Mr Dale. He started to fill out a form which lay on the desk in front of him. He looked neither at her nor at the Coopers.

Lottie managed a fairly tight-lipped hello. Mr Cooper nodded. Mrs Cooper clucked into life. 'Hello, Lottie, it's lovely to meet you at last we've seen lots of pictures of you but you're a much prettier girl in real life.' She spoke with no punctuation and without taking breath.

Lottie wondered why they had looked at pictures of her. What did the woman mean?

The woman was grinning. 'That's an awfully pretty dress do you like pretty dresses? I know most girls wear jeans and things don't they but no matter when you come and live with us you can wear whatever you like.'

Lottie's bottom lip narrowed. What did this woman mean – 'when you live with us'? Nobody had mentioned anything about living with another couple. She lived here in the home. She had a bedroom that she shared with Little Girl. She was wearing a dress simply because they had to wear a dress on schooldays.

She didn't want a couple to buy her clothes. She didn't want a home with people she didn't know. They would let her down, like Harry and Joan had. She'd been imprisoned in this home, and yet here she had found a friend in Little Girl. She didn't want that to end, not now, not today, not tomorrow, not ever.

Chapter Twenty-Eight

Frankie parked the car on Village Way next to the gates at the south of the park. She couldn't bear to go home.

This wasn't how the day should have ended. She'd been told to take her things and get out of the office. They'd suspended her pending further enquiries, and she knew that meant they had fired her. It was a question of who had said what in the room. There was no proof that Terry Breen had made his ridiculous request.

She hadn't cried. Inside, she was angry with herself. She could have played it better and pretended that she would go on a date with him. He'd probably have been foolish enough to give her the job before the date. But inside, she knew she couldn't have done that. She couldn't lie; her parents had brought her up to speak the truth. Yet this was not the first time the truth had got her into trouble.

She had let the anger wash over her like a child filling in a colouring book, daubing the figures in one colour. She'd let it push through her without a second thought. Mind you, she'd aimed a pretty expert shot with the computer monitor. The entire glass wall had come crashing down.

She walked into the park. When she saw the dog signs, she thought of driving home to collect Dimwit from Mr Jenkinson, but instead she set off down the No Dogs side to one of her favourite benches. Alderman Parkin's bench was in a peaceful place on a little terrace by the edge of the lake.

She watched the moorhens, the grebes and all the birds she'd learned to identify from the large noticeboard at the water's edge. She wasn't sure how long she sat there. She must have closed her eyes and fallen asleep.

'I expect I'm the last person you want to see.'

Frankie opened her eyes. The first thing she saw was a snatch of the green-and-yellow coat. She wondered why Cora wore it almost every day. Not for the first time did the red hair, the coat and this morning's yellow training shoes with a hint of orange bring to mind the clowns Frankie had found so unfunny and frightening in the circus as a child.

'Hello. Not sure I'm good company. Not been the best of days.'

'You'd better tell me all about it, then,' said Cora, settling herself on the bench next to Frankie. 'After all, that's what friends are for, isn't it?'

Cora listened to Frankie's story. She could see her flick between anger and despair: anger that she'd let Breen put her in such a position and despair at feeling so helpless. She finished the story.

'Thanks for listening.' Frankie suddenly became more tearful.

Cora didn't do touching; she found it painful to console and hug people. Her entire body tensed as she laid a hand on Frankie's forearm and patted it. She didn't know what to suggest. She found it hard to understand why Frankie was so distressed. Surely there were other jobs? Not that Cora knew much about work. She found it hard to comprehend Frankie's

127

behaviour. 'Is it a good time for a pot of tea?' she asked.

Frankie sniffed, nodded and stood up. Together they strode along the side of the lake. They were turning onto the central path up to the north gate when a crocodile of young children came towards them. They stepped to one side to let them pass. The youngsters all wore red sweatshirts and black shorts or skirts. There were four adults wearing the same red shirts with yellow hi-viz jackets with the words *Teaching Assistant* on the back. The crocodile moved in an exceedingly orderly fashion, rippling with animated chatter as the children continued their afternoon trip into the park.

Once it had passed, Cora stepped onto the path and they headed towards Deli Do.

***

'That's something I'd like to do,' said Frankie, tipping another spoonful of sugar into her cup.

'Teaching assistant?' Cora sipped her tea. 'But you've got three marvellous children.'

'I know, and I love them, but I don't get paid for looking after them. Imagine if I did. What if I had a job where I got paid for doing something I do well and I enjoy? Something where I didn't have to deal with idiots who don't know their USB from their arsehole?'

'I certainly know what the latter is,' said Cora.

Frankie spluttered into her tea. She liked Cora and loved the fact that she could still surprise her.

'You'd like a job working in childcare?' asked Cora.

'Yes, I would. I don't have a chance of getting one, but it's what I'd like.'

'Don't give up before you've started. Think positive.'

Frankie laughed. 'With three kids and no cash coming in, it's hard to jump for joy.'

Cora finished her tea and picked up her bag. 'Things to do, people to see!'

Frankie stood to embrace her. She felt Cora stiffen. 'Thanks for today, Cora. And I'm sorry about this morning.'

Cora pulled back out of the embrace and laughed. 'I think cranberry juice can bring out the worst in all of us.'

***

Back in her flat, Cora gazed out of the window while she waited for her computer to boot up. She loved watching people in the park through the trees, moving around like little ants, scurrying along their own path with no pattern or reason. She was far enough removed to be a passive observer, untroubled by their strife, but knowing that, like ants, they were so easy to trample.

The computer flickered into life. It was getting past its sell-by date. Everything took a bit longer than Cora would like. Clicking onto her Frankie Baxter document, she checked what was now three full pages of text. Then she started to type:

Childcare.

Job.

Opportunity …

Chapter Twenty-Nine

It was five days later when the email arrived. Frankie's contract with the Techno Factory hadn't ended, but she'd cleared her desk when she left and had not been back. Nobody had requested her to return the company laptop she used at home, so the kids were using it. She allowed Shannon and Henry access for a couple of hours each night under the pretence of doing homework. Jonny had managed to invest in a Smart phone and tablet. Frankie knew she should have asked where he'd earned the money to buy them but she wanted him to know that she trusted him, so she decided to let sleeping iPads lie.

Now her days advising people on how to deal with hardware and software problems were over, Frankie didn't spend much time on the laptop. She did online banking and would occasionally look things up, although she preferred the kids to do that on their phones. Once a day or so, she opened the laptop to go through her email. That was when she saw it: a little red number six clinging to the outside of a blue circle on her menu bar.

Once she had turned down offers of limitless wealth from Nigeria, three phishing emails from a bank and an imaginary building society, and an offer to sign up to meditation apps for inner calm, there was one unopened email.

Childcare assistant vacancy application PU 791F, it said in the subject box. She knew all about not clicking on strange emails but the subject matter caught her attention.

Jonny had told her about a programme he'd watched on TV revealing how your phone could listen to you. 'That's how they know what adverts to send,' he'd told her.

She'd been sceptical. 'I think my phone listens to me about as much as you three do,' she'd said. Now, seeing the email, she thought about her phone resting on the table in Deli Do last week while she'd chatted to Cora about being a childcare assistant. Was she putting two and two together and making five? There didn't seem to be any other answer.

Sure enough, the email contained a dream job opportunity.

Develop your career in childcare in our award-winning day nursery!

Are you looking for a new rewarding and challenging role? We are seeking a confident, knowledgeable and enthusiastic candidate to join our friendly, passionate team and continue our high-quality provision.

The right candidate will have a strong work ethic and be enthusiastic about learning new skills. You will complete your childcare qualification with Langley Training, who will work closely with the nursery to support you through your course.

This is a full-time position working 42.5 hours a week between 7.30am and 6.00pm Monday–Friday.

We have an amazing learning environment which includes 10 playrooms, a sensory room, a sports hall, a large outdoor learning environment, a baby garden and sand pit. We are just a three-minute walk from Langley overground station.

These posts are covered by the Rehabilitation of Offenders (Exceptions) Act 1975. If successful, you will be required to apply to the disclosure and barring service for an enhanced disclosure.

The job description made Frankie sit up. Getting paid to do something she loved and was good at? Wasn't that what she'd said to Cora? It was a dream in an email. And training was provided for the successful applicant!

She clicked on the link at the bottom of the mail and, sure enough, it took her straight through to the website for Langley Park. It looked like too good an opportunity to miss; now there was just the problem of writing a wonderful application letter and dazzling CV that would secure her an interview.

There comes a point in the life of most mothers when they realise that they don't know their daughters. Few have remained unsurprised by their female offspring, no matter how close they are. Over tea at the kitchen table that evening – oven chips and a fairly divided steak and mushroom pie – Frankie mentioned that she was thinking of a change of job and would need a CV. None of them seem surprised at the news.

Henry asked, 'Does that mean we've got to move, Mum?' and needed reassuring that it didn't. Then Shannon uttered what had to be the most remarkable sentence Frankie had ever heard her construct. 'I could make your CV for you, Mum. On the computer. I know how to do those.'

'Can you?' Frankie tried not to sound too astonished.

'Yes. I've made them at school. I did one for Mr Betts, the chemistry teacher, when he was leaving. I want to work in a publishing and graphic design when I leave school.' She shovelled another eight chips into her mouth.

'Thank you, my love. That would be great.'

Later that evening, Frankie sat at the kitchen table watching in awe as Shannon's fingers whizzed across the keyboard, moving page borders and headings, changing font sizes, and producing what in Frankie's eyes was easily the most professional CV she'd ever seen. After another half hour spent completing the online application form and attaching the document, Frankie pressed send.

Shannon mooched through into the living room and flopped onto the sofa.

'Thanks love. That was really helpful,' said Frankie.

The reply, unintelligible as it was, established that Shannon had reverted to full grunt mode.

***

'And you've applied?' said Cora

'About four or five days ago. Haven't heard anything yet. Don't think I've ever spent so much time checking my email.'

'Good luck. It sounds right up your street, exactly what you're looking for.' The two of them were trying out Snifters, a wine bar at the bottom end of the high street opposite the park gates.

'I left Jonny in control. I had to tell somebody I've done something about it. All my mates were people from work and I don't see them any more. And as you and I were talking about jobs the other day, it seemed right to let you know.'

Cora smiled. 'Well done you.'

They spent the rest of the evening finishing two bottles of an expensive Pinot Grigio Cora had put on the table when Frankie had arrived.

'Better make sure that Jonny's got the other two in bed.'

Frankie slurred her words. A night out with a mate and a bottle of wine each was not something she was used to. Cora seemed fine, but Frankie tripped on the step leaving the wine bar and then on the kerb outside the park. They parted at the gates and Cora headed up the hill.

Frankie didn't actually know where Cora lived. She talked of living by the park, but there were lots of houses and blocks of flats along Parkside, some of them rather grand. Perhaps next time they met, she should try and get an invitation?

Frankie stumbled along the pavement, following the outside of the park towards the south gates from where she could turn for home. The evening had tipped into darkness and along this particular road it was a question of moving from pool to pool of streetlight.

She'd been walking for about five minutes when she heard a noise behind her. Not sure whether she should turn and check, she stopped and bent down, pretending to tie her shoelace and steadying herself with a hand on the railing. As she did so, she peered back over her shoulder. The street was empty, the three pools of light behind her clear, their edges defined by velvet darkness.

She set off once again and, sure enough, there was the noise again. It was from a hard shoe, not a stiletto but something low, clicking on the pavement. Frankie crossed the road, glancing back from where she'd come. Bushes poked through the park railings and the darkness beyond seemed forbidding and impenetrable. On the other side of the road there were a number of driveways and gardens bordered by hedges. Lots of places for someone to hide, she thought.

It might have been the wine, but she felt very nervous and

alone. She could see the main road ahead of her. That was where she needed to be so she would feel safe.

She quickened her step, taking comfort from the knowledge that if someone rushed at her she could run up to one of the houses she was passing and bang on the door. She hurried forward and was almost at the main road with its well-lit pavements when she heard a metallic clash and a stifled groan.

Stopping dead in her tracks, she turned. Something about the sound was familiar. She took a deep breath. 'You'd better come out. I know who you are.'

Chapter Thirty

Frankie had a sore head. She managed to burn the toast and give Henry the wrong cereal. She couldn't recall the last time she'd had a hangover, but there was something satisfying about it. Part of her knew this was what her soul had been missing, some 'me time'. Although loving her children was still the fundamental reason for her existence, she realised she'd do it better if she had a little happiness in her own life.

Her stumbling around didn't pass unnoticed.

'Are you ill?' asked Jonny. Remarkably, all three children were ready to leave the house and Frankie was still sitting, clutching a cup of coffee.

'No, I'm fine. I went out with Cora. We had a bottle of wine. Two, if I'm being honest.' She chuckled. 'I was a little merry. Cora had to escort me home.'

***

Having been called out as the mystery stalker, Cora had stepped out of a nearby driveway. 'I knew it was you.' Frankie started to laugh. 'What on earth are you doing?'

'Someone has to make sure you get home okay. You were a bit of a sight crossing the road when you left me. I thought a walk round the block would do me good and let me keep an eye on you.' Cora moved into the light.

'I'd hoped you *were* a stalker.' Frankie giggled. 'Come to get me.'

'Of course not. Well, not yet anyway.' Cora laughed and reached out to steady her. Frankie hooked arms and they wandered along the street, Cora trying to provide a steady anchor for Frankie's wobbling.

'Do you need me to come in with you?' asked Cora as they arrived at the corner by Frankie's flat.

'God, no! Kids should be in their rooms. I'll just go straight to bed. Promish.'

Cora watched her struggle to find the keyhole and close the door behind her. She remembered the times she herself had been the worse for wear. Not for a long time now, though. She began the brief walk home.

***

Frankie was extra careful driving Shannon and Henry to school, and her head seemed to clear on her return home. She gave a little yell of pleasure when she saw that her parking space remained unoccupied.

Walking across the grass to the front door of the flat, she heard her name. 'Mrs Baxter, could we have a word?'

***

'No sugar, thanks.' Detective Sergeant Webb watched Frankie put the tea in front of him and slide the sugar bowl in his direction. She'd ladled three spoons of sugar into her own cup. In the corner of the kitchen stood the junior constable, PC Ashley.

DS Webb debated whether to try the steaming drink. 'I'm

sorry we haven't been in touch for a while. We had a couple of things to sort out.'

Frankie nodded and looked at them suspiciously. He hadn't told her the purpose of their visit.

'But I'm happy to tell you, we're a little less inclined to consider you as a leading suspect in the case of Mrs Steadman.'

Frankie couldn't help letting out an audible sigh of relief. 'What's changed your mind?'

'I'm not at liberty to tell you everything, Mrs Baxter.' Webb sipped his tea and winced at the heat of the liquid. 'We have the time you left the building logged onto the CCTV. It seems that Mrs Steadman may have taken a call on her mobile phone after that.'

'So it doesn't take Inspector Morse to work out she was alive when I left. Which is what I said all the time.'

DS Webb moistened his lips and looked at the tea again. 'Could I have a spot more milk in this, love?'

Frankie reached into the fridge, smiling to herself. Within the last five minutes, she'd moved from 'suspect' in a murder investigation to 'love'. She poured a large glug of milk into his tea, hoping it would cool it down quickly so he could drink it and go.

'I do have one question for you though,' Webb continued. 'Yes?'

'The incident in the supermarket car park. You had someone with you. Who was it? Robocop didn't get a note of it at the time.'

PC Ashley sipped his tea and avoided eye contact with anyone in the room.

'That was my friend, Cora,' Frankie said. 'Cora Walsh. She'd been shopping with me.'

Webb took a substantial quaff of the cooler tea. 'You wouldn't happen to have an address for her by any chance?'

Chapter Thirty-One

Little Girl felt her heart would crack when Lottie told her about Mr and Mrs Cooper's visit. She couldn't bear the thought of being separated from her best friend. She needn't have worried; a few days after the interview in Mr Dale's office, Lottie was told by one of the senior staff that her move into foster care wouldn't be going ahead. The Coopers had failed some test.

Lottie found herself torn between the expectation of a fresh life and staying with her dearest friend. The possibility of being separated seemed to have intensified their intimacy and they spent every hour they could together. Up in the attic room, they told each other about life before the home. Neither of them attempted any explanation for what had brought them there, but both had memories of happier times. Lottie, never having had proper parents as such, listened with envy to Little Girl's story.

'I knew they didn't like me, but I always thought it was something I'd done wrong. Nobody told me what it was. They were kind in their own way. We had a wonderful day at the seaside once, the only one I can remember. A long drive in the car and a walk across some fields to a tall white building that stood next to the sea with two little white houses at the bottom with green windows. It was the most perfect place. I hoped that one day I could live in one of the little white houses and stand in my garden and watch the sea.'

'You've seen the sea? You saw the real sea?' Lottie asked.

'Yes, and it's big and it goes on forever, although Mummy said that if I looked hard I could see France. When we grow up, we could both go and live in one of the white houses with the green windows.'

Lottie nodded. 'And we could make all our own rules and look after ourselves.'

'When I remember that day, I think the people who looked after me tried their best.' Little Girl held Lottie's hands. 'They were my real mummy and daddy, but I felt they only wanted me some of the time.'

Sharing stories made the two girls inseparable, yet Lottie knew it was not forever. The deputy warden's words echoed in her head: 'They will find you somewhere. Somebody will want you.'

'I don't want fostering.' Little Girl spat out the word as though it had a bitter taste. 'I had proper parents. They didn't want me. I don't want anyone else.'

The girls loved their life in the home, but as they grew older the outside world pushed its way in. Now they went to a school down the road every day. They were in the same class, and sat next to each other, and did their lessons together, and shared their homework, and flatly refused to make friends on their own, yet the gentle harmony of the friendship changed.

Lottie started noticing boys.

Chapter Thirty-Two

It was a week before the reply to Frankie's email arrived. She now had more time to spend on her home computer and she logged on every day. She checked her emails every hour. She knew they had a phone number for her and every so often she checked for a missed call. She'd done nothing about any other job.

The Techno Factory had called and told that they could no longer offer her work due to her inappropriate behaviour. There was a negligible sum of money owing but, because of the nature of her flexible contract, she wasn't eligible for anything else.

Frankie was glad that it was over. When things blew up in her face, she had always run away; she didn't hang around and sort out the mess. Now her hopes lay with the childcare job and, for the time being, she didn't pursue the possibility of any other compensation. She hated the snotty condescension of the staff in the job centre, jumped-up little managers with half a GCSE, who themselves were only one step from unemployment.

'I don't think you'd be eligible for anything anyway,' said Cora at their next coffee meeting in the Deli. 'It's a minefield trying to claim against a company. It could end up costing you money.' She paused for a moment. 'I know it's a little rude, but is everything okay in that department?'

'I'm managing. Just about. A couple of cash in hand shifts at the launderette. I don't want to have to go and sign on. I hate doing that. I've always worked. I'm holding out for this childcare post – and at least I don't have to pay for the coffees.'

Cora smiled. 'My pleasure.'

'It's very generous of you. I do think about it, you know, what a lucky chance it was, you bumping into Henry and bringing him home. I don't know what I'd do without you.'

***

Frankie put the laptop on the kitchen table and opened the email.

Dear Mrs Baxter,

Thank you for your recent application for the post of childcare assistant. We are pleased to say you have been put through to the next round of the application process. Please see the attached questionnaire which you should complete and return to us by 18th October.

Yours sincerely,
Sheila Ferguson.

Frankie couldn't believe her eyes. She picked up her phone and dialled Cora.

'I can't take your call at the moment. Leave a message. I'll get back to you.'

Frankie hated leaving messages on phones, but she had to share the news with someone. 'It's me, Cora. I've got through to the next round. On that job. I am so buzzing. I'd love to meet up for a bottle of wine. And I'm paying.'

**

Frankie made sure she arrived at the wine bar first so she could do what she'd promised and buy the wine. She chose a bottle of house white, much cheaper than the stuff Cora bought. She hoped it would be okay. The chunky barman brought the bottle and two glasses over to her table, and she poured herself a glass and took a generous sip.

She thought about how strange this relationship was with someone she knew so little about. Yet in many ways that was why it worked: no history, no keeping up appearances. Cora seemed happy to take her as she was. She knew nothing about Frankie's ex-husband, father of Jonny and Shannon, or about the disastrous liaison that had brought Henry into the world. Cora only saw the results, three children of whom Frankie was inordinately proud.

Every day she asked herself how she'd managed to have them, what she'd done right. There had been so much upheaval and disruption in her life, so much unwillingness to commit to anything. But once she'd held Jonny in her arms, she knew all would be well and she would give her life to protect him.

Cora came through the door exactly on time as always, her green-and-yellow coat swirling dangerously near other people's drinks as she passed their tables. She unbuttoned it to make it easier to sit down and, as she did so, Frankie caught sight of a lanyard dangling from Cora's neck. How strange she'd never noticed it before. It was bright yellow plastic with a printed card inside. 'What's the lanyard for?'

Cora poured herself a glass of wine and clinked Frankie's glass. 'First things first. Cheers and well done you.' She took a sip and Frankie was sure she saw her flinch as she tasted the wine. She held out the lanyard so that Frankie could see the card. It had what looked like a recent photograph and the words *Langley Social Services Assessment Officer.*

Frankie wasn't clear what Cora meant her to think. 'Is that your job, then?'

'Well, it's not my preference in jewellery.'

Frankie laughed. 'It's just that I've never seen you wear it before.'

'And you wouldn't have seen me wearing it tonight if I hadn't been so keen to get here and celebrate your good news. It's not important.'

'But it is important.' Frankie put down her glass and lowered her voice. For some reason, she didn't want anyone to hear what she was going to say. 'Langley Social Services are behind my job offer. You know, the people who are asking somebody to apply. They put me through to the second round.'

'I didn't want you to know.' Cora spoke softly but clearly, almost as if she were talking to a child. 'I didn't see your application. Whoever assessed it put it through to the second round because it was a wonderful application. Okay?'

'Yes. But what now? What are you saying?'

'What I'm saying is that your application falls under my control. As long as you don't mess up the next stage, I'll do my best to make sure you get the job.'

Frankie's heart thudded in her chest. There were no words to cover her joy or surprise.

Cora went on. 'It will be my decision. I have to make sure

that I'm employing somebody who can do the job, but if that somebody is my friend, an individual who I know this job means a lot to, then I'd be happier if they got it. Get my meaning?'

Frankie poured a large splash of wine and downed it in one. This was all too much to think about. A dream job that she'd applied for and been lucky enough to get through to the second round, and now here was her friend saying she could decide whether or not Frankie would get it. 'They sent me a questionnaire.'

'Yes, I know. When you've done it, send a copy to me. I'll check it over.'

'Are you allowed to do that?' Too many times in her life Frankie had fallen foul of silly mistakes, misunderstandings. What if this was illegal in some way and she lost her chance of the job? She couldn't bear the thought of that.

'It's not illegal. If it were, I wouldn't be doing it. I'm offering some informal guidance to a preferred candidate for the good of my department.' Cora picked up her glass and held it out. Frankie raised hers to meet it. 'After all, I want what's best for everybody.'

Chapter Thirty-Three

Lottie wasn't sure when she first noticed Craig Heaton, but it wasn't long before she was in a group of girls who were seeking his attention. He was one of the tallest boys in his year and even occasional acne, lank black hair and a beak of a nose didn't prevent him being the apple of many female eyes.

Seated together as they were during many of their lessons, Little Girl was often irritated by the amount of time Lottie spent trying to catch Craig's eye. 'You do know he's done it with Janet Happs, don't you?' she whispered during a boring English lesson about Jane Austen's *Mansfield Park*. 'It's not only Fanny who's been doing it behind the ha-ha.'

Lottie, who'd been paying no attention to the lesson, didn't get Little Girl's reference. It was the rumour that Janet might be ahead of her in the race for Craig's affection that displeased her. 'She's a slag. That's why she's done it.'

Little Girl applied herself to the novel in front of her, something that Lottie did little of. Although the girls were still close and spent evenings together in their attic room doing homework, more often than not this consisted of Lottie copying Little Girl's notes at the last moment.

'You do know people say they've done it and often they haven't.' Lottie always made sure she had the last word. Boys were her latest addiction. First there had been ponies, which involved lengthy walks for both of them to a nearby farm where she fed apples stolen from the kitchen to a dismal old nag of a horse. Then there were computer games. The common room had a PlayStation which the children could use each evening for an hour. Lottie quickly gained a reputation for forcing other children out of the way in order to play on it. Twice she was banned from using it until, after several fights had broken out, they removed the machine.

Now her focus was sex. She'd done kissing and been willing to go a little further on more than one occasion. All this was for her own benefit, just to find out what it was like – the boys involved had not interested her. Now she'd made up her mind that if Craig Heaton wanted to go the whole way with a girl, she was going to be the first.

Little Girl couldn't see the point of it all. She liked school and she found her lessons interesting. Someone had said that knowledge was power, and power meant control. Little Girl had already made up her mind that she would be in charge of the rest of her life.

Lottie started hanging around the boys at morning break. Craig Heaton held court on the edge of the school playing field round the back of the science block. Several girls would arrange themselves a short distance away in the hope of catching his attention.

Lottie strode straight over and perched on a railing near him.

'Whatcha doin'?' he said, trying to raise his eyes from her breasts, which were still a curiosity at this stage of his life. His mates whooped around the two of them like dingoes circling a kill.

Lottie was delighted that he feigned surprise. She could see full well how much he loved the attention. 'I'm doing whatever you fancy.'

'And how do you know what I fancy? Bet you're just another prick tease like Janet Happs.'

Lottie jumped down and stepped close to him, so close that she could have reached out and burst one of his pimples. Instead, she studied his face with eyes full of mischief. 'Try me.'

By Christmas, she was pregnant.

Chapter Thirty-Four

Clutching the envelope, Henry walked through the gates at the top of the park and out onto the high street. This must be how spies felt, he thought, delivering secret information to contacts they didn't know. Except that he was taking his mother's job application to Cora.

He wasn't sure why it had all been arranged like this. Mum had filled out the questionnaire on the computer last night and then asked Henry if he would meet Cora outside Snifters wine bar and give her the envelope.

'Why do I need to do it, Mum?' he'd asked.

'Because.'

'Because what?'

'Because I say so, Henry Baxter.'

It was Cora who'd told Frankie it wasn't a good idea if anyone saw them together until the whole job application process was over, but Henry knew none of this. This brief foray into the world of espionage was filling an otherwise boring half-term afternoon.

As soon as he came out of the park gates, he saw Cora in the green-and-yellow coat, the only thing she ever seemed to wear. She was standing on the corner by Snifters. He hurried across the road, narrowly missing a cyclist who yelled at him.

'Mum said you want this.' He looked around quickly to make sure no one saw him hand over the envelope.

'Thank you, Henry. Though you do seem to have a problem crossing the road when I'm around.' Cora laughed and ruffled his hair. He jerked his head away. She placed the letter in her shoulder bag and then, without another word, headed up the street.

Henry had turned back towards the park when a thought occurred to him. No one knew where Cora lived. He knew it must be by the park, near where he'd met her on that dark evening of his lonely expedition. Mind made up, he scurried along the pavement after her.

She was about a hundred yards ahead of him and it was easy to follow her thanks to the coat. Every so often she stopped and Henry dived into a shop doorway. A little further along the road, she turned into Parkside. As soon as she disappeared from view, Henry quickened his pace. Reaching the corner, he turned into the road after her.

To his surprise, there was no sign of Cora. The road was deserted. In the failing light of the autumn afternoon, Henry could see the gate set in the railings where he'd made his secret entrance into the park with Cora's help. She must live in one of these blocks of flats.

He walked along the front of the blocks of flats that made up the other side of the cul-de-sac but there was no sign of anyone. No door closing, no gate swinging open.

One of the blocks, Parkside Tower, was eight storeys high. It had large, white-railed balconies on each floor from which the owners could no doubt look down onto the park. Henry gazed up, wondering how exciting it would be to live at the top of such a building. The ground-floor flat in which they lived had no such views; it overlooked a shaggy piece of grass on the corner of a major road. Buses stopping outside often blocked the view from their living-room window. This was different.

Henry walked down the drive and peered through the enormous glass door into the hallway. To the right he could see mailboxes, little light-blue painted cupboards, each with its own letterbox and lock. Further back, he saw the lift. The number five was illuminated above its door. No wait a minute ... six, seven. The lift stopped on the eighth floor. Had someone just gone to the eighth floor? Was that where Cora lived, on the eighth floor of this tower overlooking the park where they had often met?

Henry tried the front door of the block but it was locked. He walked along the front of the building. Down one side was a driveway with four cars parked next to a wooden fence. At the far end of the drive, past the gardens, were garages and parked in front of them was a car.

Henry was sure it was the one Cora was driving on the night he'd narrowly missed causing an accident. He looked up at the tower. More balconies on this side, too. One, two, three ... he counted eight floors up. There were four windows on the eighth floor.

He was wondering if the windows belonged to one flat or more when he caught a movement behind the glass. He peered up through the darkening afternoon but the window was empty. Was it part of the spy game he had been playing? Or had someone been watching him?

Chapter Thirty-Five

How long did it take to deal with a job application? The more days passed by, the more Frankie's hopes fell. Cora had rung her after Henry had delivered the first attempt at filling out the questionnaire. She'd spent an hour giving corrections, changing sentences and pointing out how Frankie could phrase her answers in the sort of language a childcare organisation would understand. It both delighted and baffled Frankie; she was delighted that someone would take so much time to help and yet baffled as to why.

'How does Cora know that these are the right answers?' Shannon was entering Frankie's notes into the online application form. Frankie knew her daughter would do it better than she could herself.

'She knows what they want. That's what it's all about at this stage. It's not about whether you're any good for the job, it's all about what you say.'

Shannon and Frankie crossed their fingers on the mouse together and clicked 'Submit'.

'Good luck, Mum.' Doing the job application together had given them a new closeness. Shannon would now string words together and almost make a sentence. They had what might be called snatches of conversation. Frankie loved this. If the worst came to the worst and she didn't get the job, at least she had a chattier daughter.

But she wanted the job, she wanted it more than she'd ever wanted anything. Her money from the launderette only went so far and Christmas was coming. If all went well, she'd borrow enough from the bank short term to get them through Christmas. Then, with a higher wage and a new job, things would be easier all round.

The older they got, more expensive the kids became. And then there was the car. It was such a generous gesture from Cora, but she didn't actually pay for the running of it and it did seem to be more costly to keep on the road than Frankie's old banger. She needed this job.

She'd filled her time since leaving the Techno Factory doing odd jobs. She'd done shopping for Mr Jenkinson in return for dog sitting with Dimwit, helped out one evening a week at the Cub Scouts pack where Henry went reluctantly when he could be persuaded.

What she missed most was Cora – a wine-bar catch up or coffee at the Deli. These were things she'd grown to love. Losing them while waiting to hear about the job was hard.

When her phone rang and the display told her Luke Buchanan was calling, she answered the call with a huge smile in her heart.

'Hello…' She got no further.

'Is that Mrs Baxter?' The voice was unfamiliar and sounded thick with cold.

'Yes. Who's this?'

'I'm Luke's mum. I think he looks after your kids sometimes.' There was a loud sniff and cough.

'Yes. He's great and they …' Frankie stopped. Something was wrong.

By the time the call was over, Frankie could hardly believe what she'd heard. Poor Luke. A faulty gas heater in rented digs. How awful. And worst of all, she would have to break it to the kids.

She made herself a cup of tea and sat at the kitchen table thinking of all the laughs they'd had around it on the evenings Luke had been with them. Whatever was she going to say to Henry? Her phone range again. 'Unknown caller' was displayed on the screen. She picked it up.

'Could I speak to Mrs Frances Baxter, please?'

'Speaking.' This was odd. It sounded like Cora.

'Mrs Cora Walsh calling from Langley Social Services. I need to verify a few of the answers that you've given on your job application and have a brief chat about your suitability for the situation.'

This was bizarre. Frankie had understood Cora's reasoning as to why they shouldn't go out together before she interviewed her for the job, but this was a phone call. Was someone listening? Was Cora doing this for the benefit of someone else?

'That's fine, Cora.'

'Thank you, Mrs Baxter.' Cora sounded very formal. She raced through questions about date of birth, previous job, family situation, all of it information Cora must have already known.

'You've written a personal statement as to suitability. I understand that you lack the qualifications necessary but would be willing to undergo the appropriate training, which we would provide?'

'That's right. No formal training. Just a mum of three,' said Frankie, playing along with the questions.

'You've made no mention of a criminal record.'

Silence.

'Is there one? Is there anything we should know about?'

Frankie held the face phone away from her face. This was taking whatever game Cora was playing too far. It wasn't what they'd talked about. She'd thought someone else would interview her and, if they approved, Cora would rubber stamp the application.

'It's nothing personal,' Cora continued, 'but if there were any criminal offences still in place it would be difficult to get the approval you'd need.'

Frankie took a deep breath. *I've made so many mistakes I wouldn't know where to start*. Telling Cora everything would be so easy. 'My record is clean.'

'That's good. We've done a full search and nothing came up. It's always good to ask, just in case, Mrs Baxter. I'll be in touch as soon as I can.' And with that, Cora hung up.

Frankie put down the phone and gazed out of the window. A bus pulled up and people spilled from it, coming home from work. In some shady corner of her thoughts, a thin sliver of sunlit memory flashed on a recollection that Frankie couldn't place. It hung out of sight.

The conversation with Cora had certainly been strange. Had she changed her mind? Was there something wrong?

Chapter Thirty-Six

The one fact of which Lottie was certain was that she was keeping the baby. From the moment she knew a life was growing inside her, her sense of responsibility changed. She'd slept with Craig Heaton twice. The first time had been such an unqualified disaster on his part that she'd wanted to reassure herself that sex might possibly be enjoyable. It wasn't the case. There was an awful lot of energetic thrusting from him, while she seemed to have no part in the proceedings.

At the home, the girls had regular medical check-ups as part of the welfare programme. Lottie wasn't sure why the nurse had insisted she take a pregnancy test, but she could see the result written on the nurse's face before she saw the thin blue line on the piece of white plastic.

'Now there's nothing to worry about.' The nurse dropped the test kit into a bin by her desk. 'This will be easily dealt with.'

Lottie had already decided what would happen: she was going to become a mother. How much it concerned other people was up to them.

'You can't stay here, you know,' said Little Girl. 'You'll have to go to someplace else. A young mum's home. Either that, or they'll take it into care.'

'No sympathy there, then,' thought Lottie. Racing upstairs

to their room to share the news, Lottie had so wanted Little Girl's reaction to be one of joy and excitement.

A sticky silence ensued as neither girl knew what to say next. 'I suppose it's Craig Heaton's?' Little Girl sounded haughty and aloof.

'It's nobody else's. What do you think I am?'

'I think we know that.' Little Girl's face boasted a sick, smug, self-satisfied smile.

'I'm not getting rid of it. They won't be able to make me get rid of it if I get married.' Lottie watched the smug smile disappear from Little Girl's face.

'But you can't! You're sixteen.' she pleaded.

'Watch me.'

At morning break next day, Lottie marched up to where Craig was occupying his regular position on the railings. A couple of other fifth-form boys hung around. 'I need a word.' She wasn't sure whether Craig knew how awful he was at sex. She assumed that, as he'd got what he wanted, her thoughts hadn't entered into his head. 'I'm pregnant.'

Craig fell off the railings. Two of his mates standing nearby burst out laughing. He got to his feet and dusted down his trousers, doing his best to recapture his cool. 'Fuck off.'

'It's yours.'

'You can't be sure.'

She reached out and snatched the knot of his tie, pulling him towards her. Craig made a futile attempt to splutter his indignation but she spat the words into his face. 'It fucking is yours, and you can do something about it otherwise people might think it's rape. Got it?'

The minute she'd said it she regretted it, but words had

deserted her. This was the beginning of her fight to keep this child – *her* child – and if marriage to Craig Heaton was what it took, then that's what she would do.

That evening Little Girl laughed out loud at her. 'They won't let you do that. They definitely won't let you do that.'

But they did. There was a certain amount of relief on Mr Dale's face when she announced her plans. Things moved quickly, almost as if the home couldn't wait for her to leave.

Craig and his mother came for a meeting. They agreed that Lottie would live in the spare room at Mrs Heaton's and there would be a registry office wedding as soon as they could arrange it.

Lottie told Little Girl of the plan. A tear rolled down Little Girl's face and, for one moment, Lottie felt sad about how she had spoken. Little Girl was the best and only friend she'd ever had. Now she would be alone.

***

The day she was to move out was the last day of term at school. Lottie's belongings occupied one enormous suitcase and two battered cardboard boxes. Mrs Heaton loaded them into the back of her car while Craig sat in the passenger seat looking out of the window, any touch of swagger gone.

Lottie shook hands with Mr Dale at the top of the steps and turned to Little Girl, who was standing next to him. 'Thanks,' she whispered. Little Girl kept her face turned away.

Lottie walked down to the car and, as she opened the door, glanced back one last time. Little Girl stood watching her, her eyes full of heartache and her heart full of hate.

159

Chapter Thirty-Seven

As the days grew shorter and winter neared, the harder it was to get Jonny, Shannon, and Henry up and out to school in the morning. By the middle of November, it was proving almost impossible.

Frankie was finding it tougher to fill her days with useful activity. The strange phone call with Cora seemed an age ago. Frankie was beginning to lose hope. She made herself a cup of coffee on her return from the school run and sat down at the kitchen table. How could she fill the day? Pop her head into the launderette to see if she could pick up a few hours work around lunch time?

She savoured the smell of her coffee. It filled her head with visions of the success and money the job could bring. It was a brief pleasure, but these moments alone were precious to her.

A sudden sound broke into her reverie, a loud knock on the door. She wasn't expecting anyone, so she was surprised to see PC Oliver Ashley standing outside, cap in hand. She liked Oliver, but her stomach still flipped in the way it always seemed to do on catching sight of a police uniform.

'Good morning, Mrs Baxter.' He sounded far too cheerful to have brought bad news.

'Would you like to come in, constable?'

After she'd made him a cup of coffee, she sat down with him at the kitchen table. 'Should I look worried, constable?' She grinned at him.

'I was wondering if you might be able to help me. It's about that telephone number you gave us. Cora Walsh.'

Frankie's stomach tensed. 'Is there a problem?'

'We don't seem to get any answer on it. There is a woman's voice with a message, but no name. We're not even sure if it's Mrs Walsh's number.'

Frankie thought quickly. With the job application pending, she didn't want Cora any more involved than she already was. Cora never answered the phone; Frankie always left a message and Cora got back to her. If she wasn't returning the call from the police, she must have her reasons.

'It's the only number I have for her.' Frankie took a little breath. 'She's not a great one for using the phone. I never arrange anything with her by phone. She calls round or we set another time when we meet for coffee.'

PC Ashley looked a little puzzled. 'You have no way of contacting her in an emergency?'

'Why would I? She's not family, just a casual acquaintance. In fact, I haven't heard from her for a couple of weeks. I'm a bit of one for keeping myself to myself. If Cora wants to meet for coffee or anything, she pops round. I leave it to her.' Frankie wondered how convincing she sounded.

'And you don't have an address?'

'No. I told Detective Sergeant Webb. I think she lives by the park somewhere but I'm not sure.'

PC Ashley sipped his coffee. 'To be honest, I got a bit of stick from the sarge. He said I should have taken more than a mobile phone number and that I obviously wrote it down incorrectly. This is the number, isn't it?' He thumbed through his notebook and showed her a page.

Frankie checked what he had written with the number on the card in her bag. 'Yes, that's the number. She can be a little reclusive. Difficult to get hold of – but I think that's how she likes it.'

'Thing is, we've done a bit of digging. Detective Sergeant Webb's annoyed because my records aren't actually complete. The Sue Steadman case is still open, and there's a gaping hole because I never interviewed both of you. Perhaps I should have questioned Mrs Walsh at the time of the original incident with the car.'

'She would have told you the same as me. Neither of us had met the woman before. It's a bit worrying that you still link the argument in the car park to what happened to the poor woman.'

'We don't, not any more. I'm just tying up loose ends. A full check of the electoral roll and no Cora Walsh, or any initial. No address by the park. In fact, not on the local register at all. Strange, isn't it?'

'I'm sorry I can't help.'

'No problem, Mrs B. As I say, we are working to tie up loose ends.'

The constable put his cup back down on the table. He stood up and put on his hat , which made him seem too tall for the kitchen. 'Thanks for your time, Mrs Baxter. And the coffee.' He paused at the door. 'Sorry, I almost forgot. The postman gave me these as I was coming up the path. Not sure I should be doing his job for him.' He plucked two envelopes out of his pocket and handed them to Frankie. 'Bit creased. My fault.'

He headed off down the path. Frankie looked around to see if anyone was watching. It wasn't good to have police coming out of your house too often; people began to talk.

Once he'd gone, she turned her attention to the envelopes. A brown official one from the DVLA, which she ripped open. The car tax was due. She'd only paid six months' tax when Cora gave her the car because it was all she could afford. The time had gone by too quickly. Yet more money that she had to find.

A sudden thought hit her. If the car had been Cora's, she would have registered it and that would require a name and address. Frankie could tell the police about the car. They'd be able to access records of previous owners.

'Let sleeping dogs lie,' was advice Frankie seldom took but now she understood it might be the wisest choice. The last thing she wanted was the police poking around in her affairs while she was waiting for the outcome of a job application.

She picked up the other envelope. It was of a much more expensive type: crisp, white, and with no window for her address. It didn't look official, yet her name and address were clearly typed and there was a Langley Borough Council frank over the stamp.

Frankie went back inside and sat on the sofa clutching it. Once opened, she knew there was no return; while the envelope remained sealed, there was hope.

She took a deep breath. Unfolding the contents, she started to read. There was the letterhead for Langley Social Services. In one moment, this letter could smash all her hopes. How many times had she opened envelopes with the kids' reports in them, trying to be confident and teach them to be brave when getting terrible news? Yet here she was, scared to unfold the rest of the paper.

She saw a reference number and then her own address in bold type on the left side. She read on.

Dear Mrs Baxter,

Thank you for your recent application for the post of childcare assistant in our day nursery.

After careful consideration of your online questionnaire and telephone interview, we are pleased to be able to offer you the post of …

She caught her breath and skimmed down the rest of the letter without taking any of it in. There it was in black and white, signed by Senior Assessment Officer, Cora Walsh.

Tears formed in her eyes, blurring the words. She wiped them away with her sleeve. The job was hers. To convince herself, she told the coffee table, 'I've got the job.'

She, Frankie Baxter, had achieved this. After all her disappointments, after all her mistakes, she could put this on a win list.

She read the letter once more. This was just a formal communication; details, training manuals and other information, including a starting date, would arrive by email in the next couple of days if she accepted. There was no mention of references. Was this Cora's doing, knowing as she did what had happened at the Techno Factory with Mr Breen?

Catching a glimpse of her reflection in the window, Frankie gave herself a beaming grin. Outside, a small queue of people stood at the bus stop. They were total strangers but she couldn't resist an exuberant wave; an older woman waved back with a bemused smile. Frankie wanted to run outside, hug her and tell her the news. She wanted to scream it at the whole queue.

Picking up the phone, she was about to dial Cora's number when she realised that there would be no answer. She cancelled the call and sent a text: *Thank you. You know what for. Thank you.*

***

Cora sat at the table in the window. She tapped away at her keyboard, entering figures into a spreadsheet, then she sat back, looked at what she had written and smiled.

Her phone pinged with an incoming message. Picking it up from where it lay on a crisp pile of good-quality white envelopes with no windows, she read the text.

How nice to be able to help a friend. Now the fun could begin.

Chapter Thirty-Eight

Lottie stared out of the window across the road at a row of identical houses mirroring the one in which she was living. She couldn't recall any stories that she'd read as a child where the prince and princess married and lived in one room with their baby in the prince's mother-in-law's house.

There was a moan from the cot behind her. Lottie glanced over but the baby seemed to settle again. She breathed out, a whisper of relief. Everything had a baby odour. Dirty nappies and talcum powder.

She loved their child. She swore she could see her heart glowing in her breast with that love, love for the one connection she had with her husband. But the baby didn't keep its own space. It spread like a virus, infecting the lives of all the people connected with it. It bound the family together, whether they wanted it or not.

A rust-red car, more rust than red, pulled into the street. Lottie imagined herself clambering out of it, as she'd climbed out of the Heatons' car when she'd arrived here. Mrs Heaton, a woman seemingly composed of two isosceles triangles, had stood on the pavement watching her struggle with suitcase and boxes until Craig offered to carry the smallest box into the house. Lottie followed, dragging the suitcase which held her world.

If only she'd known then to run. How she wished she could have got back in that car and driven away, had her baby somewhere else, anywhere but here. Yet she had never had that baby and now here she was with its replacement, loving it with all her being. Trapped in a prison of her own making.

***

'I know you're …' Mrs Heaton had struggled for words when she'd brought Lottie into the house for the first time. 'I realise you're already friendly with Craig, but you won't be sharing a room.' She pushed open the door of a tiny bedroom and Lottie struggled in with her case. 'Craig's still at school and needs space for homework and study.'

Lottie found it hard to imagine anyone in their year at school less likely to spend an evening studying, but she remained silent.

'Would you like a cup of tea?' Mrs Heaton pursed her lips with the effort of asking the question.

'That would be nice,' said Lottie, more out of the need to respond than a desire for tea.

'I'll leave you to make yourself at home.' Mrs Heaton pulled the door closed behind her. As Lottie remembered it, that was the last time she'd set foot in Lottie's room.

Although she kept her distance, Mrs Heaton was keen to make plans. Craig was struggling through his last few weeks of school. Being older than Lottie, he could escape after his GCSEs or continue on to sixth-form college. Lottie knew he wasn't the brightest of boys, and his mother took considerable pleasure in pointing out there were plenty of jobs he could get that would be satisfying and would bring a wage into the family.

'If we're to have a baby in the house, we'll need money coming in. You can't waste your time at college. Lottie will need to be here, so you'll need a job.'

There was an interview with someone from social services almost as soon as she moved into the house. Lottie remembered Craig's eagerness to please during the interview, how his bullishness had disappeared and something akin to tenderness had taken its place for a few moments.

Lottie had painted a picture of teenage lovers who wished to settle down and raise a family, of two young people who'd been a little too eager. It seemed to work; there was no talk of prosecution and, other than regular checks by social services, no talk of separating mother and baby.

'And have you thought about the wedding?' Mrs Heaton had dropped her own particular bombshell into conversation with Lottie one morning after Craig had left for school. 'I just think it would be best. For everyone concerned. Even after my own particular calamity with Mr Heaton, I think everyone should try to have the best start as a family.'

Lottie looked up from her breakfast. She was pretty sure Mrs Heaton meant that it would be best for herself, but she kept her thoughts to her Weetabix.

'I'm not talking about a big do. The three of us. I could get Sylvia Cutts to be a witness. Have a little lunch afterwards on the top floor of Cole Brothers. They do a nice scampi.'

Since finding out she was pregnant, Lottie's thoughts roamed no further than the birth. The baby separated her from the world that she knew, from her best friend and only place of safety. Marriage had been her plan but doubts had grown. 'I'm not sure.' She saw immediately how disappointed Mrs

Heaton was. 'Perhaps it should be baby first and then we'll see,' she added.

Her hesitancy was not going to deter Mrs Heaton. That morning, when Lottie had gone out to pick up some shopping for supper, Mrs Heaton rang the home.

'We did try to contact her previous carers about a year ago,' said Mr Dale, 'but there was no response.'

'Does that make me her legal guardian then?'

'I'm afraid not. Given that her adoptive parents dumped her with us, and we've never seen them since, in effect we are her guardians. It shouldn't be difficult for us to get a special notice for you. I know people in social services and, quite frankly, they'll be glad to get her off their books. Leave it with me.'

Three weeks later, Mrs Heaton, Sylvia Cutts and Mr and Mrs Craig Heaton sat at a window table in the fourth-floor restaurant of Cole Brothers ordering lunch.

Sylvia, who'd already consumed most of one bottle of sparkling wine, raised her glass. 'I suppose, being best man and bridesmaid all rolled into one, it's up to me to make the toast.'

Lottie smiled at her as best she could. There was enough of Sylvia to roll a whole congregation into.

'To Craig and Charlotte.'

Mrs Heaton raised her glass. Craig had a small glass of wine as a token gesture. Lottie had been told that wine was bad for her and had a glass of sparkling water.

The scampi and chips arrived in small cane baskets. Lottie smiled and wished they'd ordered soup. The chips were cold.

The pain started about one in the morning. Lottie had gone to bed early. Mrs Heaton, several glasses over her personal limit, had been ill in the bathroom when she got home and fallen on her bed shortly afterwards.

With his mother unconscious, Craig had made a sweet, if futile, gesture to Lottie and asked if they might spend some time together in his room. Lottie took his hand. 'Let's sit on the sofa and watch some TV together, shall we?'

With no sign of Mrs Heaton, she'd made them cheese and ham sandwiches and a cup of tea, then given Craig a gentle peck on the cheek and gone to her room.

It wasn't Craig's fault. She'd felt rather sorry for him during the wedding. They were partners in crime, co-conspirators who hadn't even looked at one another as they mumbled their declaration in front of the registrar.

The ring was something Mrs Heaton had found in a jewellery box. 'Belonged to my Auntie Lorraine,' she said. Lottie thought it looked as if they'd prised it off Auntie Lorraine's hand in the grave but said nothing.

***

Lottie wished Craig were here now. The stabbing, ripping pain in stomach wasn't good. She pushed her head into a pillow to muffle a cry. Something was wrong. She felt she would collapse if she tried to stand, but the searing spasms continued. Telling herself she should get to the bathroom and call for help, she slid off the bed. She pushed herself upwards and grabbed for the door handle. With the sheets peeled back, a red smear covered the bed where she had been lying.

'Please, no.' Her voice stuck in her throat, the pain in her stomach pulling it back inside her. She stumbled across the hall, reeling from wall to wall. As she pulled the cord in the bathroom, the noise of the extractor fan filled the room and the light made her shield her eyes. She fell forward towards the toilet, pushing up the seat, trying to find a way to turn and sit.

A shard of glass ripped through her innards and she fell backwards against the wall, calling out Craig's name. She slid down onto the side of the bath, holding onto the taps to keep herself upright.

It wasn't Craig who answered the call. Mrs Heaton appeared in the doorway looking much the worse for wear, still in the remnants of her wedding outfit. She stood transfixed by the bloody mess that lay on the floor between them. And she knew that it was Lottie's fault.

Chapter Thirty-Nine

Good luck speeds up life. Happiness makes the days fly by. It seemed like only yesterday that Frankie had opened the letter telling her that she'd got the job, yet so much had happened since. Having left a message for Cora, who hadn't rung back to speak to her, Frankie couldn't wait to tell the kids on their return from school. She waited until they were all sitting down, plates of ham, egg and chips in front of them, before she revealed anything.

'You remember that job I applied for? The childcare one?'

Three heads looked up. Being of the *X Factor* generation they were all too familiar with the protracted pause Frankie made before she told them. When she simply couldn't hang on to the announcement for a second longer, she yelled at the three of them, 'I got it! I got it!'

The three of them replied with a terrific cheer – and tight hugs from the boys –before returning to their supper. Shannon gripped her mum's hand. 'That's brilliant, Mum. You've done real well.'

Frankie was more touched than words allowed her to say. It was good to see Shannon pleased and proud after she'd helped out so much. 'I couldn't have done it without you sorting out that CV and questionnaire and everything like you did.'

Shannon blushed and returned to her chips.

'Girl power,' whispered Frankie in her ear as she stood up to make some drinks.

***

Cora did send an email. It was surprisingly formal; reading it Frankie couldn't determine whether Cora had picked up her message or not.

To: frankiebaxter@gmail.com
From: cwalsh@infomail.langley.com
Subject: Childcare assistant appointment.

Dear Mrs Baxter,

I'm pleased that you are able to accept the post of childcare assistant as offered. It's a pleasure to welcome you on board. We attach a registration form to this email to gain further details from you and to advise that your initial assignment will be an online training course which you should complete before Christmas. We will include this in your salary payment in January.

I will send details of your position prior to your commencing on site work on January 4th.

Yours,

Mrs Cora Walsh

Senior Assessment Officer

Frankie replied as formally as she could, sending the details they had requested: date of birth, bank account, address, etc. She gave her name as Baxter. She'd never changed it back to her maiden name after leaving Jonny and Shannon's father.

She was registered at the Techno Factory as Frances Baxter and had paid tax in that name for a long time. This might not be the moment to point out that technically it wasn't her name

Frankie took Shannon on a trip to a large office supply store in the local retail park. Shannon was anxious that her mum looked the part in every way when she turned up for her first day at the office. They filled a trolley with packs of A4 paper, folders, marker pens and a smart leather attaché case in which Frankie could keep her paper work. Frankie thought her employer might supply all this when she started, but Shannon said it would be better if she had it when she turned up.

Frankie's savings had run dry and Christmas was coming, so the next port of call was an interview at the building society. Here she proudly produced the email about the job and the raised salary from January. She had an excellent record on her account despite always trying to keep her head above water regarding money, so an overdraft of £2000 until the end of January, when she received her first salary payment, was no problem.

The overdraft was going to give the four of them a wonderful Christmas. She might even buy a present for Dimwit. When the children were small, the dog had always received an annoying jangling toy or a packet of doggy chews. As they had grown older, they had thought less about presents for their pet and more about what they were getting themselves. This year, Frankie hoped she could buy the things they wanted.

Her online training would consist of five modules which Frankie had to read through and then fill out a multiple-choice questionnaire at the end of each section. Somebody would mark this; as long as she received a pass grade of sixty percent for each module, she could start in January. Much of the training was common sense, things she'd picked up as a mother. But as she progressed, the material became more specific and involved the basic procedures that any childcare provider had to address.

She targeted herself to finish the course in the week before Christmas and get it marked. It would be no problem starting on the fifth of January. First day back at school for the kids, first day in a new job for mum.

Even the simplest of tasks, such as going down to the launderette to do her lunchtime shift of service washes, had Frankie walking on air. 'I won't be available to do any of the shifts after Christmas, I'm afraid, Mrs Demetrio. By that stage, I will be a fully-qualified childcare assistant.'

Mrs Demetrio, the manageress of the laundrette whose face was equal parts beaming smiles and hairy moles, gave her an enormous hug. 'Is good for you yes? Proper job. Pay taxi.'

'Taxes. That's what I'll be paying.'

Frankie knew the launderette ran on a cash-in-hand basis. The Iranian owner, Mr Lankarani, whom she had met once, came in every evening to empty the machines. He gave a tiny portion to Mrs Demetrio for the staff. The rest of Mrs Demetrio's income came from running the service washes and tips.

Frankie grinned as she loaded another machine, knowing she was leaving all this behind. She tipped another basket of sports gear into the tumble dryer. Proper daily employment, proper hours, a proper wage, a proper job, would all be hers.

Chapter Forty

Lottie could never forget the look of horror and disgust on her mother-in-law's face as she stared at the mess on the floor. Her cries had disturbed Craig, who stood next to his mother not knowing what was going on. Mrs Heaton did nothing. She told Craig to call for an ambulance, but she refused go to the hospital with them.

When they discharged Lottie the following afternoon, it was Craig who was waiting for her. 'We don't have a baby then, do we?'

Lottie glanced at his pitiful face. She didn't want to talk about what had happened so she nodded. He placed his arm around her and they started walking towards the hospital doors. 'Got married for nothing, then, did we?'

'I don't know,' said Lottie, tears crowding her eyes. 'I suppose that's up to us.'

Mrs Heaton wanted nothing to do with them. Craig put on his pinny to make some tea. The following morning, his mother announced she was off to stay with her sister for a week or so. 'Violet's invited me, and I do like to go. It's nothing personal. I think it's better if I'm out of the way for you to sort yourself out. Goodbye, Lottie.' Her words sounded final. Lottie knew Mrs Heaton didn't expect to find her in the house on her return.

Lottie hated herself for failing. Whenever she did anything, she needed to see it through to the end. She'd been trying to work out how best the surgeons could operate on Joan. That was all.

From the moment she'd discovered she was pregnant, she'd wanted to be the best mother possible. Suddenly all that seemed out of reach. To begin with, Craig had never been part of her plans. Yes, he was the father, but Lottie didn't see a role for him. Yet pushed into living with the Heaton's and marrying Craig, she had started to understand why the best upbringing for a child was with a father and a mother. Separated from his braying pack of acne-covered mates, he was a different person.

She saw his genuine concern at the loss of his baby. His emptiness was as great as hers. He made her meals. He took her for short walks to the end of the path and back. He held her hand when it all became too much and the tears came. He learned sometimes that words weren't enough and that his silence was the best gift he could offer. Slowly they became closer.

A week later the front door opened and Mrs Heaton stepped back into their lives. If her painted eyebrows could have risen any higher, they would have left her face. She made her feelings clear. 'We gave you home for a reason, because you were the mother of Craig's child. If there's no child, there's no need for you to be here, is there? It's about time you packed your bags.'

'Where would you like me to go?'

'You can get back to that shithole of a place we had to rescue you from. That'd be a start.'

Craig stepped in front of Lottie. 'Lottie's not going anywhere. She's my wife. And whether we got a child or not, she stays here. If you don't like it, why don't you find somewhere else?'

Mrs Heaton's upper lip curled and the lower side of her right eye twitched. She fought to hold in her reaction, then turned to pick up a bottle of gin from the sideboard and disappeared into her bedroom. It was the last time they saw her for two days.

***

Lottie snapped out of her reverie and watched the red car pull up outside the house and Mrs Heaton climb out a little unsteadily. She was back from another supposed visit to her sister's, the excuse Mrs Heaton used to leave them for days at a time. Lottie watched her pick her way up the front path and heard the key make several attempts to find the lock. Lottie had no desire to step out of the room and greet her mother-in-law.

She looked at the cot in the corner and smiled at her child. Mrs Heaton kept a distance from the baby when possible. She had brought Craig up as a single mother and, although she'd been keen to take in Lottie and keep the young family together, she had no wish to be part of it. Most evenings she went out and returned the worse for wear. Lottie and Craig had space to themselves to watch television, Craig playing games of Snake on his phone and lifting his eyes every so often to catch up with the programme, Lottie half-listening to the presenter and half-listening to the baby monitor plugged into the wall next to her.

It would take most of the evening to change and feed the baby and then settle him back. Loneliness seeped into the cracks of her life so easily.

When she had lost the baby, it had brought them together. Craig had changed. He had barely left Lottie's side, making meals for her and running errands, almost as though he had something to make up for. Lottie had felt stranded. Living in their home without a purpose, married to a man she had never fallen in love with, and yet she felt her best option was to give him a chance.

Once he'd left school Craig had got a job at Marks & Spencer. 'Good promotion prospects there, love,' slurred Mrs Heaton. 'You'll be a manager by the time you're twenty-three. He's got a wonderful sense of organisation our Craig, hasn't he, Lottie?'

Lottie smiled and nodded. She wondered how different her life would have been if Craig had been able to organise a condom.

'He's a diamond in the rough, is our Craig.'

Lottie knew what she meant, but she saw Craig through new eyes. To her, he had simply become a diamond. Their world could be as rough and unpredictable as the choppiest of seas, but it never seemed to affect him. She saw him shine with an inner beauty that had never been there in the schoolboy, and that was what had won her over. Lottie loved his sparkle. Suddenly the poser on the fence from school seemed to have turned into a man who adored her. And one evening, while Mrs Heaton was out in search of gin and company, she rewarded his adoration.

Craig played the role of father to be to perfection. When the time came, he held Lottie's hand and burst into tears of relief and joy at the sight of the baby. Through her exhaustion, Lottie smiled at him then looked at the baby laying on her bare skin. She cried the sweetest tears, knowing this was the happiest moment of her life.

On their arrival back home, Craig's mother kept her distance from both of them. Lottie realised that Mrs Heaton didn't expect the couple to spoil her life for much longer. Within weeks of the birth, she started reading aloud ads for flats in the local paper and often commented about having 'looked in the newsagent's window' for nice cheap accommodation.

One Tuesday afternoon she returned triumphant. 'I've found you somewhere to live. A lovely studio flat. Its got its own little entrance. I think you'll like it. If you're careful, with Craig's wage and your child benefit you should manage just fine.'

Lottie wasn't sure what to say. Although occasionally she'd dreamed of having her own home with Craig, at least there was her mother-in-law to interfere. In their own flat she'd be on her own with the baby for the entire day while Craig was away at work. Not for the first time, Lottie felt a little sick at the thought of the solitude.

'And then as soon as he goes to nursery, Lottie, you could get a couple of hours work at a supermarket or something.' Mrs Heaton had booked a viewing to see the flat that afternoon.

The studio flat was a bedsit in all but name, one sizeable room at the back of a Victorian house with its own front door at the end of an overgrown path to the side of the house. Opening the door, Lottie's heart sank. Painted magnolia and sparsely furnished, the room had a large double bed shoved into one corner. A battered chest of drawers was propping up a wardrobe that looked as if it might collapse as soon as they hung anything in it. A sofa with an odour of wet dog stood against one wall and, in front of it, a small scratched dining table and three chairs. There was an enormous bay window that overlooked the rear garden of the house; it made the place feel exposed to the ragged unkempt lawn and forbidding hedgerow of trees.

In the far corner of the room was a recess with a compact kitchen. A huge old American fridge stood in the corner of the living area. Off the hallway was a bathroom with a toilet, sink and a shower and some sort of pink mould on the tiles. The only thing in the place's favour was its price.

**

Lottie scrubbed the flat from top to bottom. She put the baby's cot in the bay window. As cash was scarce, she visited local charity shops and found two mismatching curtains, some cushions and a rug. Mrs Heaton gave them a few pieces of crockery which didn't match, and a belated wedding present of a second-hand microwave.

It was a brief walk from their new flat to a parade of shops which had a small convenience store, a chemist's and a newsagent's. Often that was as far as Lottie felt like going. When the baby needed to sleep, Lottie felt like sleeping too, but often this was the only time she had to do her cooking and cleaning.

Craig became less and less involved in the family. He was trying to do his best in his job, but Lottie wished he had a little more time for his child. Sex was perfunctory, both of them seemingly having lost the desire for it. Afterwards Lottie would lie still and let loneliness wash over her while Craig showered. She would cry for her misfortune, for the things that had brought her here. She felt as if concrete were drying in her chest, but she forced herself up from the bed to attend to the baby or put something on a plate in the microwave for Craig's dinner.

One day she woke up feeling calm after the reboot of sleep. Craig had left early and her day stretched ahead with possibilities. After she'd done her jobs, she longed to get out of the flat for a long walk. She bundled up the baby and pushed the pram past the shops and up the hill into town. After a while, she realised she would pass the home where she had spent so much time with Little Girl.

She stood on the opposite side of the road and looked at the house, remembering how large it had seemed when she'd first arrived all those years ago. A cool wind blew and she pulled her coat around her. A chill of memory. The passing time had made the place look smaller and much less daunting. Here she was, a mother with a child, no longer a helpless girl climbing into a car and trying not to look back.

She pictured Little Girl standing on the steps and felt a sudden rip of sadness. There was no joy inside her and she wanted to walk away and leave the past behind. Something in her stomach told her she had done wrong.

Taking a deep breath, she pushed the pram up the steps and rang the doorbell. An unfamiliar motherly figure in a green overall came to the door. 'Can I help you?'

'I was wondering …' She asked for Little Girl by name.

'Nobody here by that name. But then I've only been here two months, love. You wait a minute.' She disappeared.

Lottie gripped the handle of the pushchair. If Little Girl was here, would the sight of Lottie's baby heal the rift that had torn their friendship apart? Could she say sorry? Should she?

The woman returned. 'Sorry to keep you waiting. I know who you mean now. I've checked the records. She's no longer with us, not been here for a long time now.'

The disappointment welled up in Lottie's throat. She nodded and drew the pram handle towards her.

'But we do know what happened to her. Nothing nasty.' The woman beamed with pride. 'She was one of our success stories. A lovely couple came to meet her and fostered her. Special people. She went to live in Dubai.'

Chapter Forty-One

On the Wednesday before Christmas, Frankie spent the early part of the afternoon at the retail park Christmas shopping for the children and starting to collect the mountain of food she knew they'd devour over the four days of the holiday weekend.

As she was loading the car with groceries, she noticed a new shop in the far corner next to B&Q. Pet Zone: the perfect place to pick up something for Dimwit that the kids could get some fun out of. There were numerous toys with squeaks and bells in them, but she knew from Christmas's long ago how these irritated after a short while. Then something hanging up in front of her caught her eye and made her smile. It was a little doggy coat made to look like an American football jersey.

Pleased with what she'd found, she headed back to the car. She picked up Henry from school. Shannon was staying behind for a Christmas carol concert, and Jonny had announced at breakfast: 'Be in later, Mum.'

Henry helped her take the bags into the kitchen. With the food stashed into what was now a very full fridge, Frankie was putting the remaining items in the kitchen cupboards when Henry noticed the bag from the pet shop. 'What's this, Mum?' Before she could stop him, he'd pulled the item out of the bag and was holding up Dimwit's doggy sweater. 'Oh wow! How cool is this? It's the best thing. I'll even take him to the park wearing this.'

Frankie laughed. Dimwit was Henry's responsibility, something he managed to forget most of the time. The dog had become another box to tick on Frankie's list of chores.

'Can I try it on him now, Mum?' he asked.

'It's a Christmas present. You're supposed to wait till then.'

'Oh please, Mum, please! Just let's see what he looks like in it. Then it can go back in the bag. The others will get to see it at Christmas.'

Frankie knew Henry would get his own way. 'Okay. Go next door, collect him from Mr Jenkinson and let's have a look.' She carried on putting the groceries away as Henry opened the door to the small yard.

There was an ear-splitting scream. Henry stood stock still in the doorway. Frankie couldn't see what had stopped him but pushed past to look for herself. She clutched at her mouth but not quick enough to prevent herself bringing up most of her sandwich lunch. 'Oh, God.'

Henry stood silent and still, his mouth stretched wide in horror as tears began to cascade down his face.

'Inside, darling. Go inside, please.' Frankie pushed Henry back into the kitchen, closed the door and took a deep breath.

She picked up her phone and started to dial the number PC Ashley had given her. Her hands were shaking, and she had to start dialling again. She couldn't get the picture out of her mind, the picture of blood-stained sheets on the washing line flying in the wind and below them Dimwit, staked to the ground, slashed open from throat to tail.

Chapter Forty-Two

The day after Lottie left her, and while her stomach was still curdled with despair, Little Girl met her new foster parents. She sat in Mr Dale's office, knuckles white from clenching her fists too hard. Her hunched body exuded animosity. Mr Dale started to explain the situation. 'These very kind people want to look after you. They want you to become part of their family.'

The couple smiled at her. They might have been picking up a puppy from a rescue home. Little Girl's face was red with suppressed rage; when Mr Dale touched her on the shoulder, she swung round ready to snap. But her strength had gone. She was alone here now and her heart told her that being here without Lottie was not what she wanted. She turned back to the couple sitting in the chairs in the window and pushed her face into a smile.

***

After her new foster parents, Erich and Marta, had filled in all the forms, attended all the interviews and were deemed suitable, one Friday afternoon they took her to a flat in the city. She had her own bedroom and they looked after her extremely well, yet from the beginning she knew something was wrong. Erich seemed utterly unconcerned with her. Given how her father had acted towards her so many years ago, that didn't bother Little Girl – but it did make her wonder why he and Marta had chosen to foster someone. She'd always thought that if she was lucky enough to get foster parents, they'd be people who genuinely wanted her to be part of their family.

Erich was Dutch and she couldn't help thinking he looked like an older version of the guy in a film who'd been the robot. Handsome but craggy, with the fearsome gaze of a tiger. Looking at her, he constantly made her feel as though she had done something wrong.

Erich worked in international finance and said he lived in London in the flat where she was staying, but Little Girl started to doubt that. The flat had remarkably little furniture and there were few belongings. It was uncomfortably large, more of a hotel foyer. There was a polished concrete floor, white walls and a set of cream furniture on which Little Girl was hesitant to sit. There was room here for dozens of children, yet she doubted if even one would be welcome. She was due to spend a weekend with them before an appointment on the following Monday with a new social services officer.

On the Saturday, Marta took her shopping. They bought lots of clothes – bright clothes, expensive clothes, clothes for a holiday. It was so long since she'd been anything new that Little Girl didn't complain. Marta seemed happy to hand over a credit card at every opportunity, and Little Girl took great pleasure in collecting more and more bags.

Marta dressed with tremendous style; that was the first thing Little Girl had noticed about her. Her blonde hair was swept back from her face, she wore very little make-up, but she was striking. Her tailored clothes fitted perfectly, right down to the T-shirt and culottes she wore around the flat. Little Girl thought she might have been a model at some point, or an air hostess, and was dying to ask if this were true.

On Saturday evening, Marta produced an enormous suitcase and told Little Girl to pack all the new clothes and any other belongings she wanted to keep. Little Girl thought this odd but pushed as much as she could into the case. When she'd finished, Marta opened a bottle of wine and pushed a glass across the kitchen counter to her. Little Girl picked it up and sipped at it as she had seen people do. It was tart and bitter, but she held her face tight so as not to show her unfamiliarity with it.

Eric arrived home carrying a large brown envelope. He tipped the contents onto the kitchen counter. There was a small red booklet, which Little Girl picked up.

'Careful,' said Eric. 'Hot off the press that.' He laughed and looked at Marta.

Marta took the booklet from Little Girl's hand. 'It's a surprise, my darling. Tomorrow we're all going away for a little while. Somewhere special.'

Little Girl saw them exchange looks and smile. One thing life so far had taught her was to grab any opportunity with both hands when it came along. To her, elegant Marta and sexy Erich looked like one hell of an opportunity.

***

The plane touched down in darkness. Marta told her the time was after midnight, though Little Girl's new watch still showed eight o'clock. A man holding a sign saying 'Skura' met them in the airport. Little Girl wondered if both Erich and Marta shared this name, but she had no time for further thought as they followed the man down a long white corridor past a glass booth where a handsome Arab in white robes held out his hand.

She handed over her red booklet, as instructed by Erich, and the man gave it the most cursory of glances before handing it back. They moved on.

The car they got into outside the airport was the biggest Little Girl had ever seen, so grand that she thought she could make it her home. Ice-cold bottles of water stood on a narrow rack circled by blue-neon lights which stretched along the side of the door under the handles. Little Girl felt as though she were sitting in a spaceship. The driver took the bags and she clambered into the back with Marta. Erich sat up front with the driver.

Little Girl remembered a film they'd all watched on television one Saturday evening in the home. It starred Harrison Ford and it was all about robots and people who weren't real. What she recalled most was the fantastic city where it was set, a mix of an old town market and huge skyscrapers. If anyone asked her to describe where she now lived, that's what she would say: 'I live in a film. That's Dubai.'

Whichever way she looked she saw cars rushing past along the widest road she'd ever seen in her life. Sometimes little rundown shops huddled together in the shadow of glass towers that spiralled out of sight into the night sky.

The car was cool, but when they pulled into the driveway of a sizeable house hemmed in by high white walls, she stepped out into a hot bath of desert air.

Marta went first, turning on lights as she moved from room to room. The house seemed vast, all the rooms leading off from one huge central space. One wall consisted of sliding glass doors that looked out onto a garden where Little Girl could see a fountain sparkling under lights that illuminated exotic-looking trees and bushes. She wanted to explore at once.

'It's late, darling, and you need to sleep. Everything will still be here for you to explore in the morning.' Marta opened a door and ushered her in. 'Here is your bedroom.'

Little Girl stepped into a simply decorated room with one tiny window, too high for her to see out of. A vast bed stood in the centre of the room on a glossy wooden floor. White sheets, a fur coverlet and a mountain of pillows adorned it. Tiny recesses in the walls on either side, shaped like the towers of the minarets they had passed on the ride from the airport, held small coloured lights. On the walls hung silk tapestries. It was like a princess's palace and, for a moment, she was playing with her dolls once again at her parents' house.

To her delight, a second door opened into a private bathroom. An enormous bathtub stood in the middle of a marble floor with a large rain shower hanging above it. Someone had arranged bottles of potions and creams around two sinks, and a pile of white fluffy towels stood two-feet high on a wooden stand. This was to be her kingdom; this would be her genuine delight.

Marta kissed her good night and closed the door. Little Girl heard a key turn in the lock. She was familiar with the sound and it no longer frightened her. The bedroom was her palace; here was safety. This was no prison. Within this mystical place she could be happy.

She opened the suitcase and started to hang the clothes Marta had bought her. She placed her paltry things from the home around the room but they looked wrong, cheap. She swept her arm across the top of the chest of drawers, knocking them all into a bag and hiding them in the bottom of the wardrobe.

The action made her realise how tired she was. It had been a long and strange day. She had moved to another world and now sleep called. She went into the bathroom, prepared herself for bed then settled between sheets. These were the finest sheets she had ever slept in. She rested her head on a marshmallow pillow. She thought of sweets purchased from a shop on the way home from school, Flumps, soft and doughy. She remembered her dolls and their tea parties. She saw the early light of a summer's evening through the curtains of a childhood bedroom.

As her eyes closed and she tumbled into slumber, one thought echoed in her mind: 'I'm safe here.'

Chapter Forty-Three

As a child, Frankie had longed for Christmas Day to go on forever. This year she couldn't wait for it to finish. Her plans to make it extra special and to give the four of them everything they wanted had been destroyed. She couldn't get the picture of Dimwit, cut open amidst a mess of blood and entrails in the yard, out of her head.

After shoving Henry back into the flat, she'd dialled the number PC Ashley had given her. To her surprise, he was at the door within half an hour with WPC Barbara Something who, while looking a little less friendly, seemed to understand how distressing the sight of their family pet had been. Frankie put the kettle on and started making cups of tea, her universal cure-all.

'And the dog was with Mr Jenkinson?' PC Ashley asked.

'Yes. He takes him all the time and in return we do a bit of shopping for him. Drop the dog off in the morning, pick him up after school. I think George – that's Mr Jenkinson – likes the company.'

PC Ashley nodded and tipped his head in the direction of next door. WPC Barbara stepped out of the kitchen door and left the flat. PC Ashley went into the sitting room where Henry sat huddled up at one end of the sofa.

The constable sat down next to him, his knees lifting high from the low sofa. 'I'm sorry about this, Henry. Whoever did this is wicked and cruel. I can't make any promises, but we will do our best to find out who it was.'

Frankie stood in the doorway, carrying a mug of tea, and saw how Henry gazed up at the young constable as though he were some sort of superhero. In her heart, she knew they might never find out who'd done this. 'Tea, constable?'

The two days leading up to Christmas seemed interminable. Even an email with the results of her online training, a welcome to the job and starting details for early January did little to cheer Frankie up. Her supervisor, Victoria Adams, looked forward to meeting her at the principal office in Langley Park.

Frankie put the letter to one side and started to wrap the presents she had bought. She opened a bag and pulled out the little jacket for Dimwit. Her eyes filled with tears as she held it in her hands. How could someone do something like that? Ever since she'd become a mother, she'd always hoped that the world into which she'd brought her children would be better than the one she had experienced as a child. Sometimes it seemed an absurd idea.

She put the little doggy jacket into a plastic bag and placed it in her shopping bag, making a mental note to drop it off at the charity shop on her first journey into town after Christmas. Shannon had wept a great deal and Jonny had remained silent, not sure how to react. The burgeoning man wanted to be big and strong and try not to let it affect him, but the little boy inside him was just as distraught as Henry at the loss of their family friend.

It reminded her that she still hadn't told the three of them the truth about Luke. She'd had the best of intentions, but the moment had never seemed quite right. She said that he'd gone away for work. The most depressing thing of all was that now even Henry seem to have forgotten him.

'Lying is a form of love, you know,' Cora had told her when she'd asked how she might explain Luke's death. 'It's good you've told them something positive. Children tend to hang on to bad memories.'

Christmas Day came, full of films and food. By the end of Boxing Day afternoon, Frankie had had enough of being cooped up in the flat. Dimwit would have provided the perfect excuse for a walk, but that was no longer possible. 'Going for a walk in the park. Anybody fancy it?'

Jonny shook his head and shifted his attention back to the science-fiction film he was watching. He lay sprawled out on the sofa with Henry curled up by his brother's feet. He shook his head too.

'I'll come, Mum,' replied Shannon.

As they walked into the park, Frankie wiped the corner of her eye on seeing the sign which divided the path into Dogs and No Dogs. She was about to turn to the No Dogs side when Shannon caught her sleeve. 'We can still go this way, Mum. Even without him.' Frankie linked arms with her daughter and the two of them set off defiantly down the Dog path.

As they walked, there were places where Frankie remembered trying to control the little bundle of mongrel energy that had been Dimwit. She remembered how her heart had leapt into her mouth on the afternoon when Dimwit raced back towards them with no Henry on the other end of the lead. Without a word, she sat down on Ivy Tillotson's bench and looked across the reeds to the still, black waters of the lake.

Shannon perched on the bench arm next to her. 'How did they know where to put him?'

'What, darling?' Frankie turned and saw her daughter's baffled face.

'Dimwit was with Mr Jenkinson all day in the yard. Somebody who was just being cruel and horrible would have done what they did to him in Mr Jenkinson's garden, but they didn't, did they?'

Frankie realised what her daughter was getting at. 'Which means they must have known he was our dog.'

Shannon started to weep. Frankie moved along the bench and flung her arms round her. She held her tight while Shannon's body was wracked with sobs.

'You're a truly clever girl,' said Frankie. 'They put him in our garden because they knew he was our dog.' She sat holding her daughter as darkness fell around them.

When she spoke to PC Ashley after the holidays, he told her what Mr Jenkins had reported to WPC Barbara. 'Evidently he let Dimwit into the yard and then fell asleep in his armchair in front of the television. The next thing he knew, Barbara was knocking on his front door. So we can't be certain when it happened.'

Frankie told him what Shannon had said.

'Can you think of anyone?' he asked.

Frankie laughed. 'Who hates me enough to want to rip open my dog? I'm not always an easy person to get on with, constable, but I think that's a bit over the top. I don't suppose there's any news.'

''Fraid not,' said PC Ashley.

Frankie pictured him sitting on their sofa that disastrous afternoon comforting Henry, his shoulders rounded in disappointment. 'Thanks for coming so quickly and helping me deal with it all. The body and burial and everything.'

'No problem. And if there is anything at all, call me, Mrs Baxter. Please.'

The family were going to spend New Year's Eve together. It was what Frankie wanted and, although Jonny had made arrangements with friends, he seemed to have no problem in cancelling them so they could be together. Frankie had rung Cora and invited her, but there was no reply to her message. Cora was being extremely serious about having no informal contact before Frankie started her job.

They had a favourite evening meal of garlic chicken Kiev with chips and a sherry trifle, which Frankie had done her best to assemble in the afternoon. Then they played a game where each of them put a card in a band around their head and pretended to be a historical character and the others had to guess who they were. Jonny proved unusually skilled at it, guessing when Henry was Baby Spice, a fact that Henry detested. There was a lot of laughter.

Frankie let Henry dilute some of Jonny's beer into a shandy as midnight approached. They toasted each other. 'Here's to a big, bright, better year for all of us,' she said.

'And here's to Mum's new job and lots of money and a new dog,' said Henry.

Frankie winced at the word 'dog' but thought this wasn't the best time to question it. They raised their glasses again and laughed. It was almost two in the morning when Frankie persuaded them all to go to bed.

She finished the last little bits of washing-up and stood looking out of the window. A night bus pulled up and deposited a few revellers on the pavement. Judging by the noise, they'd had a good time. She watched them stagger across the road, thinking how strange these days were when everyone should be having a wonderful time, when every family searched for happiness and wanted to celebrate together.

She recalled the ghosts of Christmas past when there hadn't been people or presents. She had so much now, for which she was grateful. And New Year was a time for new chances, for fresh starts, and that was exactly what she intended to have.

Chapter Forty-Four

Lottie cleared away the fragments of Christmas toys that were still scattered all across the living-room floor. One child produced an awful lot of junk. Every night since they'd unpacked their Christmas stockings, Lottie had cleared away the plastic and the cardboard and the dressing-up outfits. Each day, a new piece of toy had gone missing. Now, on New Year's Eve, with her child in bed at long last, she needed the house to be as perfect as possible before Craig arrived home.

There were no New Year celebrations for her other than a bottle of beer she'd found in the fridge. She hoped to be in bed before Craig returned from wherever he'd spent the evening. That was the simplest way of handling things. His mother would be round in the morning to wish them Happy New Year, and to cast her eye over the house to ensure it was all spick-and-span. For a woman who drank as much as she did, Mrs Heaton had superior standards of spick-and-span.

'The fact is Lottie,' she said on the day they unpacked their few boxes of belongings into the unfamiliar council house, 'this place will be your responsibility now. Craig is out there making money. He'll expect to come back to a lovely home every evening. Won't you, my darling?'

Craig found his mother's attention no less embarrassing than

Lottie did, but he smiled and returned to the *Daily Mirror*.

The bedsit in which Lottie and Craig and baby had struggled to coexist for nearly eighteen months was clearly too small for a second child. Mrs Heaton had surprised Lottie by taking charge of the search to find somewhere new.

'A baby on the way and one to look after. You can't all be staying in this shit hole.'

A shit hole, thought Lottie, that Mrs Heaton had been all too willing to dump them in after the first baby had arrived. The constant pestering of 'someone with influence on the housing list' ultimately produced results, a modest two-bedroom brick box on the Park Crescent estate, rented from the council but at such a reasonable cost that, with Craig's increasing income, it looked like they might actually have a bit of money in their pockets at last.

That had been the decision behind her second baby, although Lottie was not sure it was a decision in which she'd had any involvement. Craig had found her contraceptive pills in her bedside drawer, pills she'd asked the doctor to give her in order to buy some time after the birth of their first child.

Craig was having none of it. 'The first one might have been a mistake, but this is the perfect time for us to be settling down as a family. A brother or a sister for our little one.' He flushed the pills down the loo. Lottie had to visit the doctor later that week and explain that she'd mistakenly thrown a packet into a bin and needed another prescription. But it seemed that Craig had got lucky. Two attempts at sex during that week and now here she was, with baby number one fast asleep in a narrow bed in this dump of a house and baby number two kicking its way around her belly.

She picked up the last box of toys and shoved them into the hall cupboard. She turned off the lights in the tiny living room and was making a cup of tea in the darkened kitchen when she heard the front door.

Craig stood in the kitchen doorway. 'What the fuck you doing up? Fuck off to bed.'

'I'm going. I've just been clearing up.'

'That kid makes more fucking mess than an army.'

Lottie ignored him and finished making her tea. Craig stood blocking the doorway. One thing he'd not lost since school was weight; he filled the door, despite doing what he said were several sessions a week down the gym. Fat rather than fit were the words that came to mind when she looked at him.

He staggered over to the fridge. 'Oy, there was a fucking bottle of beer in here.' Lottie remained silent; clutching her mug of tea, she headed towards the door. 'Did you hear me? Where is my fucking beer?'

'I wanted a drink at midnight. Just something to celebrate and it was all there was.'

She couldn't remember whether she felt the scalding hot tea run down her arm first or the fist smack into her cheek. Her head cracked back against the wall and she slid down it as the tea burned and soaked into her lap.

'It was my fucking beer,' said Craig. He stepped over her and headed to bed.

Chapter Forty-Five

At what point does a dream become a nightmare? As you rest your head on the pillow and fill it with happy thoughts to steer you through the darkness, what is rotting away in the deeper corners of your brain ready to ooze through your dreams, poisoning sleep and making you yell in terror in the dark of night.

Little Girl could not recall a day where the taint of her nightmares had not soaked into her life. The morning after her arrival a single ray of bright sunshine awoke her, shooting down through the tiny window in her room like a golden spotlight waiting for the arrival of an actor in a play. Throwing back the bedclothes, she stood where the light shone on the polished wooden floor. She could sense the heat of the early morning.

Her hand reached out to open the door and she remembered the sound of the turning key when Marta had left the previous night. Was there any point in calling or knocking? Her watch said eight o'clock, but she was confused whether she had changed the time on landing last night.

She went into the bathroom and started to fill the tub. She poured bath oil and creams into the water. When it was full, she let herself slip below the surface of the bubbles to wash away the night.

Marta walked into the room while she was still soaking. 'Good morning. I thought you might still be tired and asleep. There's breakfast in the garden and you can spend the day out in the sunshine.' She smiled at Little Girl. 'But don't try to leave the house. Eric will be back this evening to talk to you.' She turned and left the bathroom.

Little Girl thought Marta sounded different. She no longer sounded as if she was playing the role of mother but seemed more like a wardress.

A small table stood on the terrace outside covered with a crisp white cloth. A silver coffee pot, a dish of fresh fruit, and some pastries and bread were laid out as a breakfast feast. To Little Girl, it was all very grand. No Coco Pops today. She poured herself some coffee and ate some bread and jam. While still munching on her breakfast, she wandered around the garden. Considering the size of the house, it was small and compact. The high white chalky walls were topped by broken glass and gave no view of the world outside. A flowerbed ran around the edges of a patchy lawn, but this was not a garden laid with love.

Once she had finished her breakfast, she went back into her room and changed into one of the swimming costumes Marta had bought on the shopping trip. She topped the outfit off with sunglasses bought at the airport. There was a bundle of magazines in the room; snatching a handful, she went to the far end of the garden where two sun beds were separated by a small brass-topped table. Stretching out, she saw herself like many of the women in the magazines and tried to believe she was on some exotic holiday. Yet so much was unexplained. The puzzle as to why she was here provoked a nervousness in her that she found hard to let go. Soon heat, weariness, and confusion lulled her into sleep for most of the day.

The air began to chill in the early evening. She crouched down to pick up the magazines strewn on the ground by her sunbed and was conscious of someone standing over her. It was Eric.

'Marta tells me you had a bath this morning.'

Little Girl smiled at him. 'I did, thank you. It was wonderful.'

'Go and take one now,' he replied. 'We have visitors coming this evening and you need to be clean.'

She always remembered that second bath as the last time she felt that she owned her body. In the time that followed, she lost count of the number of people who visited in the evening. Men of all ages and all sizes. Some were rough, some did nothing more than try to talk to her, but none were welcome. By the time darkness edged its way through the small window in her room, tears often filled her eyes. She would run to the bathroom after her visitor for the evening left, trying to scour away their touch on her skin. After a while she stopped. She realised she would never clean everything away. She would fall into a numb ache of sleep, clutching one of the pillows in a desperate embrace.

Left to her own devices during the day, she tried all the doors and windows but found them locked or screwed down. Some places she couldn't get into at all; her movements were limited to her room, the lounge, the garden and the kitchen.

When Marta was in the house, she worked in another room which Little Girl thought might be an office. Once, when the door was left ajar as Marta visited the kitchen, Little Girl caught a glimpse of a brightly lit television screen with numbers all over it. It sat on a desk covered with papers.

Breakfast was set out on the table in the garden every morning. She saw no one until the evening.

Marta acted as some kind of hostess for the visitors, but Eric was invariably the one who brought them to Little Girl's bedroom door. Some nights there were two of them, some nights there were more. One evening, there were seven. Afterwards she lay on the bed and held the pillow close to her like some long-lost lover and cried into it.

Sleep was her companion, bringing oblivion, but she was woken next morning by the scent of them in the room. Sweat and semen. She went to the bathtub and lay for hours, soaking in perfumed oils and creams. Then, having dressed, she drifted around the house looking for anything that might help her in some way. The house was spartan. There was nothing to be found other than a few magazines and the plates and cups in the kitchen.

This hunt became her daily routine. It took her a month to discover the gas canister.

Chapter Forty-Six

Frankie had taken a lot of jobs over the years. Some had lasted longer than others; some had given her no guarantee of hours or earnings – flexible working, her employers called it. No way to feed a family was how she saw it. Yet, as a single mum in ever-changing circumstances, sometimes the no-fixed-hours option was the best way to get work. Whatever the job, she always had a tingle in her stomach on the day she started. Today she thought there was a volcano erupting inside her.

Having got up early, she dressed with some thought for once, rather than dragging the first two items out of the wardrobe. Sharing a bedroom with a teenage daughter didn't offer much privacy or cupboard space. Knowing she still had weight to lose, she managed to find a pair of smart jeans with an elasticated waist, washed and ready to wear. A loose, light-blue tunic top gave her the smart ready-for-the-office look she thought she would require for her first day.

Shannon was in the bathroom, so she took a seldom-used tube of tinted moisturiser out of her daughter's drawer and applied a little, together with some blusher, which she then rubbed hard to remove. She wasn't one for makeup, but if it helped then it was all to the good. You never get a second chance to make a first impression, Shannon claimed. Internet wisdom, no doubt, but Frankie thought it as good a motto as any for her first day.

She studied herself in the mirror. This was it. The start of a fresh life. Regular money, good money, to give her some freedom and to provide her and the kids with a better life. She was pulling her stomach in and holding her breath to try to give herself the silhouette she craved when Shannon burst into the room. 'Are you going to be late on your first day, Mum?'

'Oh God, sorry, love. I wish I wasn't quite so fat.'

'You're not fat, Mum.' Shannon hesitated a moment. 'You're curvaceous.'

Frankie laughed and picked up her bag. 'Curvaceous I'll take.'

They headed out and walked to the car accompanied by the boys. The atmosphere on the drive to school was boisterous and excited, all of them picking up on Frankie's nerves and letting them raise their chatter to fever pitch.

Frankie was glad when the car was empty and she was alone with her thoughts. One thing she hadn't done was any planning on where to park. She pulled into the car park behind the cinema. It was going to cost eight pounds for the day. Frankie made a mental note to ask her new workmates in the office where was the best place to leave the car, otherwise most of her new wage would be going straight back to the council in parking fees.

She stuck a ticket on the windscreen and crossed the road outside the cinema. The office she was to report to lay halfway down the high street in a small modern block. She gazed into shop windows as she strode along, imagining being able to pop out in her lunch hour to shop each day rather than being stuck on an industrial estate as she had been at the Techno Factory.

Taking one last glimpse of herself in a newsagent's window, she drew a deep breath and bumped straight into Cora. 'Hello, stranger, fancy seeing you.'

'It's not a coincidence,' said Cora.

Frankie thought she looked rather serious. 'I wanted to catch you before you go in. I wanted to wish you good luck, privately, of course.' She took Frankie's hand in hers. Holding it tightly, she looked into her eyes. 'I just hope you do well. It's everything you deserve.' A smile crept slowly across Cora's lips, forcing its way to her eyes.

Frankie swallowed hard. This wasn't the moment to get emotional. Seeing Cora made her realise how grateful she was, how the woman in front of her had changed everything. She could never repay her. 'It's so kind of you. Not only helping me apply and all, but being here this morning. Thank you, Cora. It's been a bit strange not seeing you for a while. It wasn't the easiest of Christmases, but this is my fresh start this morning.'

Cora released her hands. 'What about us having a little glass of wine at Snifters when you finish? To celebrate?'

'That would be great. I'll ask Jonny to sort the other two out after school, and it's my treat. No argument.'

Cora laughed. 'No argument. See you there.'

She turned and the green-and-yellow coat swirled into the morning crowds on the high street and disappeared.

Converted from a shop, the office they had summoned her to was where all the childcare assistants based themselves. They reported in with their paperwork before heading out to the nurseries and childcare facilities in Langley.

The ground floor of the shop was open plan. With five or

six desks and computer stations dotted around the room, the only one occupied was nearest to the door. A young man, with curled inky hair and a tanned complexion that looked like it might be out of a tube, was pumping away at his keyboard. Obviously something was wrong. He looked up as Frankie closed the door and stood in front of his desk.

'Can I help you?' He had washed-out green eyes, as if the colour had run. When he spoke, the playful tune of his voice lit up his face into a broad beam of a smile. What an excellent person to be sitting on a reception desk, thought Frankie.

'Good morning, I'm Frankie Baxter.' She smiled at the young man.

'Good morning, Mrs Baxter.'

'Ms Baxter.'

'Of course. I'm Lewis, general dogsbody and helpmate.' He stood up and came out from behind his desk. 'If you're here with an application for childcare services, you're a little early.'

Frankie loved Geordies. She hoped the job meant she saw a fair bit more of Lewis, even though he looked a good eight or nine years her junior. 'No. I'm not here for childcare services. Or rather, I am. I'm here to start work. I start today. Childcare assistant. Did my online training and I was told to be here by nine this morning.'

Lewis's eyebrows furrowed like two caterpillars doing a mating dance, a bewildered expression distorting his features. 'Let me just check, Ms Baxter.'

'Call me Frankie, please.' Frankie gave a nervous grin.

Lewis sat down again and squinted at his screen. 'Let me be up front with you, Frankie. I think someone's made a mistake and forgotten to put it in the book. First day back after

Christmas, bound to be that.' His eyebrows tugged themselves apart and the wattage of his smile increased. 'How's about I make you a coffee and you hang on until Mrs Soyinka gets in? She runs things here and if anybody is likely to know what's going on, it'll be her. Sugar?'

Frankie sipped at the remains of her coffee and put the cup back down on the corner of Lewis's desk. She'd managed to make the drink last nearly thirty minutes while feigning interest in messages on her phone. She sent a text to Jonny to ask him to collect Henry and Shannon after school. A bottle of wine with Cora would more than make up for this hiatus, a chance to thank her properly for the job. She wanted to get started, having raced through breakfast and the school run to make sure she was here on time. Half an hour of sitting around wasn't helping her nerves.

By now, more people had appeared in the office. Calling New Year greetings to Lewis, they sat at their separate desks. Frankie felt more and more uncomfortable sitting on her chair by the door as several pairs of eyes peered over computer screens at her.

She was about to ask Lewis if there was anyone he could call when the door burst open and a whirlwind of scarves and bags entered the office. In the midst of them was a sizeable woman, large to the extent that Frankie felt like a supermodel in comparison. The roundness of her face was heightened by a multi-coloured beanie hat tugged low onto her head. Several colourful, jangling necklaces gave the impression of a human wind chime. She had the widest eyes Frankie had ever seen and the most beautiful skin. Above all, she had the look of a listener. A problem solver, Frankie hoped, as she stood up to say hello.

***

'Slow down and tell me one more time.'

Frankie had been sitting at Mrs Soyinka's desk for the last twenty minutes. Even though Lewis had dispensed a second cup of coffee, she didn't feel that any significant progress was being made. 'I applied for a job as a childcare assistant at Langley nursery.' Her speech slowed right down. She was keen not to go through the whole story again. To ensure Mrs Soyinka understood it, she over-articulated in the way the English do when they're ordering beer and chips on the Costa del Sol. 'I filled out the form online and applied.'

'I hear what you're saying, dear. No need to treat me as though I'm simple,' said Mrs Soyinka. 'It's just that it doesn't make any sense. How can you be here for a job when no one has ever met you before?'

Frankie took a deep breath and gripped the desk to keep her composure. 'Look, I'm not sure I'm supposed to tell you this. My friend, Cora Walsh, is a Senior Assessment Officer. She helped me with the application.' She waited to see if there was any flicker of recognition from Mrs Soyinka at the mention of Cora's name. 'I've done everything else above board. And I've got the letters and emails from other supervisors and people who initiated my training at home.'

Mrs Soyinka clicked her mouse and swung her computer screen in Frankie's direction. There was a picture of an Indian man in his mid-forties wearing a broad smile and a light-blue shirt. He was smiling at the camera in the way people do when they don't know where else to look. 'That's Mr Derek Pravasana. Derek is the Social Services Senior Supervisor for childcare in Langley.' She contemplated Frankie for a moment. 'I'm sorry, Mrs Baxter. I've never heard of Cora Walsh. There's nothing coming up on the staff list under that name.'

Frankie scrabbled in her lap and unzipped the case she'd bought on the shopping trip with Shannon, a little embarrassed now about how cheap it looked. 'I've got the other emails.' She rummaged in her bag. 'Here. Printed them all out, just in case I needed them. Everything's here.'

She put four pieces of paper in front of Mrs Soyinka. 'These are emails from different people. One telling me I'd got through the first round, from a Sheila Ferguson. Another talking to me about my training from Victoria Adams, and a third one with all the details for starting today from Siobhan Fahy. And here I am.'

Mrs Soyinka stared at the pages and then looked up at Frankie. 'I've never heard of these people. I'll do a check on the personnel list, but something tells me that, like Cora Walsh, they're not going to show up.'

Frankie couldn't understand how this could be happening. Cora had arranged it all and led her through it. Cora was in charge. She'd organised the training and everything.

'The thing is, we don't train anybody online. If you'd applied for a job, you would have come in and done an interview, and possibly a second one. Then you would have attended a training session at one of our centres. In fact, if you'd got so far as getting a job, you wouldn't be here at all. You'd be at whichever nursery facility you were starting at.'

'But I did get a job.' Frankie fought back tears of desperation. 'Langley Park.'

Mrs Soyinka picked up her phone. 'Let me give them a call and double check. I won't be a minute.'

Frankie was aware of at least seven pairs of eyes looking at her. Lewis sat at his computer, staring in her direction. She smiled at him. 'Do you have a problem?'

His head shot back to his screen as he started to tap away on his keyboard. Noise filled Frankie's head, a sound of hedge trimmers cutting through the warm stillness of a sultry summer's afternoon. An indistinct buzzing preventing her from hearing what Mrs Soyinka was saying. She could feel moisture seeping under her arms and began to worry in case it started to show. Reaching into her bag, she took out a tissue to mop her armpits. Breathe in and breathe out. Breathe in, breathe out, just as she'd been told to do when having her anxiety attacks.

Mrs Soyinka replaced her phone. She wasn't smiling. 'Langley Park haven't advertised for a new childcare assistant in over nine months.'

'But they did,' protested Frankie, the pitch of her voice beginning to rise. 'They did. I got an email. I replied to it and that's when they sent me the online questionnaire. My daughter helped me fill it in.'

She saw Mrs Soyinka scribble on her notepad. 'There's something wrong here. You've printed out the emails, which is very helpful, but if we could see them on your computer, we might be able to trace where they came from.'

'What do you mean? They came from you. This is ridiculous. This is typical of any council organisation, your right hand not knowing what your left hand is doing. I've put a hell of a lot of work into this. Gave up my job. All 'cos I was getting this. Signed off benefits and stuff. Got an overdraft for Christmas 'cos I start this today. Now you're telling me that somebody's lost my application.'

'I'm not saying anything about a lost application, Ms Baxter.'

Frankie could hear Mrs Soyinka's patience was wearing thin. Well, that was tough. This was Frankie's fresh start, her livelihood, her big chance. Why couldn't the woman just check with her superiors?

As the thought came to her, Frankie pulled her phone out of her bag. She pressed through to Cora's number and dialled. Mrs Soyinka leaned forward. 'I'm sorry, but we don't allow people to use personal phones in the office.'

'I'm ringing Miss Walsh. I'll leave a message. Soon as she gets it, I'm sure she'll sort all this out.' As Frankie expected, the call went straight through to an answering machine.

'Cora, I'm in the childcare assistance office. I'm dealing with Mrs …?'

'Soyinka. Winifred Soyinka. Office Director.'

'Winifred Soyinka. They have no record of my application or my training, and they're not expecting me. They're saying that you don't work here. I don't know what's going on. Could you call back? I'd appreciate it.'

Mrs Soyinka looked at Frankie and her enormous smile started to return. 'This is all most unfortunate. Would it be possible for you to go home and get the laptop you received the emails on? I'm going to check things out at this end.'

Frankie nodded and stood up. 'Thank you. I'll be back as soon as I can. And if Cora calls me back, shall I ask her to ring you?'

'Please do. If she is who she claims she is, she'll have my number. I'm really sorry for all this trouble and upset, Ms Baxter. But it does look to me as if you've been the victim of some dreadful hoax.'

Chapter Forty-Seven

Lottie put her laptop into the largest of the three bags and stood at the door to watch for the taxi. The kids were both perched on the sofa with coats, gloves and scarves, looking a little bewildered. As the taxi appeared, Lottie checked around to make sure no one was watching the house, then she carried the children and the bags into the taxi and they drove off.

She should have walked out the first time Craig hit her, but with a second baby on the way she'd been uncertain what she would do and how she could support them. And she feared that it had been her fault. Craig worked hard. Had she sometimes made things tough for him? Being alone in the house all day with a child made her long for company. Had she asked too much of him when he came back home?

Things seemed to have become easier with her baby inside her. No doubt Craig was worried about harming the unborn child, so lashed out less with his fists and more with his tongue. Often he would try to make amends, holding out his arms and enveloping her in a hug. She flinched as he stepped towards her, never sure he wasn't going to grab her by the throat.

'I'm sorry, Lottie. Darling, I'm sorry. It's not my fault. I can't help it. I'm tired and sometimes it just happens.' For a while she believed him.

She'd been home from the hospital for seven weeks when he hit her again. He hit her because the new baby was wailing and she couldn't stop it. He walked out and stayed away for two days, stayed at his mother's, most likely. And that was his mistake. The empty house showed her how things could be, how she could be alone with the children. She knew it was her job to look after them, to nurture them and to give them every conceivable chance, and she couldn't do that if she lived in fear.

It took her a year to organise, talking to people, making phone calls, getting help and plucking up the courage. And now she'd done it. Here was the rest of her life. And she was going to play it by her rules.

Chapter Forty-Eight

The laptop sat on the table between Frankie, Mrs Soyinka and Mr Pravasana. Mr Pravasana clicked on an email. 'Did you ever check where these mails were coming from, Ms Baxter?'

Frankie had driven all the way home to collect the laptop. When she returned to the car park by the cinema, she saw she'd lost the parking place she'd paid for. Driving round to the high street, she found a parking bay two doors down from the office and ran back in to dump her bag on Mrs Soyinka's desk.

The man in the photograph was now waiting next to Mrs Soyinka. Once he'd introduced himself, Derek Pravasana wasted no time at all booting up the laptop and logging into Frankie's email account.

'If you click on the email address, you can see where it's actually come from. Although it does read victoria.adams@ langleycc.com, that's what tells you this office didn't send it.'

'I don't understand.' Frankie's patience was wearing wafer thin.

Mr Pravasana took great delight in explaining at length. 'We are dot gov dot uk,' he went on. 'We are not a dotcom address. This is somebody pretending to be us, or spoofing, as it's known. They've set up a fake email domain called Langley CC. I presume they hoped you would think that stands for Child Care. Then they created different email addresses for these people who have contacted you – Victoria Adams, Siobhan Fahey, Sheila Fergusson.'

He paused for a moment to check that Frankie was taking it all in. 'Mrs Soyinka is right. Victoria Adams doesn't work here. Neither do any of these other people. Because you didn't think it strange that you never met any of them, someone was able to mail you and deceive you into coming here today.'

Frankie drew in a short sharp breath and exhaled noisily. Don't patronise me, she thought, looking back at Mr Pravasana. 'Cora Walsh is an actual person. I met her just over a year ago. She exists, and she knew all about the job. I've met her on numerous occasions. She's not a figment of my imagination.'

'This job is a figment of somebody's imagination,' sighed Mrs Soyinka. 'It's the first day back after Christmas, and we've been dealing with this for over three hours.'

Mr Pravasana closed the laptop. 'I have all the files I need, Mrs Baxter. This is a case of fraud, and your friend Cora Walsh is involved somehow. I shall be reporting it to our IT security department, but it doesn't look as if there has been any violation of our own files. Someone's conned you. I'm very sorry but there's nothing we can do.'

'And that's it, is it?' Frankie spat out her words. 'Do you know how long I've been looking forward to this? Telling the kids our lives can change? Working out how I'm going to spend the money and give myself a bit of security for once? Then I walk in here, there's no job and you tell me there's nothing you can do.'

'I'm afraid so.'

'This isn't fair. Why would someone do this?' She picked up the papers and stuffed them back into her bag. Grabbing the laptop, she kicked out at the chair she'd spent most of the morning sitting on waiting for someone to tell her there really was a job and that this was all a nightmare.

Lewis jumped to his feet and Mr Pravasana took a step towards her. 'Now Mrs Baxter, it's not our fault. There's no need for that kind of behaviour.'

'It makes me feel better,' said Frankie. She swung her arm across Mrs Soyinka's desk, sweeping the contents to the floor.

'I can't begin to understand how you feel.' Mrs Soyinka stood calm and still, ignoring the stationery around her feet. 'Someone's played a cruel trick on you. At the moment you want to get back at them. I do understand that. You want to make sure they get the punishment they deserve. How about you go home and have a cup of tea? I promise you, we are going to look into this. I'm going to call you tomorrow if we find out anything.'

Mr Pravasana made an attempt to speak, but Mrs Soyinka held up her hand to silence him. 'And that's my promise because what's happened here is horrible.' She unleashed her widest smile.

Frankie hugged the laptop to her chest. 'Thank you.' She walked out through the door to the car. A traffic warden stood on the pavement next to it, tearing off a ticket ready to place under her windscreen wiper. 'Excuse me,' she exclaimed as she strode over to him. 'I've only been here forty-five minutes.'

'It's not the time, love. You don't have a blue badge and this is a disabled bay.'

It was at that moment that Frankie threw the laptop through the childcare office window.

Chapter Forty-Nine

She knew what the little blue canister was as soon as she found it. She'd seen them on picnic outings as a small child. Little blue bottles of gas for the picnic stove that cooked sausages and made tea on damp summer afternoons in a lay-by.

Little Girl couldn't work out why they would conceal a single canister of picnic gas at the back of a cupboard in the kitchen. She simply knew that it might help in some way. Picking it up, she took it and stashed it at the back of her wardrobe. Would Eric or Marta notice it was missing? Days passed by and no one mentioned it.

Each day, during the time she was alone, she became a little braver in her exploration. On certain mornings, she woke to find a woman cleaning the villa. The woman wore a veil across her face and Little Girl could see her eyes peeking at her across the room. At first she was afraid and kept clear of her but one morning she decided to say hello.

She was sure the woman's eyes were smiling but, when she introduced herself, they widened as if in terror. The woman turned away and proceeded to dust and clean. Going back into her room, Little Girl left the door ajar and watched her work. After a while, the woman moved into the kitchen. Little

Girl changed position so she could still see what the woman was doing.

The woman took a bunch of keys from her bag and unlocked the only room Little Girl had never been able to gain access to. A few moments later she came out, locked the door and put the keys back in her bag. From then on, Little Girl made sure she always said hello to the woman. Sometimes she didn't turn up and it was ten days or so before Little Girl had a chance to see her.

The night-time visitors showed up at weekends. On those days, Eric and Marta were in the house. There was only the briefest conversation between them – Eric was especially silent. Marta smiled at Little Girl and sometimes brought her an iced drink if she was in the garden in the afternoon. It was Marta who went into her room after she had woken up, stripped the stained sheets from the bed and prepared it afresh for another night.

The woman who cleaned never did this; she never went into Little Girl's room. Little Girl was sure she had been told to stay away.

The solitude and physical pain produced an apathy that Little Girl fought to keep at bay. She knew any chance of changing her situation relied on not floating around the house in a stupor.

One morning she woke early. There had been no visitors the night before, so she was alert and wide-eyed.

The woman was out on the terrace, wiping down chairs and tables and scrubbing the tiled floor. Little Girl walked into the kitchen to make breakfast. There, on the kitchen island, the woman's bag was lying open. Little Girl saw the bunch of keys with the key for the cupboard. She had no idea what might be in it but she had to try and find out.

Checking that the woman was still busy on the terrace, she picked up the keys and crossed to the cupboard door. She put the first key that came to hand into the lock. No luck. She tried a second, but that didn't open the door. The fifth key she tried turned and the lock clicked.

The room turned out to be a large pantry. On one side shelves were piled high with pans, plates and dishes, and on the other, oils, vinegars and packets of staples. Little Girl thought it odd; Eric and Marta never cooked and she couldn't understand why they would need a room such as this. Someone delivered their meals and the food in the massive double door refrigerator was basic stuff such as cheese, fruit and salads.

These pans and plates looked as though they had come from an old-fashioned Victorian scullery in a picture book: heavy cast-iron frying pans, copper-bottomed saucepans. Little Girl's eyes alighted upon a shiny old pressure cooker at the far end of the bottom shelf, the sort that her mother had steamed puddings in for her.

She wasn't sure why, but she knew that she needed to keep the key to this room. She tiptoed back into the kitchen. The woman was still washing the terrace. Little Girl took the key from the ring, slipped it into her pocket, and placed the rest of the bunch back where she had found them. She made herself a cup of coffee and some toast, picked up a magazine and sat on one of the sofas to keep an eye on what the woman was up to.

Having cleaned the terrace, the woman came back inside, averting her eyes. Little Girl looked up from the magazine and smiled and the woman's eyes flickered. She disappeared into the room off the main hallway that served as an office.

Little Girl finished her coffee and put her cup in the sink. She stood near the bag on the kitchen counter. The keys were now lying at the top of it, in plain view. The woman came out of the office and, as she picked up the bag, they fell to the floor. The woman looked at Little Girl and made a sound from behind her veil.

Little Girl bent down, picked up the keys and held them out. The woman took them and put them in her bag. A smile filled her eyes and she left the house.

Little Girl stared at the cupboard door. She needed to think a little more. Often, on nights when there were no visitors, Eric spent the evening in the office and Marta retired to bed early. When Little Girl had first arrived, Marta had accompanied her as she settled into bed, but lately she'd taken to looking round the door and then locking it without a word. Some nights Little Girl fell asleep before Marta did this and the couple left her undisturbed until the morning.

It took a week to formulate the plan. As it fell into place, it filled Little Girl with panic, so she tried to think of it as a mischievous thing a child might do. If they kept her confined, then this was how she should behave. Her passiveness when the visitors came was not something she could continue forever. Somehow she would show that she could fight.

The following Friday there were no visitors. Little Girl said goodnight and retired to her bedroom. She dressed in a pair of jeans and a dark T-shirt. Opening the bedroom door, she saw Marta sitting out on the terrace enjoying a glass of wine and the last of the day's sunshine.

Little Girl grabbed a heap of clothes from the wardrobe

and packed them under the duvet to resemble her sleeping self. It wasn't very convincing, but it would have to do. She put the gas canister into her bag, slipped out of the bedroom and crossed the kitchen. Opening the cupboard, she stepped inside, locked the door and sat down in the blackness to wait. At any moment she expected to hear someone call her name. What if this was the night that Marta didn't just peep through the bedroom door but called in for a bedtime kiss?

Minutes ticked by, and Little Girl dozed a little with her back pressed against the lower shelf. Unsure as to when she could safely unlock the door and step out into the kitchen, she waited until her watch showed it was a little after two in the morning. Fumbling with the key, her fingers rigid on the metal to muffle even the slightest noise, she knelt in front of the door and turned the key in the lock. Through the tiniest of cracks, she saw that the lounge was dark. There was no light coming from Erica and Marta's bedroom. She waited, holding her breath, to see if anything moved.

Slipping back into the pantry, Little Girl picked up the metal pressure cooker from the shelf and put it on the front ring of the big gas stove. She placed the canister in the centre of the pressure cooker, then returned to the storeroom to collect an enormous bottle of cooking oil. Listening for any sounds in the rest of the house, she slowly filled the pressure cooker. The glug of oil as it dropped into the pan seemed to echo around the space and call out for attention.

She placed the empty bottle at the side of the stove. Remembering how her mother prepared bland stews and pungent soups, she placed the lid on the pressure cooker and twisted it until it engaged, then took the heaviest of the weights for the cooker's lid and fastened it onto the valve.

It took her two attempts to light the blue flames under the pan. As they flickered, they cast a weird glow across the kitchen. Little Girl looked at the pan, hoping she had got it right and the oil was starting to heat, then tiptoed into the front office as quickly as she could.

The last time she'd seen her passport, it was in the top drawer on the right-hand side. 'Let it still be there, please!' she prayed. She slid open the drawer. Night streamed through the window and it was hard to see the contents in the half-light, but finally she pulled out the little book she'd held in her hand on the flight so many months ago.

She looked around. Two letters addressed to Eric lay on the desk. She pushed them into her pocket with the passport and stepped into the hallway. The pan was hissing on the stove like some strange predator. She moved to the terrace doors and wrestled with the handle, but they didn't move. The hissing of the pan built in volume. She went back into the office and shut the door behind her. Here, too, the window was locked.

Her heart sank. She'd hadn't thought about what to do when the pan exploded. In her fear-filled planning, she'd thought she would hide at the end of the garden or by a door, and hope that people would arrive after the blast. Now, here she was in Eric's office by the window, holding on to a desk chair, waiting for what she was certain would be a disappointment.

She heard the hiss and noise from the pan as though gas were filling the room. She tightened her grip on the chair and lifted it from the floor.

When it came, the explosion was anything but disappointing. A huge tight fist of red flame filled the house. The office window shattered. Little Girl flung the chair aside and threw herself through it, propelled by the intense heat. The air filled with smoke and fire and the pungent smell of oil.

She clambered into the front garden as flame and glass and stone and wood rained down around her. She crawled towards the road and tried to stumble to her feet; as she did, she felt another enormous explosion at her back which flung her down onto the stone kerb, cutting her knees and smacking her hands onto the tarmac. A wave of excoriating heat passed over her face and she screamed with pain.

Rolling onto the side of the curb, she looked back at the villa. Whatever had exploded, it wasn't only the primitive device she'd placed on the stove. Flames now licked around the entire place, and a thick dark pall of smoke was seeping out of the windows and through the roof.

She thought of her doll's birthday party, the little figures burning away. She heard her mother's screams and her own laughter. She knew Eric and Marta were in the flames. As she clutched her face in pain, she started to laugh once more.

Chapter Fifty

Frankie was discharged from the police station just before six o'clock. It had been a long afternoon, tearful, frustrating and, above all, puzzling. The traffic warden had carried out an heroic attempt to arrest her after she'd thrown the laptop through the window but she had resisted. She would have been able to get into the car and drive away were it not for the traffic warden spotting the rare sight of two constables out on patrol on the high street.

Within half an hour, Frankie was in the back of a police van heading down to the station. The last thing she saw as she looked out of the window was the self-satisfied traffic warden fixing a ticket to her car.

The desk sergeant looked familiar. 'You'll be wanting to book a room here,' said Sergeant Chescoe.

Frankie gave him a weak grin. 'Suppose there's no point in me saying this is not my fault?'

'You're right.' Chescoe turned to his computer screen. 'Now stand on that white line while PC Crocker and I get you booked in.'

PC Crocker, the taller of the two constables who'd arrested her, who to Frankie's eyes looked like an effeminate version of Stephen Merchant, stepped up to the counter and gave details of the time and nature of the offence.

Frankie practised her breathing. In … One, two, three, four. And out. It seemed to help. She managed to stay silent, only speaking when requested to answer the sergeant's questions.

'You're lucky, Mrs Baxter. Your friend DS Webb is on this afternoon. I'm afraid we've got to put you in a cell for a while until he's free to interview you. After that, it should all be pretty straightforward – providing you behave.' He added particular weight to the last three words.

PC Crocker and his unnamed companion led her down a blue and cream corridor of heavy doors. It was the sort of place she'd seen on television a hundred times. Pulling open the door of cell number four, PC Crocker asked her to remove her belt and shoes. She perched on a thin ledge under the window, which she assumed served as a bed. There was a rancid smell in the room; once PC Crocker closed the door, Frankie saw the open-plan toilet arrangements in one corner.

She'd started the day ready to begin a brand-new job and now, five hours later, she was trying to calm herself in a room smelling of shit. She pulled her knees up to her chest and hugged them close.

There had been many times when she'd taken what life had given her, so why hadn't she been able to do that today? Why hadn't she been able to deal with it reasonably? She knew why: she needed to be heard.

There had been four hours of discussion in that office about a job she knew was hers, a job that two people she'd never met insisted didn't exist. She was pretty sure they had doubted her sanity by the end of the morning. As soon as she walked out of the door, they would forget all about her.

She couldn't allow that. The squeaky wheel got the grease; to get the answers, she had to create a noise. That was just what she was doing when the laptop sailed through the office window – although that might prove a problem with Shannon or Henry when they started looking for the computer to do their homework.

She'd lost track of the time when the cell door cranked open and the ferret face of Detective Sergeant Webb appeared round the door. 'Well, well, well. Look who it is.' Frankie fought hard not to tell the sergeant that he should have opened the door with, 'Hello, hello, hello.' He didn't seem in the mood for jokes. 'Follow me, Baxter.'

She was pretty sure it was the same interview room in which she'd spent time when she'd met Detective Sergeant Webb before. It was heartening to see the familiar face of PC Ashley waiting at the interview table. He nodded when she entered the room but stayed silent.

The sergeant went through the routine with the recording device and then looked her in the eye. 'You're not doing badly, are you, love? Session in here as a possible suspect in a suspicious death enquiry and now damage to council property. What's going on?'

Frankie took a deep breath. Was it worth explaining? The tone of his voice suggested he would be impervious to any form of excuse, but she knew she couldn't give up. 'Something odd is going on, sergeant, and it all seemed to come to a head this morning.'

'You'd better start explaining to me before we get the charge sheet out.'

Frankie bit back her response. Her stomach tightened and

she exhaled slowly while trying to find the right words. She told him about the job application, the emails, the online training and how she'd turned up at the office this morning, as requested, and found it was all a lie or some kind of malicious trick.

'I'm no expert on Internet fraud,' said Sergeant Webb, 'but it all sounds a bit extravagant just to get you to turn up for a job that's not there. A bit of a prank, if you ask me.'

'A prank?' The word hit Frankie in the face as if he'd slapped her. 'Somebody's fucked my life up, sergeant. That's how much of a prank it is! Somebody's built up my hopes that for once I could achieve something, that for once I wouldn't be scrabbling around in the bottom of my purse for loose change to buy something for supper. Just for once, I wouldn't be having to fill out endless benefit forms to supplement what they call a flexible hours contract. Somebody has taken my miserable fucking life and hung it out to dry.'

Webb relaxed his gaze and looked down at the table for a moment.

'And if you could feel one bit as stupid as I do,' she went on, 'then there's a slim fucking chance you'd understand.'

PC Ashley squirmed in his seat.

Webb looked at her. 'Right, you can make a formal request for an investigation. I have to inform you that there is very little actual evidence. What we are here to sort out is the damage to the childcare office while you were doing your impersonation of Fatima Whitbread with a laptop. Leave it with me. Detective Sergeant Webb leaving the room.'

A soon as the door closed, PC Ashley leant across the desk and pushed a button on the tape recorder. 'Just pausing the recording for a moment.' He smiled at her. 'Nothing you say is being recorded now, okay?'

Frankie looked a little bewildered but nodded her head.

He moved round to Frankie's side of the table and sat next to her. 'I think someone has targeted you for this. Someone wanted this to happen.'

Ha! The incisive police mind at work, Frankie thought. She remained silent, her heart pumping as she realised what he was suggesting.

'Have you any idea who it might be?'

The answer was straightforward. 'No.'

'None at all? You did tell me about the circumstances that caused you to leave your last job. The guy who propositioned you. Wouldn't be the type to want to get his own back, would he?'

'He *did* get his own back. I got sacked. I don't believe this. I keep myself to myself. Me and the kids. I've had enough shit in my life. Once Henry's dad pissed off, I made a promise that it was me and the three of them together. Everything I do, I do for them.' She snatched a pause for breath. 'I've no idea why somebody would go to such lengths to set me up. My friend Cora sorted this job. Why would somebody want to make me jobless? They've made me a fool of me. I owe the bank all the money we spent over Christmas, and now I'm sitting in a police station facing charges of criminal damage. And you think that someone somewhere is getting a kick out of this?'

'I don't know.' PC Ashley stared at her. 'But with your permission, I want to try to find out. I can't do anything today – the sarge will be back in a minute – but I could call round.'

Frankie was having trouble taking everything in. 'If you do, could you not wear uniform? I'm sure the neighbours are sick of police turning up at my door.'

PC Ashley laughed and moved round to the other side of the table as the door opened. Sergeant Webb came in. 'Right, we've had a call from a Mr Pravasana who is the guy running the place where you went bananas in this morning. I'm not sure why, but it looks like you struck gold. If you agree to meet the costs of the window replacement, they'll agree not to press charges. If I were you I'd grab it, otherwise, you're going to have a criminal record.'

Walking back up the street to the car, Frankie pondered the events of the afternoon. She'd no idea where she was going to find a couple of hundred pounds to pay for the window. The only positive thing was a brief flicker of hope from PC Ashley. If she could find out a bit more about what was going on, this might all make a strange kind of sense.

She turned onto the bottom end of the high street and saw the lights on in Snifters wine bar. A few people were sitting at tables in the window. Cora had asked to meet her there that evening for a drink after work. Would she turn up? There was no sign of her at first glance.

Frankie found a table near the back of the room and ordered a bottle of the cheapest house wine, the sort that would make Cora splutter if she tasted it. She thought of what Cora would say when she found out what had happened. She'd had no response to the phone message she'd left, but that wasn't unusual. Surely she was nothing to do with this? She'd given them a car. She'd shown them endless kindness. And yet something was wrong. Why had she said she was the boss, when nobody at the office knew who she was? And why did she never answer the phone? It was what Sherlock Holmes might call a two-glass problem.

As Frankie downed her second glass of wine, things became clearer. Cora had an enemy. Someone had realised what she was up to and resolved to make her plan fail. They'd interfered in the job allocation process and wiped Frankie's records from the scene.

Another glass, and that didn't make any sense. Cora had waited outside this morning to wish her good luck. Cora must have thought she was going into a job. But then nobody at the childcare office had heard of Cora. Had she lost her job? Had she been too afraid or embarrassed to tell Frankie about it? Was she lingering there assuming Frankie would be fine, though she herself no longer had a job?

More wine didn't make her thoughts clearer, but Frankie knew that somehow this involved Cora. She glanced at her watch. It was coming up to eight o'clock. Cora hadn't shown up. Frankie suspected she wasn't going to and, at this moment in time, Frankie had no way of getting hold of her. And she should be at home with the kids.

She emptied the last splash out of the bottle and, beaming at the chunky barman, she paid the bill. As she stumbled out onto the pavement, Frankie realised she was more than a little tipsy. It was quite a walk home, especially in this condition, and the car was just up the street. Should she chance it? It was a straight road home; with the windows down to get some fresh air and music playing to keep her alert, it would all be fine. Wouldn't it?

She held her breath and set off, walking slowly even though her legs were telling her otherwise. She swayed and stumbled forward with a feeling that, no matter how many steps she took, she was no closer to the car.

All at once she found herself standing outside the childcare office. They'd boarded the window up and there was no sign of her car.

Chapter Fifty-One

Lottie stood on the cliff edge, staring out at the endless sea. She'd been told many times that France lay thirty miles across the water but she found it hard to accept. Standing here, it felt like the edge of the world.

She loved watching the waves rolling in to shore; breathing in time with them brought her a calmness she could never explain. She often strolled up here in the afternoons with the kids in a pushchair if either one of them decided they were too tired to walk.

The seaside town below her curled around the bay, the little harbour providing refuge for the few remaining fishing boats that still set out each day just as this tiny town had given shelter to her when she most needed it.

Bundling your two small children and worldly possessions into the back of a cab and setting off to an unnamed destination was a massive act of faith, but the alternative had been staying and enduring the physical abuse from Craig.

She could remember Mrs Heaton's voice like tyres on a gravel driveway.

'He has a long day working, does our Craig. He does that so that you and the kids get what you want. I know you've got two little ones to look after, but it wouldn't hurt you to get off your arse and think about bringing in some money.' Mrs Heaton had put an envelope down on the kitchen table. Lottie knew it would contain money to buy her silence. 'So what if he is a bit short-tempered at times? You just remember. He does it for you.'

Lottie had called a phone helpline and done as they'd told her: packed an emergency bag, bought a new burner phone and ordered the taxi from a firm in another town. They'd identified her as 'being at risk', and the social worker told her that they would help her and the children get to a place of safety. The day the taxi took them to the station, someone met them with rail tickets and the train had brought them here. She'd stepped off the train, bags and children in hand, with no idea what to do next.

A friendly faced woman strode down the platform towards them. 'Charlotte? Is it Charlotte?'

'Yes, though friends call me Lottie.'

'I'm Daisy. I hope I may get to call you Lottie.' She had the kindest eyes Lottie had ever seen and a wide smile that seemed attached to her heart. Lottie knew at once she would become a friend. Her cheap jeans, green T-shirt and hooded jacket were the sort of thing that Lottie might wear herself. Her greeting offered no hint of authority, just a hello.

Daisy stooped down and picked up Lottie's bag. 'And look at these two little lovelies,' she said in a comforting country burr that made Lottie feel warm and welcome. She introduced Daisy to the children and the little party set off down the platform.

'It shouldn't be too far for the little ones. It's between here and the sea. We'll get you all settled in, then you and I can have a natter and I'll explain how everything works. How does that sound?'

Lottie thought it sounded perfect, though she wasn't sure she'd heard anything after the word 'sea'. When they had clambered aboard the train, Lottie hadn't noticed where they were going. She knew they had to get off at a station called Queenscliffe Bay. It sounded a little unusual, but to be by the sea, far from Craig, was breathtaking.

'Here we are,' declared Daisy. They stood outside two grand Victorian houses with enormous bay windows. This was to be their home.

There were eleven other women and three staff living in the refuge. Like Lottie, two of the other women had children. Every morning a staff member looked after the youngsters in a nursery at the rear of the house. This gave Lottie time to talk and to listen and, above all, to realise she wasn't alone.

For the first time since the chats in the attic room with Little Girl, Lottie sensed she had friends. Daisy would ask the women to form a circle with their chairs and then lead the conversation. It was a safe space where Lottie could talk through what had happened. There were some tears. What her past held scared her, and memories pricked her skin like needles. With no way of fighting back, she endured the pain as a picture of Craig's face flashed through her mind. But, little by little, she felt the weight lifting from her.

The days gave her a routine that she adored. Staff put meals on the table and everybody ate together. It was one big, noisy, dysfunctional family or, as Lottie heard one of the little boys describe it, 'It's a family with too many mummies.'

Lottie liked this family with too many mummies. She couldn't remember how long she was there before Daisy explained there was a time limit on how long she could spend in the refuge. She made it clear that they would never push Lottie out, but that the staff at the refuge would put her in touch with social services in Queenscliffe Bay. 'They'll do their best to find you and the little ones somewhere to live.'

'Here? By the sea?'

'I don't think it will have a sea view, and it might be a bit of a squeeze. They do tend to come up with bedsits or small flats, but I know people who've made them into lovely comfortable homes,' said Daisy. 'Remember, we never know what's round the corner.'

Lottie liked Daisy a great deal; she was like an eager head girl at the kind of school Lottie had read about as a child. She was always smiling, a smile which came from deep inside and lit up her eyes. Lottie could hear the smile in her voice.

Sometimes, in the evenings when Daisy had left to go to her own family, the women gathered in the lounge around the television. Lottie thought about the journey that had brought her here, about the decisions she'd made. In the programmes they watched on television, everybody talked about their journey – their journey to stardom, their journey to business success. Lottie knew that she'd made some wrong turns on her own journey.

The refuge brought happiness for nine months. One morning, Daisy called Lottie into the office. 'Social Housing have been in touch. They've got a pretty little flatlet they think might be just the place for you and the little ones. Shall we go and have a peek?'

It had two rooms and a bathroom. One was a bedroom with a pocket-sized double bed and a single bed pushed into a small alcove; the other room had a battered sofa and an extremely basic kitchen corner with a gas ring and tiny fridge. In the bay window stood a dining table with a couple of rickety chairs.

'The splendid thing is that it's clean and everything comes with it.' Daisy waved her hand to indicate the colourful pots, pans and crockery. But for Lottie, the best thing of all was standing on one of the wonky chairs in the corner of the window and catching a glimpse of the sea.

'It's wonderful,' she said, and Daisy enveloped her in a tremendous hug.

Everyone was so helpful. They arranged her benefits and two of the other women helped to move things from the refuge.

Daisy called round on the afternoon of the first day with a cake. 'Here's to your new home,' she said cutting two large slices, one for herself and one for Lottie. They had tea and Daisy fussed around plumping some cushions and straightening sheets on the bed. It took several long hugs before she left. 'And do keep popping in and letting us know how you are. Success stories like you encourage the other women,' she said.

Lottie watched her walk away, before climbing onto the chair to take a look at the sea. Then she set about helping the kids settle into their new home.

***

Queenscliffe Bay was a town of two halves. Along the promenade on the seafront were the shops to attract the day trippers and holidaymakers, and the large houses that had been turned into bed and breakfasts. On the clifftop overlooking the harbour were new developments of glass-fronted palaces and apartment blocks. These were homes for people who'd discovered the joy of a town like Queenscliffe after life in the city.

The further back from the sea you walked, the older and grubbier the houses became. It was an urban landscape of faux-Victorian architecture that bore grudges. Shops fought to sell their goods for under a pound, and houses meant for one family now housed four or five in small, ill-fitted flats. This was now home for Lottie and the kids.

It was a squeeze for the three of them in the flat. Lottie felt as though the children were on top of her all the time. Daisy had managed to find an old TV set, and Lottie promised she would get round to buying a licence for it. Plonking the kids in front of the set for most of the day, she missed the interaction with the other women at the refuge. Two or three mornings a week, she found herself heading back there to catch up with everyone. She might be able to catch a glimpse of the sea, but she felt like she couldn't see the light at the end of the tunnel.

A week or two after moving in, she met Andrea who lived in the flat at the back of the house and had a three-year-old boy called Sharma. Andrea had also come from the refuge. They took to sharing a pot of tea in each other's kitchen during the morning and taking the children round the shops together to fill the afternoons. Lottie would catch sight of them in shop windows as they passed past and smile at herself: Lottie, short and growing more than a little plump; Andrea, a tall blonde beanpole who looked even taller teetering on her heels with her hair pulled into a ponytail to give her the Croydon facelift she was so proud of.

One morning Andrea knocked on the door. 'I've come to ask a favour.' Although it was barely eleven o'clock, she had squeezed herself into a pair of jeans that had given up the fight.

On the looks front, she ticked boxes where Lottie felt she didn't even have boxes.

'I was wondering if you might be able to babysit Sharma for me tonight. I said I'd have a drink with someone, and I can't leave him on his own. Babysitter's let me down.'

Andrea's son Sharma was a sweet little boy whom Lottie had adored from the first moment she saw him. 'Yes. I mean, if you're happy with that, then yes.'

That evening Andrea knocked at the door once more. Lottie had never seen her looking so glamorous. High heels, the skinny jeans from the morning, shiny pink wet-look drop earrings and more makeup than was necessary or wise. Clutching her hand was a little angel in pyjamas.

'He'll be ready for sleep soon. Put him down on the sofa or something. I won't be long. An hour. Two at the most.' With that, she teetered off into the night.

Lottie made Sharma comfortable on the sofa. Her own children were already in bed. Lottie thought that was the best way of making sure that none of them stayed up too late. She needn't have worried; by the time she'd made herself a cup of tea, Sharma was curled up fast asleep. Lottie smiled. He looked so peaceful as he slept that it made her pop into the bedroom to look at her own children. Both of them were fast asleep, one in the double bed that she shared and a tousled head peeping over the bedspread from the single bed in the alcove. Lottie let happiness soak into her bones.

The babysitting was a splendid success and Sharma became a regular fixture on the sofa. Andrea stretched her one evening out to three or four hours. One night when she was collecting Sharma, she stood holding him at Lottie's door. 'I could do this for you too. Your two could come to mine and you could have an evening out. You deserve it.'

Lottie shook her head. 'I'm not sure where I'd go. But thanks. I'll think about it.'

It was another five weeks before Lottie plucked up the courage to accept the offer. She underwent a quick make-over session, which consisted of Andrea applying cosmetics and Lottie wiping them off with the back of her hand.

With what might best be described as a natural look, Lottie found herself walking into the Lamb and Flag one Thursday evening.

Chapter Fifty-Two

'You think Miss Walsh may have a set of keys?' PC Oliver Ashley picked up the mug of tea Frankie had given him and blew across it. Frankie made a cup for herself, then left it untouched. She was still feeling the effect of last night's wine.

'I have to say,' he went on, 'you and Miss Walsh do seem to have remarkably intertwined lives. All this mix up with the job must be something to do with her. Now a car disappears, which she's got keys to and that she gave you as a gift.'

Frankie threw a couple of soluble paracetamols into her mug of tea and sat down opposite the constable. He looked different this morning. As requested, he'd not turned up in uniform. In his white T-shirt, pale-blue denim jeans and trainers, he resembled a slightly older version of Jonny. He had shorter hair but was similar enough to make Frankie understand the saying about feeling old when policemen start to look younger than you do.

'I don't suppose you've heard from Miss Walsh, have you?' he asked.

'No. I left her some messages yesterday. We'd made a tentative agreement to meet in the wine bar, but she didn't turn up and hasn't called back.'

'Have you done anything to upset her?' Oliver made a

second attempt at sipping the scalding hot tea.

'I haven't seen her since I applied for the job. As it was a position in her department, she was very keen to keep everything above board. Nobody was more surprised than me when she turned up yesterday morning to wish me good luck.' Frankie held her hand to her mouth. 'Sorry, I'm not feeling too well this morning.'

'Big night in the wine bar, was it?'

She wondered why he had to ask. 'I finished the bottle and then got back here late. Put the kids to bed 'cos I couldn't face telling them everything then sat and drowned my sorrows in half a bottle of Bacardi left over from Christmas.'

'Have you reported the car stolen?'

'No, not as yet. I wasn't really with it last night. What with everything that happened during the day, I couldn't cope.' Frankie ran out of words.

'Take a deep breath. I'm here to help, remember?'

She looked at him doubtfully. He was a kid. She didn't have much faith in his ability to solve anything.

'I think there's a simple course of action for today. You go and have a lie down for an hour or two until your head clears. I'm going to check the car registration on the ANPR, see if anything comes up. When the kids get back from school, I think you've got to sit them down and tell them what's happened. I'm happy to help.'

Frankie smiled at him. 'The one thing I've got right is mothering. They've all managed without their various dads, you know. Sorry for saying it, but you're barely out of junior school.'

'We need to speak to Miss Walsh. As we found before when we were checking up on the Mrs Steadman incident, she doesn't seem to be on any records. The sarge should have followed up on that.' He paused for a moment and contemplated the hot tea. 'I don't know whether there's anything in this, but it might be worth me taking Henry for a walk this evening to see what he can recall about the night he met her. Something that could help us work out where she might be.'

***

'Why would Cora take the car? She gave it to us,' said Henry.

PC Ashley, now back in uniform, leaned across the table. The kids had been made to sit down for a family conference in the kitchen on their return from school. Between them, Frankie and Oliver were taking them through the whole story.

'We don't know she has taken it, Henry. We do know that she still had a set of keys and somehow she's involved in this job application business.'

Shannon slipped her arm around Frankie's waist. Frankie hugged her tight.

'You don't need keys to start a car, you know?' As soon as he'd spoken, Jonny realised his mistake.

'And how would you know that?' Frankie asked, scowling at him.

Jonny tightened his jaw and looked at the constable.

Oliver smiled. 'Seen it on the telly, have you? Hot wiring and all that.'

'Yeah, and it's on the Internet,' added Shannon. 'There are YouTubes about it. I think they're supposed to be in case you lose your keys, but it's the same thing, innit?'

'Why would Cora do this, Mum? Wasn't she always nice to us?' The cold waters of the Brighton sea filled Henry's thoughts.

He shook his head and shivered.

Frankie held out her arms and he got up and went to her. 'We don't know that she has darling.' She ruffled his hair.

PC Ashley put down the glass of milk he'd asked for after his encounter with the scalding tea that morning. 'It could be that Miss Walsh is in some sort of trouble herself. That might be the reason why she hasn't got back to your mum. I wondered if you wanted to help me take a look around the park, Henry. See if you could recall anything about when you first met her.'

Henry looked a little unsure.

'It would be an enormous help. Sort of unofficial police work.'

'Oh, lucky you, Henry,' said Shannon. 'You can be a copper's nark.'

Before Henry had a chance to find out what a copper's nark was, or indeed whether he wished to be one, Frankie took charge. Even though PC Ashley was wearing his uniform, it seemed as if she'd acquired four children around the dinner table. 'Right. Henry is going to go for a walk with Oliver – sorry, PC Ashley. I'm going to make some dinner and when they get back, we're all going to sit down and eat. Everybody got that?'

The room burst into activity. PC Ashley and Henry wrapped themselves in coats, and Frankie started dishing out orders to Shannon and Jonny.

'What if I don't remember anything, though?' Henry stood by the door waiting to leave.

'I'm sure you'll do fine,' said PC Ashley. 'Who knows? You could be the key to the whole thing.'

Chapter Fifty-Three

Even in a city as exotic and cosmopolitan as Dubai, the sight of a teenager sitting on the kerb clutching a British passport, skin peeling from her face, watching a house go up in flames, attracted attention. The police and the fire brigade turned up remarkably quickly. Little Girl sat undisturbed, watching the inferno, a slow smile passing across her face.

The house looked like something out of a horror movie, all twisted plastic and charred wooden posts with nothing left to salvage. The air was full of acrid burning chemicals. The street filled with fireman and paramedics.

A policeman approached Little Girl and spoke to her in Arabic. She remained silent. Prising the red booklet from her fingers, he looked at it and nodded. 'Don't worry,' he said in clipped English 'We will have somebody here to help you very soon.'

Little Girl had decided her best option was silence. She smiled at the policeman and held out her hand for the passport. The house, and everything it stood for, was no more. Time to move on.

Twenty minutes later, a wide silver limousine drew up at the end of the street and a plump, grey-haired, bespectacled man climbed out. He pushed his way through the hosepipes of the fire brigade to sit next to her on the kerb. He offered his hand. 'May I?' He indicated her passport. Little Girl handed it to him and he flipped through the pages. Sitting on the kerb was not the most decorous of places for a sixty-four-year-old vice-consul to be.

Kenneth Howe started to explain who he was. 'I think we need to get you seen in a hospital first.' He was surprised she wasn't screaming in pain. The skin seemed to have been removed from one side of her face and her cheek was charred. 'Then we'll take you to the embassy. My wife is pretty useful in tackling all sorts of dilemmas. I'm sure she'll know what to do.'

Little Girl smiled at the man.

At his age, Kenneth was within sight of a pleasant retirement on the Devon coast. The last thing he needed was a mysterious childish girl saying nothing and sitting outside a burning building.

They spent the rest of the night checking her into a private hospital. The doctors flocked around her and she was soon sedated. A doctor sat the vice-consul down in the corridor outside her room so they could talk out of earshot. 'I fear she will need some surgery on her face, Mr Howe, sir.'

'I did wonder if that might be the case. I'm afraid we don't know anything about her, but as she is British and this is rather urgent, I suggest we go ahead and sort everything later.'

The doctor smiled at him. 'You are a kind man, Mr Howe.'

For two weeks Little Girl lay in a bed in a white room. People came in and out, but she showed little interest in them. She maintained her silence and, by the time he took her back to the consulate, Kenneth knew no more about her than he had when he'd found her.

Mrs Howe sent Kenneth packing and started clucking around her. She had no children of her own. She believed children needed stability and her husband's career as a British consul with postings all over the world had put paid to that, but it didn't mean she couldn't rise to the occasion when necessary. Little Girl was settled into a beautiful bedroom to sleep and rest.

Over the days that followed, Kenneth did his best to piece together her story. The house which had gone up in flames turned out to belong to Eric and Marta Skura, originally from the Netherlands. The most interesting fact for Kenneth was that they had an adopted English daughter registered as staying with them.

He collected papers, made telephone calls and followed up on reports. The fire brigade had discovered the remains of two bodies in the house and it looked very much as though they were Eric and Marta. Kenneth talked to Little Girl. Though most of her face was bandaged, her eyes roamed the room. Her trust in him seemed to be growing.

A few occasional nods in answer to his questions told him she'd been out of the house when the fire had broken out. She'd come back home to discover the house ablaze. She wouldn't say how she had acquired the burns on her face, but Kenneth assumed that she'd been trying to get to her adoptive parents. The fire investigators reported an exploding gas cannister in the kitchen, a defect with the gas range, apparently.

Kenneth decided the best thing was to make arrangements for Little Girl to return to England as soon as she was well enough to travel.

'She's not a child,' said his wife. 'It wouldn't surprise me if she's eighteen or more.'

Kenneth sighed. Something, somewhere, didn't ring true. 'She'll be going back to England a very rich woman. Erich and Marta Skura are exceptionally wealthy. The solicitor says their wills leave everything to each other or to any dependants.'

His wife looked at him sceptically. 'Doesn't that strike you as odd when they only adopted a little while ago.'

Kenneth nodded. 'The solicitor thinks it was some sort of tax dodge. The house, the cars, all their assets transferred to the little girl's name. Bank accounts too. She was a UK resident. Evidently that was what they needed. The authorities here were chasing them for all sorts of financial misdemeanours.'

One evening, they sat down with Little Girl. Mrs Howe thought the occasion called for a glass of wine and placed three elegant glasses on the table.

Kenneth told Little Girl what they'd found out and what was planned. 'You'll be going back to the UK with a tidy sum. And we can put you in touch with people who can help you and check on your surgery.'

Little Girl knew when words were necessary. 'Thank you' she said, and the three of them raised their glasses. Little Girl took a sip and smiled at Kenneth as best as she could through the dressing on her face. It was a long time since someone had been kind to her. Not since her days with Lottie had she felt so looked after.

'I think you've been very lucky,' Kenneth said.

Little did he know, but money wasn't all she was taking back to England. The doctor had given her other news, too.

Chapter Fifty-Four

Henry's first inclination was fear when PC Ashley asked him to help investigate, but as they left the house the butterflies in his stomach turned into thumps of excitement. This was a proper adventure. He was investigating a crime – or what they assumed was a crime. No one seemed to be sure what had happened other than the car had gone missing.

Having arrived home from school after a text from his mum telling him he'd have to walk, he'd found her setting a plate of biscuits on the table. A plate of biscuits meant trouble, or at the very least meant his mother wanted something. She poured him a glass of squash. Henry used the fact that his mother was going to ask them something to get a second glass, which was not often allowed.

'It's nothing to worry about, my darling. I just need to talk to the three of you together.'

Shannon and Jonny appeared soon after, and Frankie sat at the table with them to start the family conference. A few minutes later there was a knock on the door and the policeman joined them. Henry wondered who was in enough trouble for the police to be summoned.

Now, as he walked away from the house, speeding up every three or four steps to keep up with PC Ashley who seemed to have very long legs, Henry knew that this was an adventure. Oliver, which he now knew was the policeman's name, said they needed to get to the park. It was getting dark and the streetlights were coming on as they strode to the roundabout and across the road down towards the park gates. Henry found it more than a little difficult to keep up.

Peering through the railings into the park, the only illumination was the pale path stretching into the wooded gloom. There was no movement. Without a word, Oliver set off again along the front of the railings towards Parkside. Henry thought he would know which way to go because he was a policeman. They wandered a street or two away from the park and Henry did his best to keep up.

Eventually they turned into Parkside and Henry stopped. 'This is where I bumped into her car.' He looked up at the policeman, but Oliver was standing under a streetlamp which produced an orange halo that made it difficult for Henry to see his face. He couldn't see whether the policeman was smiling or not.

'And you didn't get hurt?'

'No, not a lot. Just a bruise. She got out of the car to say she was sorry. I told her what I was doing, and she said she had a key to get me through that gate.' Henry pointed to the gate in the fence about fifty feet away.

'She had a key to that gate?'

Henry nodded.

'And the key opened the gate?' Oliver asked.

Henry accepted it was the job of a copper's nark to answer even the most obvious of questions. He nodded again.

'Do you remember if she had the key with her, or did she

have to go and get it?'

Henry paused for a moment. He was always being told at school to think about his answers before he spoke. 'That way,' said Miss Bentham, his teacher, 'you give better answers.'

Henry counted to three in his head. 'She went to get the key, and she came back and brought me a sleeping bag and cushion.'

'Next question then …' PC Oliver had turned towards the entrance of Parkside Tower. Henry could see he wasn't smiling. 'Where did she go?'

Henry wondered if he should tell Oliver about his previous visit to Parkside Tower. But then he would have to tell him about following Cora through the town and how he'd met her outside the wine bar and given her an envelope. Oliver might think it was suspicious, and it might get Mum into more trouble.

'It might have been this one,' he said, staring up at the white balconies and the picture windows and recalling the movement he'd seen at one of them.

'I'll tell you what,' said Oliver. 'You have a quick scout down the driveway and see if you can spot anything familiar. I'll go up to the front door and check names on the bells and try to have a look in the hallway. Okay?'

Relieved that he wasn't being questioned further, Henry nodded and set off down the driveway at the side of the building. He expected a light might turn itself on as it detected movement, but nothing happened. In the darkness the trees sighed as they peeped over the wooden fence. There were several parked cars but none that he recognised, neither the one they were looking for nor the one that he'd bumped into.

What he was looking for? Cora had gone away and returned

with the key and the sleeping bag, that was all. But he wanted to impress Oliver with his keen investigative skills, so he wandered round what appeared to be a garden. Should he walk around it again before going back to Oliver to report that he'd found nothing?

Henry stood stock still for a moment, thinking about what to do. There was a sharp blow to the back of his head. As he started to turn, he lost his balance and fell to the ground. And then there was darkness.

Chapter Fifty-Five

Lottie and Andrea's babysitting system seemed to work well. Andrea went out on Wednesdays and Saturdays and at first Lottie happily limited her excursions to Friday evenings. It seemed best that the kids stayed with whoever was babysitting. When Andrea was out on the town, Sharma slept head to toe in the single bed in Lottie's bedroom, and the reverse happened when Lottie was out on the town, with her kids tucked up on Andrea's sofa.

Lottie found nights out hard work at first. It was a long time since she'd socialised but the crowd at the nearest pub, the Lamb and Flag, were sociable and it wasn't long before there were some familiar faces to talk to when she stepped through the door.

A tall, red-faced, curly-haired landlord called Derek was the centre of all the bonhomie. She spent her first visit perched on a bar stool chatting to him and revealing selected parts of her life story. That was the trouble: what could she say to people without revealing who she was and where she'd come from? She'd enjoyed her time at the refuge, yet it wasn't something she particularly wanted to talk about and certainly not if it might make people ask questions about her past. A children's home, failed marriage, abusive husband and taking flight with two children to the seaside was not the stuff of bar-stool chit-chat.

She told Derek that her parents had died and left her a little money. As she'd always wanted to live by the sea, she'd moved down here to see how she liked it. Yes, she had children, but her husband had walked out and that was part of the reason why she wanted to start again somewhere else.

'Missus left me too, you know,' said Derek, getting her a second vodka and orange. 'You've got to suit this life, letting everybody into your home all the time. They all know what's going on. She didn't like it – no privacy – and she hated being behind the bar. The thing is, it's the only job I can do. My dad did it and my grandad before him. Anyway, I'm better off without her. And I've got our Gary. He's an enormous help.'

'I bet he is,' said Lottie, looking over at Gary, who was working at the other end of the bar. There was no doubt about it, Gary Hackett was fit. His tight-fitting, short-sleeved polo shirt revealed tattooed arms and a curling snake creeping out of his collar and up the back of his neck. His hair was shorn – he'd been in the Army evidently – and he had sturdy footballer's legs. He had a similar rosy complexion to Derek, but it gave him an apple-cheeked innocence. Lottie knew he'd looked up once or twice but, as yet, he hadn't approached her.

In truth, she wasn't sure what she'd do if he did. Nothing had happened in that department since Craig. She wasn't averse to the thought, and one of the reasons she sat at the bar was to watch Gary reaching down to pull bottles from the bottom shelf. He had well-muscled buttocks, just the sort you'd like to grab and pull towards you. She took a large gulp of her drink and caught sight of her blushing face in the mirror behind the bar.

She asked Andrea about him. 'You know anything about Derek Hackett's son, Gary, at the Lamb and Flag?'

'Not really, love. Tell you the truth, I've not been in there for a good few weeks. Now we've got this lovely arrangement, I go further into town. More bars, more choice, more guys.' She threw her head back and laughed.

One morning, when Lottie knocked on the door to return Sharma, Andrea opened the door a tiny crack. 'Give me half an hour, love?'

Lottie said she would, but she had the kids on a promise for a walk along the cliffs and half an hour was the limit. Fifteen minutes later she heard the front door slam and caught sight of a tall, well-built guy in a denim jacket with spiky boy-band hair scurrying away from the house. Andrea's date, no doubt. Lottie knew the type Andrea went for.

For a moment, Lottie felt her chest tighten with resentment. Part of the agreement was that neither of them would bring men home with kids around. But perhaps one good deed deserved another.

'This one's on the house.' Gary grinned at her as he slid the vodka and orange across the bar.

'Not busy tonight?' The Lamb and Flag hadn't yet sold its soul to become a full-on gastropub. While it served meals and had gone for the stripped wood, teal walls and bare-floor ambiance, it still felt like a local boozer. On fine days they did Sunday lunch in the beer garden, and one week Lottie had brought the kids down. It had all been a bit much but then she'd seen Gary smiling at her. She knew she was in with a chance if she wanted to make a move.

There was a gentle drizzle in the air. A smoky wetness had

kept most people at home. Two or three regulars huddled at their table nodded a welcome as she stepped inside, but the place wasn't busy. With no sign of Derek, it was Gary who settled in for a chat with her at the bar.

By closing time, Gary knew everything there was to know about Lottie – or certainly everything she felt happy to confess. Lottie was determined to know a little more about Gary too, not about his family but whether his thighs were as strong as they looked and was he a wonderful kisser?

A mingling of hesitation and promise flooded through her as he called time. Gary turfed out the five or six other people who'd braved the weather and slid the bolts in the doors. He poured himself a drink and came to sit on the stool next to her. 'You do this often then, do you?' he asked. 'Hang about after time looking for a bit of fun?'

It might have been because she'd consumed four vodka and oranges that he thought sex was on the cards. He seemed to have changed; this side of the counter, he was a little less subtle. Still a looker though, thought Lottie, with his apple cheeks and broad shoulders. She began to wonder if that was enough to justify a quick fumble.

He reached across and stroked the side of her face, sweeping his hand down her cheek. 'Bit special you are.'

She giggled. Shit, that must be the drink, she thought. He got off the stool and stood next to her. Leaning forward, his moist, full lips brushed hers. A schoolboy's kiss. She pulled away, her breath shaking and shallow. His eyes reminded her of children's paintings, too much water added to the green which had run and faded.

Unable to hold back any longer, she took his head in her

hands and pulled him into a fierce kiss, nuzzling and gnawing at his lips. Her hands worked their way around his body, feeling each contour of his perfect physique. Then she pulled away and opened her eyes. She was right. He was a superb kisser.

Afterwards, Lottie decided she didn't want to stay the night. She felt cramped in his single-bedded room above the pub with the bed pushed against the wall, a wardrobe and a juvenile mix of football and pin-up girl posters.

Gary fell asleep almost instantly, but she lay on the bed awash with physical satisfaction and self-loathing. He had lived up to her hopes – not too forceful but rough enough to show who was in charge. He'd spent time making sure she got what she wanted. It'd been a long time; in fact, she couldn't recall a man ever having spent that much attention on her needs.

Yet somehow, lying there in the bedroom above the pub in the tepid sodium glow of a streetlamp, she knew it wasn't enough. She feared the urge that had encouraged her to do this would never go away. She thought of her kids and the sacrifice they'd made for her to have this night out, one of them curled up on Andrea's sofa, the other tucked into her friend's bed just so that she could have her pleasure. She loved those kids. She knew whatever else happened, she'd always put them first.

She slipped out of bed and started to pull on her clothes. Her phone had ended up on the bedside table. As she picked it up, she noticed a packet of condoms lying there. Unopened. How could she have let that happen?

Picking up her shoes, she stepped out of the bedroom. Downstairs, after pulling on her jacket and shoes, she unbolted the side door to the pub. She would have to leave it open. She'd have to hope that no one tried it until the morning. Hope Gary would be lucky. Given the unopened condom box, she'd have to hope she was lucky, too.

Chapter Fifty-Six

'What do you mean you've lost him?'

'I mean …' PC Ashley removed his cap and looked rather shamefaced '… that he's disappeared.' He stepped into the kitchen.

Frankie reached for the kettle, her automatic reaction in times of stress.

'No. Nothing to drink, thank you. I called in to see you first. I've got to go down to the station and make a report.'

Jonny and Shannon crowded into the doorway. Oliver's appearance always heralded news of some kind, and they were anxious not to miss anything. Jonny was more than a little envious that Henry had been the one singled out to do the investigating.

'We walked around the park. There's a block of flats called Parkside Tower. Henry said that it was there that he hit her car.'

'He did what?' Frankie was trying her hardest to breathe calmly and not scream at Oliver.

'He didn't tell any of us when it happened and, come to that, neither did she. Nothing serious, but he ran out into the road and caught the side of her car. That was how he met Miss Walsh.'

Frankie shook her head in disbelief. Tears were forming in

her eyes. 'I wonder what else he didn't tell us.'

Oliver continued with his version of events. 'I said I'd take a look at the hallway of the block, see if there was a name on the mailbox or anything. I suggested Henry had a look down the drive at the side in case he recognised any of the cars. It seemed to take him quite a time, so I went around the back of the building and there was no trace of him.'

'He wouldn't have done anything stupid like he did last time, would he?' asked Frankie. 'He's not run away and hidden in the park again for some silly reason, has he? We've got to get people out looking for him.'

Jonny pulled himself upright from slouching on the door frame. 'I don't think he's done anything daft, Mum. Something's happened. It's not like Henry. If he was planning something again, he'd have told me like he did before.'

'What do you mean, he told you?' Frankie lashed out with her hand, intending to clip Jonny around the head, but he proved too quick and darted away from her in Oliver's direction.

'He told me he was playing a Facebook dare and he'd be away from home for a night. Said he'd be okay, and I wasn't to tell anyone about it.'

Frankie took several rapid breaths. 'You saw how worried we were about him, and you knew? How could you? You can tell you come from a shit brain of a dad.' As soon as the words shot across the room, she regretted them.

Jonny's face crumpled and he looked on the edge of tears. 'I'm sorry, Mum. I thought I was helping. I was looking after Henry.' He bit his lip, uncertain whether to go on. 'Thing is, he was so excited when he went off with PC Ashley. He wouldn't have run away.' Jonny turned to Oliver. 'He'd have wanted to find something and impress you. He thinks you're a bit of a hero.'

'Why would he think that?' Frankie picked up a mug from the table and threw it into the sink. It shattered into smithereens. 'Most of the time you seem to be fucking useless. Now you've lost him.'

No one spoke for a moment.

'I need to call it in at the station.' Oliver reached for his cap.

'How did you end up at that particular block of flats?' Jonny got the question in before his mother could continue her onslaught against the police officer.

'It was opposite a private gate in the railings. Henry said that's where she'd let him into the park to sleep. She'd got a key. I thought she might live in that block because they give keys to residents for after-hours access to the park on summer evenings.'

'And does she live there?' said Frankie.

'No sign of her. Nothing on the mailboxes. We've tried to trace her address before, if you remember, and nothing came up.'

'And now no Henry.' Frankie shook her head in disbelief and let out a low growl.

'What we gonna do, Mum?' Shannon took her mum's arm.

Frankie hugged her daughter. 'I don't know. What *are* we going to do, constable?'

'Let's me report it at the station. I'll give you a call as soon as I've done that. Meanwhile, stay here in case he turns up.' Oliver put on his cap and stepped outside. 'I'm sorry Mrs Baxter.' He turned back and looked at Frankie. 'It wasn't my fault.'

'Go and report it and let's pray and hope, shall we?' Frankie closed the door and dropped into one of the kitchen chairs. Tears flooded down her cheeks. 'Henry, Henry, Henry, Henry.' She called his name as if trying to conjure him up. 'Why Henry?'

Jonny and Shannon exchanged glances.

'Mum,' said Jonny, 'I think he's been to those flats before. On his own.'

Chapter Fifty-Seven

Little Girl walked into the arrivals hall and was met by a stocky dark-haired man bearing a card from consulate advisory services with her name on it. A quick car journey and she settled into a hotel room just off Gloucester Road, organised by the consulate for the next few nights. It was hardly luxurious, but it would suffice for a day or two. Mr Howe had taken great lengths to explain to her before she flew back that the Skuras' bequest made her a very rich woman.

Little Girl found it hard to understand. 'Why would they leave me everything?'

She recalled the shopping trip with Marta before they left. All her dreams answered. A couple who actually wanted her. The clothes and presents hadn't mattered, but on that day, Marta had looked excited to be with her, had seemed to care for her. How mistaken she'd been. From the moment they'd arrived in Dubai, they treated her as little more than a servant, a slave to please an endless stream of strangers. Eric and Marta had never touched her themselves but that made it no less easy to hate them.

Brought up in a home barren of love, unwanted and unneeded, had this helped her survive the night visits of the white-robed Arabs? The painful memories were like deep and horrible chapters of a book. Now was the time to leave it on the shelf to gather dust. Now it was time to choose what she wrote on the pages of her life. Today, tomorrow and every tomorrow that followed had to be wonderful. They had to be hers.

She had an appointment with the solicitors the next day. She had one outfit other than the clothes she'd travelled in, which Mrs Howe had sorted out for her before departure, a plain skirt, white shirt and tailored jacket. 'I look older,' she thought, as she caught sight of herself in the mirror. It was as if the changes to her face had seeped down into her very soul. *This is my world now. My terms.*

The outfit was perfectly good enough for today. Tomorrow would be different. Money bought you dreams. It didn't always make you happy, but it could make you content. Control money, and you could control men.

She stepped out of the solicitor's office onto the pavement and steadied herself on the plate-glass wall of the office building. What was a lot of money? She recalled how they had read Shakespeare in English lessons at school. How Mark Anthony had promised Caesar's estate to the people of Rome. 'Seventy-five drachmas to each and every several man.' They had considered how it would mean something different to every person. Yet no matter how she looked at it, £3.2 million was a fortune.

Little Girl wasn't sure where she was. Central London was unfamiliar, but she knew she needed strong coffee in a china cup. Across the road she saw a hotel with a large stone portico and a uniformed footman standing outside, exactly the sort of place where she could afford to take coffee now.

Once inside, the floor, tiled in fine marble, made her every step echo. A young woman, whose features suggested she had an unpleasant smell lodged under her nose, showed Little Girl to a table in a far corner of the lobby. She felt distinctly under-dressed but that was something she could soon remedy. For now, she ordered coffee and biscuits and endured the superior glance of the grey-haired waiter who stumbled over to serve her. *You're not good enough to be in here*, his eyes told her. *Just you wait*, she thought. To infuriate him even more, she paid in cash, asked for change and left no tip.

She walked out of the hotel and stood for a moment on the pavement. She had to call at a particular bank and produce her passport. The solicitor, who'd reminded Little Girl of her headmistress at junior school, told her the consulate had taken care of the hotel and she would receive a bill for fees. Unfolding a piece of paper on which she'd written the bank's address, she stopped a passer-by to ask for directions.

Ten minutes later, she was travelling up the escalator to the glass foyer of a private bank. It wouldn't be her bank for long. Once she'd signed all the papers and gained access to the money, she'd be setting up her own accounts, running her life and spending her time how she chose. Seven months of hell in Dubai and now she was home. And planning for the arrival of her baby.

Chapter Fifty-Eight

Jonny sat at the table with Frankie and Shannon. 'He came back one night a couple of months ago. Said you'd sent him to give her a note at the wine bar or something.' Frankie nodded. 'It sounds like you were the one playing silly games, Mum.'

'Cora didn't want me to have any contact with her. Nobody was to see us together in case they thought she was showing me preferential treatment over the job.' Frankie realised how ludicrous it all sounded, how clever Cora had been in distancing herself.

'And we know it all turned out to be a hoax,' said Jonny. 'Henry thought something was a bit wrong. After he gave her the envelope, he followed her to find out where she lived. He was pretty sure he saw someone spying on him from one of the top flats. He was convinced it was Cora.'

'Why didn't he tell us any of this?'

Shannon couldn't believe what her brother was saying. 'Right from the beginning when she brought him back, he liked Cora. And she did save him in Brighton.'

Jonny remained silent.

'She did, Jonny. Shannon is right.' Frankie didn't like the way that Jonny seemed to be shifting the whole story.

'Yes, she did. Though Henry did say that when she reached him, he found it difficult at first to know whether she was trying to pull him out of the water or push him under.'

'That's ridiculous.' Frankie was fast losing patience. 'Why would she do that? She'd hardly be likely to drown him in front of us.'

Jonny looked his mum straight in the eye. 'Nobody would have known. She would just have failed to save him. What if she was going to drown him and something made her change her mind?'

The three of them sat, unspeaking, at the kitchen table. Shannon broke the silence. 'You gotta admit it, Mum. Something's wrong. All this mystery about the job, and now this.'

'It wouldn't do any harm to go up to Parkside Tower and take a look around. See if we can find any trace of her.' Jonny looked at both of them.

'It's ten o'clock at night. Your brother is missing. The police are dealing with it. My nerves are in shreds, and you want the three of us to go snooping around a block of flats up near the park?'

***

Keeping up with Jonny and Shannon caused Frankie to break into a slow trot as they made their way over to the park. 'This is ridiculous,' said Frankie. 'I'm a mother of three acting like one of the Famous Five.'

'I think it's gonna be fun,' Shannon said as she strode ahead with Jonny.

'Fun?' Frankie fought for breath. Talking and walking wasn't a good idea. 'Your younger brother's gone missing again. This time he's been lost by a bloody policeman. God knows what's happened. I'm on the point of a nervous breakdown and you think it's fun?'

'Let's just keep our heads over this.' In the time since his revelation of Henry's previous visit to the block of flats, Jonny seemed to have grown up.

'We all know he's been there before when he first met Cora.' There was a bitter impatience in Frankie's voice.

She could see her breath making little clouds in front of her as she slogged her way up Overbury Road. They soon reached the junction of Parkside and the high street and stopped to gaze up at Parkside Tower.

'If we find anything, whatever it is, we're going down to the police station first thing in the morning. We're not dealing with this on our own.' Frankie was adamant. She'd insisted they rang the police before leaving the house. The number she had for PC Ashley had gone straight to voicemail, so she'd rung the police station. 'Langley Park police station now operates on reduced hours between 7.30am and 9pm. For urgent enquiries outside these hours, please redial and call 999.'

'I don't believe it. The police station is on bloody voicemail.'

There were one or two lights on in the hallway of the block in front of them. Up on the top floor, a light glowed behind curtains. They crossed the road and stood at the entrance to the driveway. The glass doors were closed.

Frankie was not happy. Out of breath from the walk, and now no way in. 'I said this wasn't a good idea.'

'Sssh.' Jonny waved his hand at Shannon and Frankie. They crouched down behind the wall. The front door to the flats opened and a man left the block in the opposite direction. Scuttling across the grass like a member of the Special Forces Boat Squad, Jonny hurled himself at the front door and managed to get a foot inside to stop it closing. He turned round and whistled loudly. Two heads peeped over the wall.

'This is all getting silly,' hissed Frankie.

Shannon jumped up and ran across the grass to join her brother in the hallway. Frankie took a deep breath and wobbled after them.

They stood in the centre of the hall. On the wall on the right-hand side were mailboxes with flat numbers and surnames. No box had the name Walsh on it, and two of the boxes had no names at all.

'We don't know her name was Walsh. It could be any of these flats.' Frankie felt this was wrong. Anxious though she was about Henry, she had a sudden chill that it would result in no good.

'We can only try.' Grabbing a handful of flyers from the ledge above the mailboxes, Jonny pushed the button on the lift. When the doors opened, he jumped in. He turned to his mum and sister. 'You coming?'

Chapter Fifty-Nine

'It's my baby. I don't want you in his life.' Lottie stood in the doorway of the bedsit, tears streaming down her face, trying to make Gary understand why she didn't want to let him in.

'Most bloody women would kill for a man who says he'll stand by them. What the fuck is wrong with ya?'

'There's nothing wrong with me.' Lottie pushed the door again but his foot was firmly in place to stop it closing.

'I want to spend some time with my son. That's all I'm asking. That's not fucking unreasonable, is it?' Gary leaned against the door frame.

This is what happens when they want their way, thought Lottie. They get into your space. They get too close. It's always the same, Craig was the same. And when they've got near enough, they hit you.

'Just give me some space – a week or two. Let me get myself sorted. Two kids and a baby isn't easy, and I got benefits to sort and all that. When I'm fixed, I'll let you know.'

He reached into his pocket, pulled out a handful of notes, and thrust them at her. 'I don't want him wishing for anything. Take this. And there's more.'

Lottie wanted to snatch the money out of his hand and shut the door, but then he'd be buying his way into her baby's life.

Since moving to the town, she'd kept her circle of friends small: Andrea, Daisy and some of the girls at the refuge, Derek the landlord at the Lamb and Flag and, until making the fateful mistake of sleeping with him, Gary Hackett. To be honest, she'd enjoyed the sex, enjoyed one night of merry freedom.

She'd never felt at any moment that the baby was a mistake. How could the gift of a child be wrong? Her trouble was that she didn't want to share him. He was her child, part of her tribe. She was the protector. Two children growing and happy and looked after, despite all that the world had thrown at them – and now a third. Another chance to prove that here was something she could do well. She was a good mother.

She didn't tell Andrea about her plans to move, but she did visit the refuge and talk to Daisy. 'I just don't want him in their lives. I don't want to have to deal with a man.'

Daisy held up her hand as if trying to pull the stress out of her. 'He has rights. Given your past experience, I understand why you'd choose to run away. He may let you or he may decide to follow you. If he went to court, it's highly likely they would give him access.'

'He's gonna have to find me first.'

Daisy could see how determined she was. 'Have you thought where you'd go?'

Lottie smiled. 'It's not fair if I tell you. I need to lose myself again, me and the three of them.'

'I get it. I'm not suggesting you're right, but I do get it.'

Lottie saw Daisy's wonderful smile, a smile which shone light into her heart. 'Thing is, will you help me?'

Chapter Sixty

The lift jerked to a halt, the doors slid open and Frankie, Jonny and Shannon stepped out into the eighth-floor corridor. Frankie wasn't sure what she'd expected but she was disappointed to see plain magnolia walls and four dark wooden doors, two on each side of the lift.

'Eight-zero-two didn't have any name on the mailbox,' said Jonny. He strode across the corridor and pressed the bell.

'What are you doing?' Frankie grabbed Shannon, alarmed at Jonny's hare-brained action. He signalled with his hand for them to step back into the recess at the top of the staircase next to the lift and hide from view.

There was the rattle of a door chain being removed and the door of 802 swung wide open. 'Yes?' A tall grey-haired man with an outlandish moustache stood at the door in shirtsleeves and braces. 'Yes?'

The fact that the flat was occupied told Jonny it wasn't the one they were looking for, unless Cora was living with Colonel Mustard from Cluedo. 'Our pizza. Great offers on production of this leaflet,' he said, thrusting out the flyer.

'How did you get in here?' the man barked, as though he were addressing a parade ground. 'Did you ring a bell, or did someone let you in? We don't have hawkers and pedlars in the block, you know.'

Jonny didn't know what a hawker or pedlar was, but he was pretty sure he was neither. 'Sorry. Didn't know whether to leave them in the hall or push them through the letterbox, but someone let me in downstairs as they were leaving. Sorry to trouble you. Won't do it again.'

'I should hope not. Good night.' And the door slammed closed to Jonny's relief.

He walked along to the top of the landing to find Frankie and Shannon pressed against the wall. 'It's not 802.'

'This is ridiculous,' said Frankie. 'What are you hoping to find?'

'Jonny's good at this, Mum, and he's right. The other flat that didn't have a name on it was 804. Want me to try, Jonny?'

Jonny handed the pizza flyers to his sister and stepped back, dragging his mother out of sight. Shannon walked down the corridor to the door of 804. She was about to raise her hand and ring the bell when the lights went out. 'What's happened?' she hissed.

'Don't panic.' Jonny fumbled over to the lift doors and pressed a white button set into the wall by the control panel. The lights turned on. 'They're on a timer. I guess it gives us a couple of minutes every time you push it.'

'That's something we should have at home with you lot. Might save some money,' Frankie said.

Shannon rolled her eyes, making sure her mother saw, and turned to the door. Jonny pushed himself back against the landing wall as she pressed the bell for 804. She held her breath and listened. The door remained unopened. After a while, she pressed the bell again. All she could hear was her mother's breathing further down the hall.

'I don't think there's anybody in.' Jonny stepped away from the wall and joined his sister. 'I think we ought to go in and take a look around.'

Frankie worked her way back up the corridor to the door of 804. Jonny had what looked like a miniature metal nail file in his hand and was pushing it into the lock. 'What the fuck are you doing?' She reached up to pull his hand away from the door. 'Stop that now.'

'If you don't want to know, then look away.' Jonny pulled his arm out of his mother's grasp and resumed poking at the lock.

'I've done my best to bring you three up. Where on earth you learnt all this from, Jonny Baxter, I don't know. I am not pleased.'

Jonny continued to work the slim metal file into the lock.

Frankie tried again. 'You do realise this is now breaking and entering, don't you? It's ceased to be "having a look" and it's now criminal behaviour.'

Jonny felt the file slip into the lock. Pulling the sleeves of his sweatshirt down over his hands to make sure that he didn't leave any marks, he pushed down on the door handle and opened the door. 'Step inside and don't touch anything.'

'I'm not coming in. It's criminal.' Frankie folded her arms to make her point.

'Fine, then stay out here in the corridor and make people suspicious. I'm doing this to see if we can find something that explains why my brother has disappeared. My brother. I'd do the same if you or Shannon went missing. If you don't want any part of it, why not piss off downstairs and wait outside?'

Jonny had never used so many words in one go before. He

must be angry, thought Frankie. She lowered her head a little to avoid his eyes and stepped into the flat.

They found themselves in a narrow hallway. Jonny tried the light switch but nothing happened. To the left of the front door was a bathroom devoid of any signs of life. Ahead of them was a sizeable room with a kitchen recess at one end. Even up here on the eighth floor, the orange glow of the street lights crept through the windows, silhouetting the furniture against pale walls. An enormous picture window at the other end of the room overlooked the park. To the left was an archway leading into an open-plan sleeping area with a substantial double bed stripped bare. All the furniture seemed basic. There was a small sofa, a coffee table and a dining table by the window with one single chair, but no sign of life.

There was no air of fustiness; someone had lived in this place until not long ago. Frankie could smell a hint of furniture polish in the air. No cushions on the sofa, no television, and empty cupboards in the kitchen. Whoever had been living here had gone.

Suddenly there was a loud bang. Shannon let out a small scream and grabbed her mother. 'Oh God, what's that?'

'Front door which Mum didn't shut,' said Jonny, heading back into the hall.

'Mum!' Shannon moved over to look out of the window.

'Be careful, Shannon. You don't want anybody seeing you.' It terrified Frankie that they might be discovered. She didn't want another visit to the police station for breaking and entering.

Shannon took a step back. 'You can see most of the park from here. In daytime you could see everything. Do you remember how Cora turned up sometimes when we were in the park? Remember how she got upset when we were making that film with Luke?'

Jonny walked into the kitchen and, covering his hands once more, pulled open the remaining kitchen units to find the cupboards bare. 'There's nothing here.' His disappointment rang out clearly as he spoke. 'It could have been a hideaway but, if it was, she's gone.'

Shannon stepped back from the window and bumped into the table. Turning round, she saw something flutter to the floor. Apparently it had fallen from between the table and the wall. She picked it up.

'What's that?' asked Frankie.

'It's a postcard.'

Frankie and Jonny crowded round her. There was nothing written on it. Shannon turned the card over so they could see the picture. Two white cottages with green window frames and doors basking in the sunshine; rising between them, a tall white lighthouse.

Chapter Sixty-One

Little Girl rapidly realised that having other people to do business for you made life much simpler. Money bought people and people gave you time. She stayed away from the individuals whom Mr Howe had recommended. She wanted no connection with her past and its memories. Money allowed you to disappear. Money could buy you an unfamiliar name and, with it, anonymity.

She found a small flat on the south bank of the river in a recent development which she loved for its lack of neighbourliness. She took delight in fashioning it into a home, the first place where she'd felt relaxed since sharing a room with Lottie. Most evenings she sat on the balcony watching the river slip by. Her love for the city grew as the baby in her belly grew.

The arrival of a child changed her life, but even she wasn't quite ready for the overwhelming torrent of love it unleashed in her. The child was her world now. This was what she was born to do, to raise this child, to give it the opportunities she had lacked, and the love she had craved. She would ensure that her child always felt needed and loved and wanted for nothing. She would protect it, nurture it, fight for it, if necessary.

In her life, she had failed in many things. She'd failed in childhood through no fault of her own; in the house with

Mother and Father, she had been invisible and lost her ability to love.

There had been a glimmer of hope in her friendship with Lottie. Hours spent talking, sharing deepest secrets, sharing their lives, their likes, rejoicing in their misbehaviour. When Lottie left with scarcely a word to set up home with Craig and have his child, it hurt more than when Little Girl's parents had died. She told herself she wasn't to blame when people hurt her. But was it her fault if they hurt her a second time?

Little Girl determined no one would ever harm her child. She sold the flat for a lot of money, not that she needed it. Wise investment of the money left to her by the Skuras gave her an income to live off and capital in the bank. She bought a tiny house further out of the city in a quiet tree-lined road of obscurity. The local school was excellent, and she settled into the humdrum life of a suburban existence.

Her time spent locked in that room in Dubai made it difficult for her to approach other people but now there was a crowd of school mothers. As her child grew and went from school to school, she found it easier to become part of their world. She helped out at garden parties, made costumes for school plays and served tea on the sponsored walk. She bought raffle tickets for the Christmas fayre and cheered at sports day. Always well-dressed but never ostentatiously, she succeeded in her desire not to stand out. She became invisible by choice. Hers was a supporting role to prepare a child for the world who would be proud of her as their mother. She could hide her memories for a while in another life.

Little Girl remembered how hard her own teenage years had been. Taking that journey once more, but this time as a parent, proved no easier. She learned to step back, not to interfere, to offer gentle guidance when asked and to endure the fact that, most of the time, she was alone. But birthdays brought special joy. On her child's seventeenth birthday, she arranged a trip into the city: shopping for presents, lunch at what would be a trendy, if not necessarily good, restaurant and the best seats for a hit show.

The pavements of the city were a teeming river of humanity. At times the tide carried them along and on other occasions they battled against it. Teenagers don't hold hands so Little Girl carried the packages, trying to keep an eye on her child while not being overprotective. At the top of Bond Street, they paused because crowds were waiting to cross the road. Little Girl placed her bags on the floor to adjust the strap of her shoe. When she picked them up again, she found she was alone. A shard of panic pierced her gut. She craned her neck, looking around and trying to see a familiar face. There, through the windows of a nearby computer store, was her child. She turned and fought her way against the crush of people, credit card at the ready to show her love.

Across the road, standing by the traffic lights waiting to cross in her direction, was a woman with a small child. Little Girl's breathing quickened. It had been a long time, but she knew who they were.

Chapter Sixty-Two

'I'm not sure there's anything we can do this time,' said Daisy. Her smile fell at the edges. 'Are you sure you're doing the right thing? You made such a success of moving here and the children are doing well. Gary does just want to help, you know.'

The sharp breeze on the clifftop caught in Lottie's eye, causing it to weep. She wiped it dry with her sleeve. 'It's my job. They're my children. I'm going to be their mother. I'm going to bring them up and nobody is having a say in it. If he can't stop interfering, then I'm going somewhere he can't find me.'

She bent down to smooth the blanket covering the small baby in the pushchair. 'I know what you're saying. Last time it was for my safety, this time it's because of my foolishness. But I can't have him around. I have to do this. I have to bring up these kids.'

Daisy nodded. 'I can't pretend I agree, but I think I understand. Have you had any thoughts about where you want to go?'

'I need to lose myself. I need to be some place where it's easy to be anonymous. Somewhere I can lose myself and the kids.'

'Let me see what we can do. I'm not making any promises.' Daisy fell into step beside her and they walked back into town. They stopped outside the refuge and Daisy kissed her on the cheek. 'I'll be in touch.'

Lottie nodded. There had been little goodness in her life, but Daisy was a massive part of what there was. She tugged at the blanket on the sleeping child once more and set off home.

Daisy proved as good as her word. Although she hadn't been able to get any joy out of a local authority in the city where Lottie wanted to base herself, she'd used her contacts to find a charitable trust that was able to help.

'I might never see you again, but you know I'll always be grateful.' Lottie pulled Daisy forward, engulfing her in an enormous hug.

'Last time we did this at the station, you just had a couple of bags. Now you've got an extra little person, more baggage, and a van full of stuff heading to your new home.' Daisy's smile was on full beam. 'I know why you're doing this, Lottie. Looking after the three of them means so much to you. But if that right person comes along, promise me. Let them in.' Daisy didn't wait for the train to pull away. She didn't do goodbyes.

Lottie missed the sea. While in Queenscliffe, she'd come to love her walks along the clifftop, which brought her calm and peace. Taking the children to the beach on summer days filled her with joy.

The local park near where they'd moved had an enormous lake. It was no substitute for the crashing waves of the English Channel, but a peaceable place nevertheless. Signs in the park told her it was a river widening out, but Lottie didn't care about that. She just knew that walking by water brought her tranquillity. She took the children to the park as often as she could. As they grew up, the older ones asked if they could go there on their own with friends. She knew she had to say yes, but she would sit in the flat with the youngest child regretting her decision, unable to relax until they returned.

The flat wasn't big enough for the four of them and she had to try various combinations of shared rooms and an uncomfortable sofa bed for them all to sleep. Once the children were at school, she'd been able to take some part-time jobs to supplement the money she claimed in benefits. Sometimes these jobs were on-the-fly, cash in hand. She knew it was wrong but, if it meant better meals on the table, fresh clothes at the beginning of each term and more treats for the kids, she was happy to risk it.

In the evenings. when all three children were safely in bed, she would switch on the television and fall asleep in front of it before eventually crawling into bed ready for another day of being a wonderful mum. She fought, she struggled, but she survived; as a result, the children grew and laughed and played and fought and loved life. Of that she was most proud. They were happy kids.

She searched newspapers and magazines and snipped out vouchers for discounts on attractions and places to visit, anything to make them feel special. If a birthday fell during school time, they celebrated it on the Saturday afterwards with a small party of school friends or a trip into the city.

This year, the youngest's birthday was on a Wednesday in half term. Having arranged for someone to look after the other two, Lottie planned a trip to what purported to be the world's largest toy shop. Burgers and milkshakes and then toy shopping. She added to this the excitement of the train journey and it was a perfect day out.

After the fast-food lunch, they made their way towards the

toyshop for what Lottie hoped would be as much looking and as little spending as possible. Things were tight at the moment and she'd had to set herself a budget. Perhaps coming to a shop offering so many treats was not the right thing to do. Her mind wrapped itself in thought as to just how much she should spend while they stood at the curb waiting for the lights to change.

It was if someone punched her in the stomach. A face – unmoving in the crowd on the other side of the road, staring out of the hustling mass and looking straight at her. A ghost. A memory.

She wasn't sure what to do. Little Girl obviously recognised her. Lottie raised a hand and started to make her way across the road. She felt sick. Reaching out to grab the child's hand, she pulled him away. The streets were school-holiday busy and she lost sight of the other woman. She sensed her child's confusion.

Suddenly she heard her name. 'Lottie? Lottie?'

Don't look back, she thought. Never go back. She'd moved on, that was what she did best. She'd moved on and things had got better. Little Girl was the past; Little Girl wasn't the best of times.

Reaching the next side street, she darted into the nearest shop pulling a bemused child with her. They worked their way to the back of the sales floor, hiding behind racks of expensive jackets. An assistant stepped forward. 'Can I help madam?'

'No. I'm fine. Just looking.' Lottie feigned interest in a rack of skirts, clothes that she would never wear and could not afford. She watched Little Girl pass the window and stand for a moment on the street corner, confused. She ducked down behind the clothes rack.

'Are you sure there's nothing I can help you with?'

One look at the assistant's face told Lottie she had marked her down as not the right sort for this shop. 'I'm fine, thank you.' She took one more glance at the pavement outside. Little Girl had disappeared. Lottie grabbed her child's hand and strode out of the shop. She turned left and disappeared into the tight network of small shopping streets.

Little Girl knew it was Lottie. She was plumper than she had been, but it was definitely her. Little Girl had raised her hand in the hope of a smile and friendly recognition. She'd received nothing.

When someone hurts you once, it's not your fault. If you let them do it a second time, then maybe it is.

Chapter Sixty-Three

No matter how she tossed and turned, Frankie couldn't find the right position. A dull haze of sleep lodged somewhere at the back of her mind but was too far away for her to reach. She lay there taking deep breaths in and slow breaths out, though her mind was racing like an icy wind. It was going to be an interminable night.

Shannon lay motionless in the other bed, no doubt tired by their adventure earlier in the evening. When they'd returned to the flat, Frankie had called PC Ashley's number only to get his voicemail again. She hadn't said anything about what they'd been up to and asked if she could speak to him the following morning.

Lying there now, she knew she had to get up as early as possible and head down to the station. Were they even looking for Henry? There'd been no word from anyone since Oliver had turned up on their doorstep and said Henry was missing. She should have gone straight to the police station and not taken part in Jonny's crazy schemes.

So they'd found an empty flat. What did that prove? And yet something lingered, like a faint trace of perfume after the wearer has left the room, holding itself in the air to evoke a distant memory of someone who was absent. The postcard bothered her. She'd never seen the picture before but somehow she was sure she knew the place. Two little white cottages with green window frames and the tall white lighthouse between them; it had a disconcerting familiarity. Had Frankie been more spiritual, the thought might have crossed her mind that she'd lived there in a previous life but that was a waste of time. The place was in this world.

Frankie had been on edge all the time in the empty flat. They'd no right to be there, and whatever Jonny had done with the lock to gain entry was illegal. She'd have words with him. She almost hadn't taken the postcard with her but, as she was telling Shannon and Jonny that it was time to leave, she slipped it into the back pocket of her jeans.

In spite of his burgeoning a career as a burglar, she couldn't help but feel proud of Jonny. She was pleased that his first thought had been to do something about finding his brother. He was growing up, becoming a man – something she'd always dreaded. It was the first sign she'd have to surrender her children to the world.

Two thirty-nine morphed into two-forty and time trickled by, marked by the glowing numerals on the clock. Thoughts of the previous day pushed their way through heavy blackness. The curtains were making a vain attempt to filter the orange glow of the street lights outside. Frankie sighed wearily.

She gave up the unequal struggle with sleep and sat upright on the bed with her legs outstretched, covered with the duvet. She could hear the pitter-patter of rain. The tapping of rain against the glass of the window made her feel alone, as if someone were outside wanting to come in.

She unhooked her dressing gown from the door and slipped

into the kitchen for a warming cup of tea. She was surprised to find the laptop booted up on the kitchen table, left there by Shannon, no doubt. She turned on the kettle and began to make tea. As she reached over to flip the laptop closed, there was a sharp ping and a message alert appeared in the corner of the black screen. Clicking on it, she recognised the email address straight away: it was one of the addresses used during her job application process: victoria.adams@ Langleycc.com.

Why would someone be emailing her at three in the morning? She clicked on the notification. In the subject box were three words: *Looking for Henry?*

Her throat constricted as if she were trying to swallow something indigestible. She clicked on the full screen. The lighthouse from the postcard filled the screen. A different angle, but definitely the same building. Suddenly there was a picture of Henry that looked as if it had been taken on a phone camera. It was impossible to determine from the background where he was, but there was a semblance of a smile on his face. Yet the smile did not reach his eyes; Henry was being told what to do, he wasn't smiling because he wanted to. He had an odd-coloured green cloth wrapped just under his face, rather like he was at a barber's.

Frankie stepped back from the computer in shock and her hand knocked the mug of hot tea to the floor. The scalding liquid splashed onto her skin. Trying her hardest not to yell in pain, she ran the cold tap and held her hand underneath it. A thousand needles stabbed her, yet she couldn't remove her eyes from the picture of Henry. 'He hasn't run away. He's being held somewhere.'

She soaked a kitchen towel in icy water to wrap around her

hand. Then, reaching over to the computer, she clicked on the corner of the photograph to enlarge it. The message faded from the screen. She could no longer see the mail in the inbox. She clicked furiously through her emails. Then, without any warning, the mail program closed itself down. She clicked on the icon to open it up again, but the screen started to flash. All she could see were lines ripping across the screen, alternating between neon tears and blackness.

Frankie hated these machines. Heart beating inside her chest like someone hammering on a door, she followed the IT support advice she'd so often given out at the Tech Factory: turn the computer off and turn it on again. Nothing happened. She was staring at a blank screen. There had been a message about Henry. She knew that. She'd seen it. The pain in her hand was proof of it. But where was it now?

She glanced at the clock. 3.25am. She ran back into the bedroom, opening the door as loudly as she could. Leaning over the bed, she shook Shannon and turned on the bedside light.

Shannon awoke abruptly. She blinked and, after a second or two, turned her head towards Frankie. 'What's happened? Mum, what's going on?'

'Get up, love. Come and look at this computer for me.'

'What time is it?' Shannon didn't move.

'It's time to do what I ask. Now!'

The two of them stood side by side staring at the black screen.

'I don't know what happened. It's totally dead.' Shannon could barely hold her eyes open.

'Yeah, I can see that, but I know what I saw.' Frankie took a deep breath. 'And someone mailed me a picture of your brother.'

***

'A picture postcard of a mystery lighthouse found in an empty flat that you shouldn't have been in, and mysterious disappearing email messages arriving in the middle of the night on a computer that's blown up. Are we doing *Midsomer Murders* or something?' Sergeant Chescoe laughed. His voice had the merriment of Father Christmas while his face was as welcoming as Scrooge's. 'Let's try and get things straight, Frankie, shall we?'

Frankie, Shannon and Jonny had been outside the front door waiting for the police station to open at half past seven that morning. Frankie had dragged both kids out of bed to accompany her. Arriving for work, Sergeant Chescoe barely managed to get his key in the door when the trio erupted before him. Now, safely behind his desk, he felt more in a position to investigate the stream of recollection that was pouring from the three of them.

'We've told you everything. Henry went to have a look at the flats with PC Ashley, and PC Ashley came back and said Henry had disappeared and he'd lost him. So we went for a look around and we found the picture of the lighthouse and the cottages, and I don't know how or where but I know that place, and that's what stopped me sleeping, and I woke up to make a cup of tea and an email came in and showed a picture of Henry, and he was smiling only he wasn't, and then the computer flashed and crashed and now it doesn't work.'

'Okay. Take a deep breath and let's go over it one step at a time.' Sergeant Chescoe turned to the keyboard on his desk and started some slow, two-finger typing. 'You say Henry went off with PC Ashley last night and disappeared?'

Frankie was about to launch into another outburst when Jonny leant forward. 'Yes, that's right.'

'And PC Ashley came back to the house to tell you this and said he'd report it?'

Jonny nodded. Chescoe's hand wobbled the computer mouse and he looked at the screen of his desktop. 'The thing is, PC Ashley wasn't working yesterday. He didn't report it here. There's no report of any missing child from yesterday evening – there are no reports from PC Ashley at all.'

'I think he was helping us out on an informal basis, but he definitely said that he was going to make a report. He's really fond of Henry.' Frankie didn't want to get Oliver into any trouble.

'Has he gone missing before by any chance? It's Henry Baxter, isn't it?' Sergeant Chescoe started scanning the screen.

'Can't you ring him up and ask what's going on?' Frankie asked.

'We can if we need to. Let me check something out.'

The three of them held their breath while Sergeant Chescoe continued to click and consider various screens.

'Didn't Henry go missing about a year ago? Just one night? Turned out to have been sleeping in the park and showed up fine in the morning? Would that be the Henry Baxter we're talking about?' Sergeant Chescoe turned to face them and folded his arms. He looked very pleased with himself.

Chapter Sixty-Four

Movement and darkness, always darkness. And his head hurt. That was all Henry could feel. One minute he'd been working his way around the garden of Parkside Tower, and the next he was trying to squeeze his eyes open in darkness.

His hands were tied tightly behind him and his shoulders had started to ache. His feet were free, so he shuffled round and lay on his back, which was more comfortable. Above him, he saw two tiny chinks in the blackness that flashed orange and white; together with the vibration shuddering through him and the brief noises he could hear, he knew he was in the back of a car.

A tiny, stupid part of him thought this was dreadfully exciting, an adventure worthy of the movies he watched on Netflix. And yet it hurt. Every bit of him hurt. His head ached and throbbed from where the blow had landed and, although he couldn't raise his hands to check, he was sure there was an alarming egg-shaped bump on one side of it. He couldn't raise his hand to see his watch and he had no idea how long he'd been unconscious.

They were heading somewhere at speed. Several times the unlit space tilted like some bizarre theme-park ride, and the egg-shaped bump banged against a hard surface. There was carpet beneath his hands; it was rucked up and the ridges poked into his back.

The longer the journey went on, the more nauseous he felt. Whenever he travelled in the car, Frankie dosed him with pills and he wore a special band on his wrist to help quell the travel sickness. Now he had neither of those and, as he bounced about in the blackness, he became aware of his early evening meal trying to part company from his stomach. Sickness clawed at his throat. He swallowed time and time again, trying to force down the rising bile, but it was too late. What looked like an unusually large portion of McDonald's nuggets spewed out of his mouth. His stomach started to contract even more, forcing everything up and out.

He could feel his face sweating in the pungent stench, which made him want to vomit more but there was nothing left to bring up. It was frightening how prodigious an amount of vomit an eleven-year-old travel-sick boy could produce. Tears flowed down his face, mingling with the sweat on his cheeks. Vomit covered the front of his jacket and he felt it, a seeping dampness forcing its way through his football top onto his chest. It stank. If this was some sort of Netflix adventure, Henry didn't want to be in it.

Chapter Sixty-Five

The kitchen table seemed to be the family war room. Frankie, Shannon and Jonny sat around it, working out what to do. Nothing they'd learnt at the police station calmed the fear taking hold of Frankie.

'Why aren't they looking for him, Mum?' Shannon demanded.

That was exactly what Frankie had asked Sergeant Chescoe when he'd turned back to them from his computer looking smug. 'I found a note,' he said. 'He's marked down as not high risk for the first twenty-four hours due to previous behaviour.'

Frankie fought a desire to punch the sergeant in the face. 'Who made that decision?'

'Seems like it's your friend PC Ashley. There's no report of Henry going missing yesterday, but there is a note on the file from last February that his disappearance was voluntary and future occurrences should be put on hold for twenty-four hours. Possible time waster, it says here.'

The words stuck in Frankie's throat. 'He's not a time waster. He's my son.'

At Frankie's insistence Sergeant Chescoe had made notes, though she wasn't sure how accurate they were. He muttered a word every so often as he typed. 'Email. Picture. Barber's shop.'

She couldn't understand why he was making this so difficult. And where was PC Ashley? She'd come to think of Oliver as a friend. After he'd returned to the house last night to break the news that Henry had disappeared, he too seemed to have vanished into thin air.

She looked at her other children sitting with her round the table, eager to help. The events of the past two days were overwhelming her. On Monday morning she'd stepped out of the house ready to start a new job; now, less than forty-eight hours later, she was trying to convince this old fool of a sergeant that her youngest son had been taken by a person, or persons, unknown, and was currently being held against his will.

'I know somebody has got him. I don't know what he's done, or why they're doing it, but he's in some sort of trouble.'

Jonny gave his mum a hug. 'Shan, let's see if we can look at Henry's Facebook account.'

He passed his phone to Shannon and her fingers danced across the screen. Suddenly there was Henry beaming out at them from his Facebook page. 'How did you do that?' said Frankie. 'I thought all this was supposed to be private.'

'It is, but his password's really shit.' Shannon tapped on the screen again and a list of Henry's latest posts appeared. 'He's posted nothing on here since Saturday evening. And looking back, I don't think it's a dare or anything like he did last year.'

Jonny sat staring into space looking thoughtful.

'Both of you are telling me everything you know, aren't you?' asked Frankie.

'Course we are, Mum. At least I am.' Shannon looked at Jonny. 'And you are, aren't you?'

Her voice broke Jonny's train of thought. 'What? Sorry, I

was thinking about that postcard. Why do you think you know where it is, Mum?'

'I don't know, but as soon as I saw the picture I thought I'd seen it before, or at least heard about it. I've not been able to work out more than that.'

'Give it here,' said Shannon. 'We can try and find out where this is. That might jog your memory.' She put the postcard on the table. Taking out her own phone, she photographed it and spent several minutes tapping and swiping. As if by magic, the picture of the two cottages and the lighthouse suddenly appeared on her screen.

'How did you do that?' Frankie peered at the picture. Even though it was now full screen, she still couldn't place it.

'Reverse image search. It doesn't always work. Now we stick this picture into Bing or onto Google. If there's a picture like it on the Internet, it'll match it and tell us where it is.'

'And here's me thinking I was the mother of three kids and I'm actually the head of MI5. Go on, then. Do it.'

Frankie and Jonny crowded round Shannon's shoulders. The picture disappeared and the screen changed so that the original picture was now on the left-hand side. On the right-hand side of the screen was a column labelled 'similar images' with small thumbnail pictures of white lighthouses. Shannon started to scroll down.

'There. Third one down in the third column. Click on that one,' said Jonny.

The pictures disappeared and rearranged themselves so that the one on the left was of a white lighthouse with two small cottages at its base. It was taken from a different angle to the one on the postcard, but all three of them were convinced it was the same location.

'Where is it?' asked Frankie.

Shannon swiped at the screen. 'It's a place called Healy Cove.'

Jonny was quick off the mark. He soon had a map up on his own phone to show the location. 'It's there,' he said, sliding his fingers to enlarge the map.

Frankie's eyes flitted between the photograph and the map that Jonny was holding out. She had a life devoid of photographs; the one album she owned was packed with pictures of the children at various times in their lives, but never of her. The snapshots of her life were contained inside her. She knew that this picture was in there but, as Jonny showed her his map, she knew it was not a place she'd ever been to. It wasn't a place that held her memories; it was somewhere she'd been told about.

'We had a wonderful day at the seaside once. The only one I can remember. A long drive in the car and a walk through some woods to a tall white building that stood next to the sea, with two little white houses at the bottom with green windows. It was the most perfect place. I hoped that one day I could live in one of the little white houses and be able to stand in my garden and watch the sea.'

And as she found the memory, she heard the voice.

Chapter Sixty-Six

Henry wasn't sure how long the journey went on for. He drifted in and out of a post-sickness snooze; every so often a heaving lurch of his stomach produced another small mouthful of bile which dribbled from his lips onto the pool of rancid vomit on his T-shirt.

Eventually the vehicle stopped. Henry waited and held his breath. He could hear voices outside the car, two voices at least, but it was hard to make out what they were saying. He lay still, the stench of sickness filling the gloomy space.

He started nervously as the tailgate lifted upwards and he found himself blinking in the light of a torch. Two figures, both in dark clothing and wearing balaclavas that revealed only their eyes, stood looking at him. One was much taller than the other.

Both of them immediately stepped backwards and one lifted an arm to shield their mouth from the smell. The other pulled up their jacket collar to cover their mouth. Making a few small retching sounds, they reached in and lifted Henry out of the car.

Henry stood on the ground, trying to find his balance. The fresh night air hit him like a spout of water from a hose. As the salty, misty night air did its work, he staggered, went as pale as if he'd been covered with whitewash and crumpled like a puppet whose strings had been cut.

He felt himself being picked up in someone's arms and carried across uneven ground. Looking upwards, he saw a tower with panes of glass on top of a white column. There was the sound of a door being unlocked and he was carried into the building and placed on the floor. This time his legs held out and his eyes opened.

The room was circular, with straight white-stone walls from which the paint was peeling. A metal staircase dominated the space. The smaller of his two captors grabbed his hand and led the way up the stairs, metal step after metal step. At the top, the door was pushed open and Henry stepped out onto an enclosed platform.

The breeze had picked up. Heavy with salt, the chill night air wrapped around him. He gripped the railing and peered down at the crashing surf below. The larger of his two assailants was now behind him on the platform and gestured to a small door in the glass chamber. Opening it, he pushed Henry through.

There were two large glass discs back-to-back like huge car headlamps. Henry was pulled over to one side. His hands were untied, wrapped around a small railing that encircled the lamp and tied once more.

He slid to the floor, grateful for the rest and yet fearful of what was to come. He stared out through the windows. Cracks of dawn light sent shimmering rays over the sea. He could see the white-foam tips of the crashing waves catching the pale watery sunlight. Fresh salty air assailed his nose. Henry was at the seaside.

Chapter Sixty-Seven

'We need to get to that place. The place in the postcard.' Frankie was leading the discussion at the kitchen table as though it were a cabinet meeting.

'Healy Cove?' Shannon flicked the picture onto the laptop screen once more. 'Jonny knows where it is on the map.'

'Is there a train?' Frankie looked to her son for help. Jonny started searching pages and stabbing at the screen on his phone. 'Train to Canterbury, then a connecting train to Queenscliffe and a bus to Healy Cove.' His face fell. 'Looking at the time-table, if we left now we wouldn't get there till early evening.'

Queenscliffe. Another memory punched Frankie's gut.

'What's the matter, Mum?' Shannon saw that Frankie seemed not to have heard Jonny's words.

'Nothing, darling, nothing. We need to get there. As soon as possible.'

'You sure you don't want to wait until the police get back to us?' Jonny looked at her and she heard the hesitation in his voice.

'We've got to find your brother, right? The police don't seem to be doing anything to help us. I don't know what's happened to him. Please God it's nothing bad. PC Ashley went off to report Henry missing, and that's the last we've seen or heard of him, too. And what's that miserable old fucker at the police station, Sergeant Tesco or whatever he's called, gonna say when we tell him we've looked up the postcard on the Internet and it's a place in Kent, and we need them to send police there because that's where we think Henry is being held? That old bastard will piss himself laughing.'

'Okay,' said Shannon, 'I hear all that, but how do we get there? You gotta be realistic about this, Mum. We don't have a car.'

Jonny jumped up from his chair. 'Mum, put what you think we need in a bag. I'll be back.'

The backpack sat on the kitchen table. Frankie had no idea what they needed because she didn't know what they were going to do. For some reason, she threw in some T-shirts and some spare underwear, followed by two bottles of orange crush, an enormous family pack of crisps and a torch. It would have to do; it was hardly the stuff of an SAS mission, but enough for a trip to a lighthouse.

She couldn't think straight. None of this made any sense at all yet memories kept sliding into place. Queenscliffe.

***

Jonny had never actually stolen a car before, but you couldn't live on the edges of a council estate within sniffing distance of London during your teens and not learn how to hot-wire one. It was part of the route to manhood.

Rule One: don't diss your own doorstep. He ran down their street and turned into Earlsdale Avenue. One street away and the house prices started to rocket. Large baby wagons and grand family cruisers lined both sides of the road. Mums back from the school run were now doing Pilates in front of the telly. He needed a little bit of luck; hopefully one of them had left their car waiting for him.

He trudged along the far side of the road, keeping an eye out for passers-by as he reached out to check door handles, praying that his touch was gentle enough not to set off the alarms. When a car door didn't yield, he walked nonchalantly to the next.

Stealing seemed such an old-fashioned word. His mates talked of 'twocking', taking without the owner's consent. That's what he was doing, looking for a twoc. And he'd bring it back. But today his mum's need was greater than some yummy-mummy's. He heard his mate Damien's voice: 'It's all part of an unfair system.'

Jonny repeated the mantra in his head to keep his confidence high. He had several mates for whom stealing was breathing. He'd been out with them, never taking anything himself but watching what they did. Now he had a cause and a need, and he understood that stealing to fulfil a demand wasn't a crime at all. For his generation, it was a way of balancing the books.

He made it to the other end of the street and was starting to despair when he saw something that gave him hope. A car was sitting in the driveway of a house with the front door of the house wide open behind it. 'Fucking hell,' thought Jonny as he looked at it. 'Why couldn't it be a shitting Mazda?'

The car was a metallic-blue Porsche Cayenne, not what he'd thought of choosing but if it was the only car in the avenue he had a chance of driving away, then what the hell? He walked up the driveway to the front door of the house. There was no sign of life, which was good. He stood, poised to knock on the open door and plead some fake errand if necessary. Then he saw what he wanted: lying on a side table just inside the hall was a black-and-silver electronic key fob emblazoned with the Porsche logo.

Jonny couldn't believe his luck. He knew this was a gift – a gift his family needed and he was going to take the chance. He stepped into the house and up to the table, holding his breath and ready to turn and run at the slightest sound. He leant forward, swiped the key fob and turned away.

Pulling himself into the driving seat, he closed the door.

Some bastards who lived in these vast houses could distinguish the noise of their own car driving off at a couple of hundred feet, even if they couldn't hear the sound of the bloody alarm blaring out at two in the morning. Reaching forward and pushing the ignition button, he held his breath. 'This is for you, Henry. I hope you're fucking worth it, brother.'

Chapter Sixty-Eight

'Oh my God.' Shannon's mouth dropped open as she stared out of the kitchen window.

Frankie joined her in time to see Jonny climb out of what looked like a very expensive car. He strolled up to the flat and burst through the door.

'What's going on, Jonny?' She squared up to him.

'He's nicked a car.' Shannon beamed in admiration at her brother.

'I borrowed a car from a mate. Okay?'

'Who do you know who has a car like that? They cost a fortune.' Frankie didn't believe him for a minute. She and Shannon stood side by side, pinning Jonny against the cooker.

'I thought we wanted to find Henry, so I went out and borrowed a car.' He looked suspiciously keen to avoid their gaze. 'From a mate.' He coughed. 'We can go to this Healy Cove place and find Henry. My mate would like the car back by this evening, and I'd like to return it, so this is our one chance, yes?'

Frankie opened her mouth to argue but Jonny continued. 'We can do this, Mum. Or I can take the fucking thing back right now.'

'Before anybody notices it's gone missing?' Shannon gave

him a high-five. 'Let's go, Mum.'

Jonny corrected her. 'Before anyone notices my mate has lent it to somebody for the day. Yes?'

Frankie watched them, unsure of what to say or do. There were some moments when being a mum was even harder than talking about contraception. She knew what he'd done, yet she could see how desperate he was to help. If they didn't use this car, what would they do? Memories of her own past told her she should be proud of her son. He'd taken a big risk.

'Get the bag. Let's get in the car before anybody starts asking questions about what the bloody hell a car like that is doing parked outside.'

Jonny settled into the driving seat with Shannon alongside him in the front. She fiddled with the digital console to work out how to enter the destination in the satnav. Computer whizz though she was, it took several minutes. During the process, Jonny jerked the car forward and away from the curb.

Frankie, who'd drawn lots for the back seat, let out a strangled scream. 'I know you've borrowed it, but can you actually drive it?'

'Yeah, I can. Thing is, it's an automatic. It's like driving a bloody bumper car. I forgot I had both feet down on the pedals, accelerator and brake at the same time. Won't happen again.'

Sure enough, the journey got smoother, the houses became grander and further apart and the trees more abundant as they drove out of the city. Soon they turned onto the motorway heading to the coast. From where she was, Frankie saw the speedometer hit eighty-five. She leant forward and stuck her head between the seats. 'We do need to get there alive, you know.'

Jonny slowed the car to a steady seventy. He might never have stolen a car before but he'd certainly driven cars taken by others. He was a proficient joyrider, with handbrake turns a speciality. It wasn't something he was proud of but today it might prove useful. He just wished he'd picked a simpler car. Sitting in the driving seat of the Porsche was like being on the bridge of the Starship Enterprise with flashing lights, digital readouts, hazard warnings and a message advising him not to get tired. Jonny thought the best thing to do was to ignore everything. If anything was wrong, they'd soon know. He concentrated hard on not letting the steering pull him to one side. All in all, a drive down a British motorway was much more complicated than a game of Grand Theft Auto.

In spite of all the excitement, Shannon fell into a doze in the passenger seat. Jonny clicked a button on the steering wheel and the voice of a weatherman filled the car. 'Low pressure over the English Channel will see showers turning heavy as the day progresses. Heavy rain over the south east and along the coast, with some heavy outbreaks and thunderstorms likely.'

'That's all we need,' said Frankie.

'We'll be there before then.' Jonny's attention remained on the road ahead.

Frankie sat back and stared out of the window at the traffic in the other lanes hurtling towards the city. 'Why me?' she thought. The three children were her life; if any of them was missing, she felt incomplete. She knew how hard she'd fight for them to stay together as a family.

She recalled moments of joy with each of them, yet her memories were like a jigsaw puzzle bought from a charity shop with no guarantee that all the pieces were there. There were things she'd shut out, parts of the picture she'd lost.

She knew that if Henry was at Healy Cove, the answer lay there. As the miles passed, she believed more and more that she was right. They would find him there and, deep inside, she had a horrible feeling as to why.

Chapter Sixty-Nine

Henry didn't know how many bones were in his body but every single one of them ached. His heart hurt with loneliness and his head still throbbed from the egg-shaped bump. He forced himself to his knees to try to stand up, but the rope tying his hands to the rail didn't allow that much movement.

Inside the strange circular chamber, he could see out of the windows opposite him. Looking straight down to determine where he might be was useless. An odour of damp old rope and salt filled the air.

It was Wednesday. He hated Wednesdays. Double biology in the morning, double games in the afternoon, accompanied by a vicious scrum to get into the showers and out before the bell rang at the end of the day. He never believed he'd miss double games, but now his heart yearned for the pushing and bullying and the damp rugby-shirted smell of the changing room.

He felt painfully hungry. His stomach, still sensitive, started to growl. The effects of the car sickness had worn off and now his empty belly was demanding food and drink.

A strong wind whirled round the glass panes at the top of the tower like a guard whistling and sneezing on patrol. Gulls wheeling overhead screamed obscenities.

A watery sun trying to peek through the clouds caught the

glass of one of the huge lamps and the light diffused at every angle, making Henry shield his eyes. The beam of light was like something he'd seen in a film where the hero, strapped to a table, had a laser gun aimed at him.

Henry didn't feel like a hero, despite having set out with high hopes of helping Oliver solve the mystery. He'd failed and now here he was, tied up, miserable, cold and hungry with no idea of what the future might hold.

Chapter Seventy

The traffic thinned out away from the city. Jonny, more confident by the minute in his handling of the powerful vehicle, pushed the speedo over eighty. Frankie was lost in thought, staring out of the rear window.

Jonny was wondering whether he might risk flicking on the radio again when Shannon opened her eyes. 'Can we stop? I'm desperate for a pee.'

He looked across at her, smiled and nodded. 'I could do with something to eat and a coffee.'

'Mum's got something in the bag. Crisps and orange squash!' They shared a snigger.

'Yeah. As I said, I could do with a coffee.'

Jonny slipped the car into the left-hand lane a few miles further along the road and they turned into a service area. Being near the English Channel, there were a variety of signs in English and French. Jonny drove into the car park with great care so as not to make any mistakes and attract attention.

Shannon looked back over her shoulder. Frankie was fast asleep. 'Shall I wake her up?'

'Let's leave her while we do the loo,' Jonny said in hushed tones. 'We can get coffee and come back with a drink for her. Yeah?'

'Okay, but let's be quick. Don't want her waking up to any empty car. She's had enough shocks today.'

'Do you think she knows more than she's telling us?' Shannon asked five minutes later as she and her brother walked back across the car park clutching coffees.

'I don't think so,' said Jonny. 'But it might help to get into a bit of conversation with her about it. We've come all this way because you found that postcard, yet she's sure this is where Henry is. Doesn't it make you wonder why? I think we've got about fifteen miles to go. Chat to her.'

Jonny pulled back onto the motorway and the needle crept up again. Frankie woke and was grateful for the coffee. She sat sipping it in thoughtful silence. Out of the corner of his eye, Jonny could see Shannon was working up the courage to ask a question. He pulled out to overtake. Frankie leant forward to check how fast they were going. 'Remember what I said about speed.'

Shannon turned her head sharply. 'Why do you think Henry will be at this place, Mum? Is there something you're not telling us?'

'It's not as simple as that. It's a long story. I need to find Henry. I want him safe.'

'We all do.' Jonny's voice was terse. The silence in the car was thick and heavy, broken only by the sound of wind rushing past the windows. The weather had worsened.

'Once upon a time there were two little girls,' said Frankie.

Jonny looked in the mirror. She was staring straight forward and talking to the space between them, as if wary of catching their eye. Shannon wriggled round in her seat to face her.

'Those two little girls were good friends. They promised to

always look after each other. It's easy to make promises when you're young. You don't realise how much it will cost you to keep them. What you do learn is that every time you break a promise, you hurt somebody.'

She stopped speaking. Jonny and Shannon waited. The sound of the car hurtling along the road filled the space.

'I think I've hurt somebody.' Tears started to run down Frankie's cheeks. 'I think that person wants to hurt me. That's why they've taken Henry. It's my fault.' Her tears fell freely, and she started sobbing.

Shannon scrambled about, unclipping her seatbelt. 'Oh, Mum. It's not your fault.'

'Shannon, no,' yelled Jonny as she tried to squeeze between the two front seats to give Mum the hug she needed. Jonny felt his arm pushed aside and he lost control of the steering wheel. There was an impact on the side of the car as he brushed a van in the outer lane. He grabbed the wheel with both hands and swung it to the left. The car shot forward, bouncing over the edge of the approaching slip road, hitting a grassy bank and leaving the ground.

It seemed to pause in mid-air. The jolt threw Shannon onto the back seat and she tried to grab her mother's hand. Jonny wrestled with the wheel, though it made no difference, and the wheels slammed down onto the tarmac of the slip road.

For a moment Jonny was high in the air, looking down and watching the car flip over and over, before he felt the seat belt tugging at his side as the car rolled onto its side. The noise of metal being bashed on concrete was almost deafening as the car scraped along the slip road before flopping onto the grassy verge and plunging down the embankment out of sight from the motorway.

Shannon smacked against the glass as the car crashed to a standstill on its roof.

Frankie's sobs spiralled into startled cries and screams.

'You both okay?' Jonny fought to catch his breath. 'Mum? Shan?'

'I'm okay.' The belt held Frankie upside down in her seat, and she grabbed the door handle to steady herself.

There was silence. Shannon lay still on the ceiling of the car. Jonny unlocked his door and pushed it open. Releasing his seatbelt, he half-stepped, half-rolled forward onto the grass, catching his arm on the open door. 'Stay there, Mum. I'll come and get you.' He opened the rear door. The seatbelt was all that was holding Frankie. 'Okay. Hang on to the bottom of the seat. I'm going to release your seatbelt. Then I'm gonna let you down slowly.'

Frankie didn't understand what he meant but she grabbed the seat, digging her fingernails into it. She knew she wasn't a lightweight, but Jonny seemed strong. As he unclipped the belt, she lurched forward. He grabbed around her waist, pulled her towards him, and both of them collapsed onto the grass.

'Shannon!' screamed Frankie. 'Shannon!'

Jonny picked himself up and ran around to the other side of the car. He tugged at the rear passenger door but it wouldn't move. He wrenched open the front door and clambered through the gap between the seats. He lay on his back on the ceiling next to Shannon and kicked at the door with both legs to push it open. Then he turned to Shannon and shook her.

'What?' Shannon was still dazed from being turned upside down when the car had rolled.

'Thank God.' Jonny placed his arms under her and dragged her out onto the grassy field. 'Right. Where is it that hurts?'

'It's my knee. Don't laugh, but I think I banged my knee.' She grabbed hold of Jonny's wrists and tried to haul herself up to a standing position.

Frankie ran round the back of the car, caught her and pulled them both into the biggest hug she could manage. 'Oh, this has all gone horribly wrong. What do we do now, Jonny?'

'We're about six miles away.' Jonny had taken his phone out of his pocket and was scanning a map. 'We can walk. The thing is that I borrowed this car and I meant to return it.'

'Can't you call the guy you borrowed it from? Tell him what's happened?' Frankie was pretty sure the owner didn't know Jonny had taken his car.

'You and Shannon start walking to the road. Here, Shannon, take my phone and follow the map. And don't turn around.'

They both looked at him and realised they had no choice. As they set off walking, Frankie put her arm around a hobbling Shannon. They did what Jonny had told them to do and walked away. The phone said it was 5.72 miles to the lighthouse; Shannon thought it was a hell of a walk if you had a bad knee.

They got to the edge of the field and pushed their way through the hedge onto the roadside. Soon Jonny ran up to join them. 'Keep walking,' he said.

They did as he asked but Frankie couldn't resist glancing back over her shoulder. Where the car had been, there was now a growing fire. She grabbed hold of Jonny's arm. 'What have you done?'

'Just leave it. You said this was your fault and we're doing our best to help. Let's get off this road and cut across country.

We need to get that lighthouse.'

Frankie remembered how excited Henry had been on the day they'd gone to Brighton, the day Cora had given them the car. They'd played her favourite childhood game of 'Who Can See the Sea First?'. Henry had won.

They walked for more than an hour after leaving the car. Jonny, being in charge of the route, decided it was best to avoid the town at the end of the motorway and cut across country. Looking on the map, it appeared that Healy Cove consisted of little more than the lighthouse and a few houses.

Shannon insisted that all she'd done was bang her knee. She said she was 'well up for it' when they started the journey, but after they'd been walking for a while she seemed to be slowing them down. Jonny was aware they were covering less and less ground. 'How's the leg, Shan?'

Instead of answering straight away, Shannon took a moment to stop and bend over, propping herself with her hands on her thighs to catch her breath. 'I'm doing my best. It hurts every time I bend it.'

'I think it might help if we strapped it up.' Jonny wasn't sure what they could strap it up with; they hadn't come prepared for a long hike. Since the early morning visit to the police station, they'd dressed in the sort of clothes they lounged around the house in, with a thick jumper or cardigan pulled over the top. Frankie had been the most sensible with a zip-up plum-coloured hoodie over both a T-shirt and jumper.

Jonny thought for a moment. 'Give us your hoodie, Mum.' Frankie took it off. Jonny started to rip open the top of one of the sleeves along the seam.

'Oy. Be careful,' said Frankie 'That's bloody Primark, that is.'

'Good. It'll tear easily then,' Jonny said, and it did. He ripped the sleeve clean away and handed the rest of the garment back to his mum. Taking the detached sleeve, he bent down and asked Shannon to straighten her leg. He wound the sleeve tight around her knee joint and knotted it firmly. 'There. That should help you keep the leg a bit straighter while we walk.'

Shannon smiled and hobbled a few steps forward to try it out.

'What am I supposed to do with this?' said Frankie, holding up her hoodie minus one arm.

Jonny had a big smile on his face. 'It'll keep the rest of you warm. Just keep swinging your arm about. Okay?'

The little party set off once more, heads down, concentrating on finding their footing through the furrows of a ploughed field. Had they looked up, they might have seen a last burst of sunlight catching a piece of glass a few miles away and flashing across the sky.

Chapter Seventy-One

Henry shielded his eyes. When the sun caught the mirrors on the lamps, the chamber was almost impossibly bright. Next to him was a bottle of water with a straw, and the wrapper from a Mars bar. The taller of his two balaclava-clad captors had brought them in about half an hour ago and held the water bottle while he drank. They'd returned with the bottle filled again and placed it next to Henry on the floor. By stretching over, he could lower himself to the straw and take a drink. They'd unwrapped the Mars bar and fed it to him in large bites.

Henry had never loved chocolate more, but he knew it wasn't good to be eating a Mars bar for breakfast. Mum would go mad at him and, as it was the only thing he'd eaten since the chicken nuggets supper he'd parted company with in the car, it did little to push away his hunger pangs.

Left to his own thoughts once more, Henry felt like this was some sort of adventure story. He liked adventure stories and he liked books. At school he could hold his own in conversations about *Avengers Unmasked* and *Avengers Uninterested*, but he preferred to curl up with the Famous Five or Secret Seven, a world where your uncle was always a famous scientist who might get kidnapped and held in a castle or a cave, or even a lighthouse, because they knew something the nasty men wanted.

The thing that worried Henry most was that he wasn't a scientist. They'd mistaken him. Perhaps a scientist lived in Parkside Tower, and that's why they'd taken him. They always kidnapped you when you got too close to the truth, and often you didn't realise what it was that you knew. That thought frightened Henry. If he didn't know what these people wanted, how could he help them get it? Or was he going to have to brave it out, say nothing and make sure they didn't get it? He hoped he wouldn't say anything but, if it was going to be a diet of Mars bars and water, he might have to give in.

There were places where the wind whipped around the lighthouse and seeped through the walls of the lantern room. How brilliant that Mum had made sure he'd had a warm jacket on when he'd set off with PC Ashley to investigate. The thought of his mum brought a tear and it trickled down his face. Sucking in his breath, he bit his bottom lip. Mum and Jonny and Shannon and PC Ashley would all be looking for him. They'd find him. That's what happened in adventure stories whenever somebody went missing. He'd be fine. He had to hang on.

As he waited, he heard the sound of someone outside. Footfalls gave an echoing metallic clang, and all the while the wind whistled around the tower in a howling scream. The door to the room began to open.

Chapter Seventy-Two

'Oh God, I'm sorry. I think it's nerves.' Shannon emerged from the bush she'd disappeared behind in order to find somewhere to pee.

'It's that coffee,' said Frankie, 'and delayed shock. After all, last time you went was before your brother decided to roll the car off the motorway.'

Jonny walked on. Sometimes Mum said the wrong thing. So he'd crashed the car. He wasn't getting into a discussion about what had happened. He'd driven well. It might have been easier to keep it on the road if Shannon hadn't decided to clamber through to the back seat and knocked his arm off the wheel. But now wasn't the time to go there. 'Come on, Mum,' he said. 'Let's keep moving.'

Shannon joined them on the path. 'Sorry about the pee thing. Didn't do much anyway.'

'Too much detail.' Jonny moved off again.

They walked on through a small wood, which hid them from the few scattered houses. It was far better for the limping one-sleeved trio to stay out of sight, thought Jonny, after what he'd had done to the car. Not that there'd been a choice, he told himself. They were here for Henry. It was no time to be caught in a stolen vehicle.

Luckily that last stretch of the motorway had been almost empty and there was nobody on the slip road to see what had happened to the car. The vehicle would have burnt out before anyone got to it.

The sky grew darker and the sun looked to have withdrawn for the day. Jonny suspected it wouldn't be long before the heavens opened. They'd get drenched. 'When we get out of these woods, it's all open fields and we should see the lighthouse ahead.' The trees were starting to thin out and Jonny could see a field, fallow for winter.

Frankie caught up with him. 'Have you any idea what we'll do? When we get there? Is this a stupid idea?'

'I don't think it's any more stupid than turning up for a job that didn't exist.'

Frankie's eyes fell to the ground and Jonny took her hand. 'Sorry, Mum, that wasn't fair. You've always done everything you could for us three. I know it's not been easy. You've been brilliant, the best mum any of us could hope for. Now it's time for us to do this together. I hope you're right about where Henry is.'

Frankie smiled. Rising on tiptoe, she put a hand behind his head to pull his forehead down and kiss him. 'I do find it hard to say how fantastic you are ... but you are.'

'Mum, Jonny! Look.' They both turned to see Shannon standing where the trees met the field. She took something out of her bag and held it up in front of her. Set against ominous charcoal clouds was a lighthouse, a white lighthouse with two small cottages at its base. The lighthouse in the picture that Shannon was holding.

Chapter Seventy-Three

Henry wished that the tall man had let him stay in the lantern room but, as soon as the door had opened, he'd untied Henry from the railing and shoved him out onto the narrow ledge of the gallery that ran round the outside.

The wind was blowing hard and cold up here at the top of the tower, and the darkness of the approaching storm made the place seem even more dangerous. Now Henry could see down to the ground, he realised how many stairs he'd climbed on the way up here. Below them white gravel surrounded the lighthouse, and the driveway led out to the nearby road. A grassy bank covered the other side of the road and rose to a cliff edge, beyond which was what looked like a long drop to the sea. The wind was pushing the waves into angry mountains.

The man pulled Henry around the gallery until he was facing the driveway then, using the rope once again, he fastened Henry to the gallery rail. The shortness of the rope meant that Henry had little movement.

'Why do I have to be out here?' At first, Henry didn't think the man had heard him. The wind was blowing loudly, snatching his words away across the darkening skies. But as the man was about to disappear back through the door to the staircase, he turned. Henry could feel his eyes glaring through the slits in the balaclava but he couldn't hear what he was saying. The man lifted his arms and hands in a comic shrug as if to say, 'Not my fault,' and disappeared through the door.

Henry explored the limitations of the rope. It allowed him to move barely a foot in either direction. There was no shelter. When the rain came, this would not be a good place. He looked down over the balustrade in time to see the man leave the front of the lighthouse and cross to the cottages on the right-hand side. Why had they left him out here? Surely someone would see him and rescue him? Then he realised that anyone passing by the lighthouse would have to look up and see the rope. He suspected that was a difficult thing to spot, and the wind would carry any screams for help far out to sea before they reached the ears of a would-be rescuer.

The lighthouse stood on its own plot of land and behind that was a vast, flat field. In the pre-storm light, it looked as though someone had dusted its surface with chalk, a white-covered brown stain across the landscape.

How small he must look up here, thought Henry. To any passer-by glancing up, he could be a post in the railing. He'd always looked up to Jonny who, at six foot, seemed to never stop growing. That was what Henry wanted to be more than anything: tall. But Frankie had been clear. 'You have different dads, my darling. Different genes. I don't think you'll be wearing any of Jonny's hand-me-downs.'

Standing there, battered by the wind, he wondered if he was always going to be small.

Something caught his eye. Three moving shapes on the far side of the chalk-stained field. Were they sheep looking for shelter? They appeared to be making a straight path across the field towards the lighthouse. Three of them. A mother, a brother and a sister?

Given that his hands were roped together, he wasn't able to wave. Surely it was too much to hope that those three insignificant dots moving across the field were coming to his rescue. But hope was all he had.

Chapter Seventy-Four

'Look.' Frankie pointed at the lighthouse as the three of them stood in the field. 'There's something going on up there.'

They'd started their journey across the enormous expanse of what looked like lunar terrain between the woodland and the lighthouse. Now they watched as two figures emerged onto the balcony. One was tall; behind him, half hidden by the railing, there was a tiny Henry-sized figure.

Frankie stumbled across the soil. 'I want it to be him and I don't want it to be him. What's going on?'

'We need to keep walking across this field and keep our eye on what's going on up there. We don't know anything for sure.' Jonny had taken command.

'Should we split up?' said Shannon.

'If there's something going on and they see any of us running across the field then, kaboom, it's all over,' Frankie said.

'It's a good thought, Mum.' Jonny could see that Frankie was against them splitting up. 'What if Shannon were to skirt around the outside of the field? She can keep an eye on us, and if anything happens she can go and get help.'

'I don't know what to say. I'm a bit of a mess, frankly. You two have been brilliant. If you think that's the right idea, then let's do it,' said Frankie.

Shannon peeled off to the left until she got to the hedgerow, which she followed as discreetly as she could. From where Jonny was standing, it looked like it would bring her round the other side of the two cottages.

Jonny and Frankie continued to walk in a straight line across the field. 'We still don't know what we're going to do when we get there, do we?' Frankie had never felt less in charge in her life. It was as if all her natural instincts as a mother had drained away. The one thing she was sure of was that, if it came to it, she would fight. She would fight like a lioness. These were her kids, and no one was messing with them.

'Mum, we've been playing it by ear. Let's carry on. If that's Henry up there then we know there is somebody else to deal with.' Jonny waited for her response. She smiled at him and set off.

The wind made it hard to walk forward and look upwards, but from time to time both of them managed it. They could see the little figure moving from side to side.

'Oh God,' shouted Frankie. 'I think he's tied to the railing. Please God, let's get him down.'

***

Now that she was on her own, Shannon made much quicker progress. Staying close to the hedgerow to make herself less visible, she ran along the edge of the field. Leaping over a low wall that separated the field from the lighthouse, she soon arrived at the back of the two cottages.

Built at a slight angle on either side of the base of the lighthouse, the one on the left seemed dark and uninhabited but there was a light on in what appeared to be the kitchen window of the right-hand cottage. A large dark-blue car stood between the buildings.

Shannon wondered what to do for the best. Should she creep into the house and see if she could find out what was going on and who these people were, or should she make a quick dash to the front and get to the top of the lighthouse? She was still trying to decide when the back door of the cottage opened. She flung herself into the hedge, twigs and thorns biting into her side.

Someone came out of the door and crossed to the car. A scarf and a black woollen hat wrapped around their neck meant that Shannon couldn't get an idea of who the person was, but they opened the driver's door of the car and retrieved a small bag which they took back into the cottage. Shannon relaxed and scuttled a little further along the hedgerow. She was sure the visitor to the car was not the person they'd seen earlier on the balcony, so they had more than one person to be wary of.

***

Jonny and Frankie splashed across the field. By running across to the right, they kept out of the direct line of sight of the houses. The weather continued to worsen and the dank smell of earth filled the air.

At one point, Jonny was convinced the lighthouse door was about to open. He threw himself flat on the ground, with Frankie following suit. She lay still, spluttering through a mouthful of foul-tasting soil, then heard Jonny mutter, 'False alarm,' and scramble back to his feet.

He scurried across the field, stooping low. Frankie made

herself a promise that if they got through all this successfully, she would join a gym or buy a bike or enlist in the SAS. If motherhood was going to call for these sorts of skills, she needed retraining.

As they closed in on the lighthouse, they saw the low wall circling the land it stood on, in the middle of which was a white gate. Jonny pushed it open, let Frankie pass through ahead of him, then they both crouched by the wall on the other side. It gave them a little shelter from the beating rain, and they took a moment to regain their breath.

Now they were closer, they saw that the lighthouse was octagonal. A gabled door was set into one wall almost opposite them and to the right was a small white shed. As they considered what to do next, the front door of the lighthouse opened. They moved to the left and hid behind the shed.

Frankie held her breath and grabbed Jonny's shoulder. 'What do we do?'

Jonny peered round the corner of the shed. 'Whoever it was has gone into the cottage. I can't see if there's anyone still up top, but I think we have to risk it.'

That wasn't what Frankie wanted to hear. 'Okay. What's the plan?'

'Follow me.' Without another word, Jonny set off from the cover of the shed across a path, over the green lawn and onto the white gravel surrounding the lighthouse. Frankie did her best to keep up, aware of her feet crunching on the surface as they reached the front door.

Jonny turned the handle and pushed the door. Frankie expected him to find it locked. When Jonny stepped through it, she followed him, her stomach churning.

Chapter Seventy-Five

Henry was growing colder and colder. The wind was an unbroken icy blast and now rain had started to splatter from the sky. He couldn't crouch and gain any shelter and, with his hands tied as they were, he couldn't lift his jacket hood to protect him from the rain.

There was nowhere to hide. Looking down through a mixture of tears and rain, Henry saw two figures racing towards the lighthouse door. He hardly dared to hope but he called out to them anyway, a feeble cry against the storm-battered building. They had to be coming to help him. Why else would they be running around?

Neither of his captors had returned since tying him to the gallery railing. He yearned for the comfort of the lantern room. He had long given up the battle against crying and let the tears flow freely. Somehow, in some way, this was his fault. He could only hope for a way out.

Chapter Seventy-Six

Shannon waited a little longer by the hedge in case anybody else came out of the kitchen to the car. From where she was squatting, she saw Jonny and her mum go through a gate in the wall. Her first thought was to run across and join them, but she wasn't sure that was the best thing. She knew someone was in the house, but who? Would knowing bring her closer to working out what was going on?

She scurried across the gravel, trying to make as little noise as possible. Arriving at the door, she peered through a frosted-glass panel. There were no signs of life and she tested the handle. It opened.

Slipping through the door, she found herself at one end of a dark, wood-lined corridor. The place smelt stale and unused. To her right was an open door into the kitchen. A mug of tea stood steaming on the table.

Perhaps this wasn't such a good idea after all. She hated all those girls in films who, despite knowing there was a maniac at large, still went exploring in white nighties through gloomy, creepy houses. This was her moment to turn round and go back.

That was when she heard voices.

They were coming from further down the corridor near the

front of the house. She inched along, keeping close to the left-hand wall. Coming to a door, she pushed herself back against it, squashing her backpack on the wood.

'The kid's still up the tower, yes?'

'Yeah, tied to the railings. Soaked by now, no doubt.'

'Good. If I know her, it won't be long before they're here.'

Shannon was holding her breath to the point of bursting. The sound of the second voice made her gasp and she caught her breath. She knew that voice. There was something recognisable about both of them, and yet she couldn't place where she'd heard them before.

'Did you make that cup of tea or not?'

Shannon took that as a sign someone would be heading back to the kitchen. She reached behind her and turned the handle of the door she was leaning against. She half expected to find herself in some sort of hall cupboard, but no; instead, there was a second door in front of her, indistinguishable from the first. She tried the handle and found it wouldn't move. She was in some sort of tiny space between rooms, or even between the houses.

She heard the voices again, but this time they were on the other side of the locked door. And this time she knew who they were.

***

Frankie followed Jonny through the door into the lighthouse. She didn't know what to expect but she was taken aback by the dusty little sitting room inside. Eight walls gave the room a circular feel. There was a tired old sofa and armchair in the centre. Along one section of the wall stood a small dining table with two chairs, and further along a sink, a stove and some lockers. The place was dirty and looked like it had remained untouched for a long time. Even so, Frankie thought how cosy it would be in here when the wind and the rain were battling round the lighthouse on a stormy night.

The key feature of the room was a grand, circular, metal staircase leading up through a hole in the ceiling to the next floor. At the bottom on the left-hand side was a wooden door.

They stood at the foot of the stairs. 'I think we have to go up to the top,' said Jonny.

Frankie hesitated. 'Both of us?'

Jonny nodded. 'Yeah. I know we split from Shannon, but I think you and I should stick together. We don't know who else is up there, and we still don't know if this is a wild goose chase.'

There was a sharp tap from the other side of the door. Frankie jumped. Jonny leant forward and tried the handle, but someone had locked the door. 'I did hear that, didn't I?' whispered Frankie.

Jonny put a finger to his lips and nodded. Raising his hand, he tapped twice on the door. After a second or so, two taps came back. He put his head next to the door and placed his ear against the wood. 'It's me,' he said and strained to hear. 'Just tap once.' The tap on the door came back. 'I think it's Shannon,' he mouthed to Frankie. 'Where are you?'

Frankie moved closer to the door. 'Are you in that house, darling?' A tap came back. 'Are you okay?' Another tap.

Jonny leant forward. 'Is there anybody else in there?'

Silence. Then a tap.

'We're going to try and get to the top of the tower, see who's up there. Try and meet us outside if you can.'

The message was returned with a single tap. Jonny turned and, quietly as they could, he and Frankie started to climb the metal steps.

***

Shannon listened for anything further from Jonny but all was quiet. She'd been too afraid to speak in case the people in the house heard her. Now she was aware of a commotion behind her. She heard voices again.

'Somebody's been poking around.'

Shannon wracked her brains. Whose voice was that?

'The back door is ajar. I think there's somebody here. No doubt they're making their way up the tower now.'

'Then let's not waste any time.'

A door opened, footsteps passed where she was hiding and a heavy door slammed. Then there was silence. Whoever they were, they were going up the lighthouse. Mum and Jonny were going to be in trouble.

Shannon tapped several times on the door but there was no response. No good staying here, she thought. She opened the door slowly and stepped out into the darkened corridor. There was no one in sight.

The door opposite her was open, revealing the sitting room. She took a deep breath and went in. It was empty. The room looked surprisingly modern, with plain white walls and furniture Shannon recognised from browsing through the Ikea catalogue online. A newspaper lay on one of the sofas and a half-drunk coffee stood on the coffee table. Next to it was a phone.

She leant forward and picked it up. When she tapped the

screen, 'Emergency calls only' flashed onto it. In Shannon's book, this was an emergency. She dialled 999 and waited.

***

Henry found he was more comfortable if he leant on the railings, although they were a little high and exposed his face to the lashing rain blowing in from the sea. He'd long since ceased to worry about how wet he was, but the cold was making him shiver and damp was seeping through his clothes and into his bones.

From this position, he'd seen two figures race across from the field and come into the tower. His heart thumped a little faster in hope, but now two more familiar figures in dark clothing had appeared from the cottage and entered the lighthouse. What was going on? The strange thing was that nobody had yet appeared up here on the gallery. A sinking feeling in his heart told Henry something was wrong. More trouble was not far away.

***

Jonny climbed up to the first floor and stood on a small landing just through the hole in the ceiling of the room below. He waited for Frankie, who was a little slower in clambering up the staircase. The second set of stairs was much shorter. Again they stopped on a small landing where there was a door on the right.

'Should we be looking in these rooms?' asked Frankie.

A distinct metallic clang rang out from below.

Jonny put his finger to his lips and opened the door to the room. 'Hide in here, Mum. Keep quiet and wait till you hear me yell. I'm going up to the top and I'll distract whoever it is.' He pulled the door closed before Frankie had time to say anything.

The room was a mess. It was smaller than the one they'd started in downstairs, with a stack of cardboard boxes and some broken furniture in the centre of the floor. A large metal locker stood by one of the windows. Frankie opened the doors but found it crammed full of papers, boxes and cartons, affording no space to hide.

Darting across the room, she hid behind the door in the fragile hope that anybody opening it to look into the room wouldn't see her. Leaning against the wall, she tried her best to hold her breath and calm her breathing.

As she stood there, her eyes flicked across the pile of rubbish in front of her and something caught her attention. One chest seemed to be full of old clothes that were spilling out onto the floor: a white shirt, two patterned blouses and what looked like a flash of red hair. Next to it was a coat. A large winter coat. A winter coat in green and yellow.

Chapter Seventy-Seven

Jonny sprinted up the steps of the last section two at a time. He shoved open the door and found himself on the outer gallery, blasted by the wind and rain. He turned to the left; holding onto the railings, he started to make his way around the tower. The slight figure ahead of him spun round.

'Henry!' yelled Jonny. Tears were streaming down Henry's face. 'There's someone following me,' Jonny said. 'We need to deal with these guys. Is there anywhere up here to hide?'

Henry, barely able to lift his hand because of the cold, pointed to the door of the lantern room.

'Okay, hang on there, fella. Won't be long now.'

'Please make it stop, Jonny. Please.'

Jonny rushed up to him and squeezed him as tightly as he could before stepping away and pushing through the door into the lantern room. He scuttled round to the other side of the two large glass lamps and squatted down, waiting.

Frankie heard two sets of footsteps pass the door, clanging on the stairs as they raced to the top of the tower. She knew she couldn't hide here. Jonny and the other person up there needed help. And the only person who could give that help was her.

She opened the door and started to climb the stairs as fast as she could.

Shannon assumed that this was the only lighthouse in the area. She'd rung 999 and told them that it was an emergency. They asked for her name and address. 'You don't need that!' she yelled. 'I'm at a lighthouse with my mum and brother, and something bad is going down.'

They demanded her name a second time and she hung up. Maybe that was a mistake. What if they thought she was some sort of wanker doing hoax calls? All she knew was that they were going to need help.

She ran round the front of the house and stopped at the corner. There, on top of the tower, she saw Jonny emerge onto the railed gallery running around the light. He made his way along the railings, bent down and hugged the tiny figure tied to the railing. Then he seemed to vanish. Was that Henry? Why had Jonny disappeared?

As she puzzled over what was happening, two figures appeared on the gallery and she dodged back out of sight. Were these the people she'd overheard? They broke apart and moved off in opposite directions around the balcony.

Grabbing the moment, Shannon raced across to the lighthouse, shoved open the door and went inside.

Chapter Seventy-Eight

Frankie was panting when she reached the door at the top of the stairs; speed was not her forte. Standing here behind the door was the last moment of safety granted to her. Whoever these people were, she had to deal with them. Fear coursed through her veins, making her heart pump harder and harder. There was no choice. Two of her boys were out there and in trouble; everything she'd fought for in bringing them up had led to this moment.

As soon as she opened the door, the full force of the wind and rain hit her in the face. The sky had blackened; a crisp winter's day had grown into a dark, tormented night. She stood still for a moment, figuring out which way to go.

She took a small step to the left. Further along the railing she saw a figure dressed in black tightening a rope tied to the balcony. She took a step forward and yelled at the top of her voice. 'Stop.' Her voice was carried away by the wind. 'Stop it!'

The figure in black moved aside to reveal Henry, hands clasped, tied by rope to the railings. His clothes were sodden and his hair was dripping. He saw Frankie and his eyes filled with terror and hope. 'Mum!' he screamed.

The black-clad figure held onto the rope and pulled it tighter, yanking Henry towards the edge of the balcony. Frankie shrieked at them both and lunged forward. Henry flattened himself against the railing. His assailant lashed out with the free end of the rope and Frankie pinned herself against the wall to give herself some stability.

As she fell back, a second figure, dressed in the same dark clothes but taller, came round the gallery from the left and gripped her wrist, wrenching her arm behind her and making her yelp in pain. They placed a hand around her neck and squeezed tight. Frankie started to gag as she fought for breath. She was pushed backwards through the door and she fell into the lantern room.

The taller of the two figures backed up to the door to prevent her escaping. Frankie could see eyes watching her. 'Please, tell me what you're doing with my son.' There was no answer. 'What do you want with my little boy?'

The shorter figure stepped towards her. 'I thought you would have known.'

Frankie started in surprise. She knew that voice; she knew that voice well. Daring to say the name, she looked straight back at the figure. 'Cora?'

Frankie watched as Cora pulled off the balaclava. With cropped hair and wearing a tight-fitting black top, this was not the Cora that she knew. She looked athletic, boyish and in charge, yet there was no mistaking who she was.

'Does it start to make sense now?'

'Cora?' Frankie repeated the name as if struggling to work out what was going on. 'And yet it's not you.'

'Cora's downstairs, all packed up in a box. Red hair, baggy clothes, big coat, funny glasses.' She laughed. 'I remember looking at myself the first time I created her. I thought, nobody will believe this, will they? I look like a buffoon out of some circus. That's why I added the silly shoes, almost as an extra dare for myself.'

Frankie remembered how she'd smiled on seeing the yellow trainers. Cora took a step forward. 'I always suspected you were stupid. I just didn't know how dumb you really were.'

Frankie saw the hate in her eyes. 'So the wonderful Cora never existed? And I fell for it all hook, line and sinker?'

'That's right. Henry didn't know me the night I met him by the park. The dangerous moment was when I persuaded him to let me return him home the next morning. I wondered if you'd see straight through me. But you didn't, did you?'

'No, I didn't. You look different somehow. Your face. I thought you were a strange lady who was kind. Who'd returned my son as an act of kindness.'

'Stop saying that fucking word. Kind? What does it mean?' Her eyes blazed and she spat the words at Frankie. 'We're all supposed to be kind to each other. We're forever being told that we have to be kind. At the end of the news – "Stay safe and be kind". It's meaningless. I don't want to be kind to everyone, otherwise it has no worth. We spread kindness around like manure, and that's all it is – shit. Shit that we dump on other people and we expect to get something in return. The one fact I've realised in life is that if you give shit, you get shit. That's why Cora became your friend. She had to be kind to you because if she was kind, you'd grow to love her. Like you said you loved me. And that's what I wanted you to do. And when people you love stop being kind to you, that's when it hurts. After all this time, it was my turn to hurt you.'

Crouched down behind the lamps, Jonny was a few feet away

from the three of them. He tried to piece together what was going on. If he moved a few inches to either side, he'd see all of them and they'd be able to see him. No sign of Shannon yet, and it didn't seem as though they had brought Henry inside. He moved slightly to his left so that he could keep an eye on the tall silent figure standing with their back to the door.

'What do you want Henry for, Cora? Let him go,' Frankie said.

Cora seemed surprised by Frankie's request. 'Life is a long curve of learning enough so we know why we die. I'm saving Henry having to do all that. Better to die unknowing.'

Frankie felt fear rip through her heart. This was the talk of madness. She was dealing with a woman beyond reason.

'You haven't said my name.' Cora looked away, gazing out of the glass roof to the clouded sky. 'You held so much of my life, and yet here you are still talking about Cora? It's not right, is it?'

'What do you want me to say? I'm here. I want to help, and I want my son. Please tell me what you want!'

Cora fixed her with her stare, pushed her face into Frankie's and whispered, 'I want to know why you broke your promise. That's all. I want to know why you deserted me. You were my friend, my best friend. Weren't you, Lottie?'

Chapter Seventy-Nine

Lottie ran up the stairs. It had been a great day at school, some harmless flirting with Craig, and a double lesson of art, a subject which she enjoyed and excelled at. She'd had encouragement from several teachers about the upcoming exams. Not that she necessarily believed them, but it didn't do any harm to be told you were doing well.

Reaching the top landing, she hesitated for a moment outside the door of the attic bedroom she shared with Little Girl. From inside came the sound of sobbing. Something told her to tiptoe away down the stairs and wait until Little Girl came to find her. Yet the friendship they had, the love between the two of them that they held dear in this tiny world of their own bedroom, made her open the door.

Little Girl sat on her bed under the window. Her head wasn't buried in her hands; she wasn't curled up in tears. She was staring at the door and sobbing.

For a fleeting moment, Lottie wondered whether the sobs were for her benefit. 'What's wrong?'

'Nothing.'

'Then what are the tears for?'

'Nothing.'

Lottie put her school bag down by the side of her bed. 'I'll go then. They've got the telly on downstairs and I'm starving. See if I can nab a biscuit before dinner.' She turned back to the door.

'Don't! Please don't go. I don't want to be on my own any more.' Little Girl stood by the end of the bed, shaking and wracked with tears.

Lottie moved towards her, raising her arms and encouraging Little Girl to step forward for a hug. 'You're not on your own. You're with me.'

'I'm not. You don't sit with me all the time at school now, and you go off at break. You've been hanging around with Craig and sometimes you talk to other people.'

'But that doesn't mean you're not my friend. My best friend. The friend I wake up with and who I see last thing every night when I go to sleep. The friend who is with me here.'

Little Girl laughed.

Lottie went on. 'It's just that sometimes at school there are other people. We have to get to know other people.'

The sobbing stopped. 'Do we? Why can't we be together? You know me. Pick me as the friend you want forever.'

Lottie gave Little Girl the hug she'd been holding out for. It helped her to say the words that Little Girl wanted to hear. 'I do love you and you are my friend, and I will never leave you. I'll be here. There may be moments when you look around and you can't see me, but I'll be here. I'll look after you.'

Little Girl stepped back, a lopsided smile on her face, and raised her hand to wipe the tears from below her eyes. 'That's kind of you. I don't know what I'd do if you let me down.'

It was a week later that Lottie found out she was pregnant.

Chapter Eighty

Little Girl stood opposite Frankie and laughed. 'You didn't mean it, did you? You didn't love me at all. We spent all that time together and swore to look after each other, and then you disappeared because that bastard Craig gave you a baby and you thought it was your way out.'

Frankie's brain chased random thoughts as she tried to arrange the story in order. Her past life was catching up with her and pushing at her conscience. She couldn't be the reason for everything that had happened, could she? 'I didn't have any choice. At the time it looked like the best way of building a life for myself. And it wasn't easy.'

'I know you lost the baby. I waited for you to come back. But no. You still preferred him.'

'What happened hurt and he was there to help. And I was stupid and for a little while. I fell in love with him.'

Little Girl let out a cry. 'You loved *me*. You said you loved me. You were my friend. You loved *me*.'

Frankie fumbled for words. 'Sometimes you have to put yourself first. That's what I did. For me and my kid. It was the only chance I was going to get, and I had to take it.'

'And what's with all the Frankie nonsense?' Little Girl half turned away to look at the storm through the glass wall.

Frankie cast a quick glance at the door, but the figure guarding it tensed and stepped forward towards her. She looked back at Little Girl again. 'It didn't work out, as I'm sure you guessed. My middle name is Frances. Charlotte Frances Baxter. Though why my parents gave me three names when they didn't want me, I don't know. Names you could call a boy, I suppose. Charlie, Frankie. I fucked everything up as Lottie. Becoming Frankie gave me another chance, a chance to do everything I wanted for my kids.'

Little Girl stepped towards her and spat words in her face. 'You promised. You agreed when we sat there in that miserable shit hole of a home and told me you'd be there for me. You said I could rely on you. Only I couldn't. Do you know what happened to me after you left?'

Frankie stood silent.

'Do you?' yelled Little Girl.

'I came back, but you'd gone.'

'You came back? You came back? Too fucking late!' Little Girl screamed. The figure at the door and Jonny both prepared to intervene. 'You weren't there. I had my own form of hell to face. Taken abroad, seven months of hell, exploited and buried away. I risked my very survival to get free of all that. Then, having hidden away for years, one day I see you across a crowded street. You've got a little boy and I look at you as if to say, "I've found you again, please say hello." But you can't meet my eyes and you scurry away.' Tears ran down her face. 'I wanted to be friends, and you walked away again.'

Frankie backed away against the two huge lamps in the centre of the room. The figure at the door shifted towards her. 'I'd had three kids by then. Everything I did, I did for them.

I fought to keep them together, to keep them away from one bastard man who wanted to hit me and another who wanted to run my life. Nobody was doing that. They're my kids. Whatever happened, they were staying with me.'

Little Girl wiped the tears from her cheek and laughed. 'We make a bargain with fate. That's how we get our lives. At any moment you could lose that bargain and nothing you have matters.'

'That's why I gave all my love to my kids. I didn't have any to share with anyone else. Not for a long time.'

Jonny heard his mother's words and bit his lip to push back tears. He had to help. He'd repay that love, a love that somehow had brought her here.

'I get that,' said Little Girl. 'I do. You always have to keep your kids close. Always have to keep your kids with you.' She smiled at Frankie and gestured to her accomplice. 'That's what I've done, Lottie. My son. My beautiful son.'

The figure by the door reached up and pulled off his bala-clava. Frankie's eyes widened in bewilderment.

'I think you know each other,' said Little Girl.

Chapter Eighty-One

Shannon found the room downstairs and the room on the first floor empty. She was pretty sure that whoever was in the building was up on the balcony, and that included Mum and her brothers.

She made her way to the top, trying to make as little noise as she could on the metal staircase. She put her ear to the door to listen for voices. The wind and the rain were firing on all cylinders outside, and hearing anything else was impossible. She reached behind her into her backpack and scrambled around until her fingers closed around a small metal object. She pulled it out and grasped it in her hand. Better safe than sorry, she thought. She opened the door.

As soon as she stepped through the door, she had to push herself back against the wall. It was a long way down and she couldn't breathe; it felt as if someone was choking her. Her heart was racing, and she wanted to curl up into a ball and wait for someone to save her. But she knew no one would. The merest glimpse of the ground below and all her bravado had gone.

Tearing her clothes, she pushed herself slowly along so she could stay glued to the peeling wall of the lighthouse.

***

Henry wondered what was happening. Someone had been about to untie him and then his mum had arrived. The weight had lifted from his shoulders at the sight of her. Everything would be fine now. Mum would sort out whatever was going on, he knew that. But he was wrong. They'd dragged her into the lantern room, and now he was alone again, flinching in the wind and rain. He strained to hear their voices but there was nothing.

The rope holding him in place was a little looser now. He edged along the gallery to the farthest place the rope would allow. He could look down onto the lighthouse cottage that stood nearest to the road and he could see a car by the front door of the house. A blue car he was sure he recognised. He couldn't put himself at the perfect angle to see the number plate, but he knew it was a Hyundai i10, the same sort of car that Cora had given them. The car stolen only two days ago. If the car was here, was Cora here too? And if she was, who was the person with her?

**

Jonny's legs were starting to ache. He'd been crouched down behind the lamps for quite a while and he longed to stretch out and stand up. He was working hard to piece together the conversation. In spite of the wind and rain, he'd heard every word and none of them made any sense. He knew his mother was speaking to Cora, and yet both of them were claiming they were someone else. They'd known each other as children, yet his mother had been surprised when Cora had turned up on that first morning with Henry.

Jonny had happy memories of his upbringing in a smaller

house in a seaside town, and in the flat they now called home. Those memories created a sense of warmth within him. And all because of his mum. Frankie. No other name. His mum, Frankie Baxter.

His mother was silent. He couldn't see her. Cora was talking about her children, about her son, and Mum had gone very quiet.

Chapter Eighty-Two

'Nice to see you again, Mrs Baxter. I'm sorry about the circumstances.' Oliver Ashley smiled at her and brushed his blond fringe away from his face while pushing the balaclava into his trouser pocket.

'PC Ashley? Oliver? This is crazy.' Frankie looked from Oliver to Cora and back again.

'You didn't think I could do everything myself, did you? The lamentable accident for Mrs Steadman? Your disappearing manny, Luke, after his visit from the boiler repair man? The fitting, if unfortunate, demise of the yapping little Dimwit?' Little Girl beamed at Oliver with pride. 'I had help. That's what it means to have a good son. Helped his mother, didn't you, Oliver?'

'Yes, Mother.'

'And, of course, your job offer.'

Frankie struggled not to show her feelings, not to wail with rage like a child who'd realised how unjust the world was. 'It was extremely convincing.'

'I'm glad you thought so. All those email addresses and letters took ages to set up. But the joy came in watching you fall for it. One big hoax, and you went all in.'

'I have to take chances when things come along.'

'You were foolish. Because you wanted it so badly, you didn't check. Letters signed by members of girl bands.' Little Girl threw her head back and laughed. 'Sheila Fergusson, Siobhan Fahey and even Posh Spice. I couldn't believe it. I kept making it more preposterous! That's why I turned up on the day you supposedly started your job, to see you walk in, all hopeful and keen, and to know that I was bringing your world tumbling down.'

Little Girl seemed to be enjoying telling the story. Frankie bit her lip. 'Why take all that trouble in becoming my friend again? Why not just play your nasty trick?'

'Because today we spend so much time being hateful and unkind to people we don't even know. We Tweet, we Insta, we Snapchat, and nobody cares or even pretends too. We inure ourselves. To make certain it worked, I had to become your friend again because when a friend's unkind, that's when we get scarred. A message on Henry's Facebook page to tell him about a sleeping-out challenge and a hint as to where he might do it. A casual meeting, and game on. And the fun of creating that clown of a woman! You couldn't even see through that. You were so desperate.' Little Girl's eyes grew wider, aflame with her need to explain.

'I've had my share of shit in life. Being let down and hurt. But I try so hard to take people as they come. I don't spend my time looking for people who're out to trick me.' Frankie felt her breath tighten each time she spoke. Stay calm. Reason with her. She was just another child to look after.

'And that's your mistake.' Without warning Little Girl leant forward and spat in Frankie's face. 'Trust is the tragic fault of the child. Children trust without question. It's a gift from God and we have to take away it from them. We have to teach them not to trust. We have to teach them that trust will get them abused, get them hurt, and will let them down. If you hadn't trusted, we wouldn't be here now.'

Frankie felt the saliva drip down her cheek. Her head ached as she struggled to fit all the pieces into place. Her mind was still mostly on Henry outside, lashed to the railings. 'Oliver's certainly done everything you told him to. He's a credit to you.'

Little Girl smiled, her face tightening with just a glimpse of pain.

'What are you proposing to do with my son outside?' Frankie asked.

'Oh, we're not interested in your son,' replied Little Girl. 'I assumed you'd have guessed by now, but then you were never very clever, were you, Lottie? Otherwise you wouldn't have let the class bully get you pregnant. It's not Henry we want. It's you.'

Frankie stared into Little Girl's deep-blue eyes which blazed with hate.

'Nothing to say, Lottie?'

Frankie's mind went blank and her eyes widened as she searched the room for an answer. 'I'm presuming you're a real policeman, Oliver.'

'Trained at Hendon and on the job at the local station. Surprisingly easy to do these days – they're desperate for people. And if you're six foot and white, they love you. Mother wanted me to do it, and who was I to say no?'

'Then, as a policeman, should you be standing by and letting all this happen?'

Oliver laughed. 'Mrs Baxter, isn't it a little old-fashioned to associate a policeman with somebody who upholds the law?'

Frankie saw how he held himself differently. There was a new authority about him that hadn't been evident in the policeman she'd thought was helping her.

'They're all in it for themselves these days. So little reward, they have to take what's there. Falsifying reports, getting someone to hand you a particular job. It's simple. Detective Sergeant Webb is so crooked, you could use him as a fairground ride. Even smiley old Sergeant Chescoe is much more helpful if he thinks there's something in it for him.'

'It's you we require, not Henry.' Little Girl didn't want Frankie's questioning of Oliver to go too far.

'That's it, is it? The broken promise of a teenage girl.' Frankie looked at them both. They sounded so sure of what they were saying. 'For what it's worth, I'm sorry. I'm sorry for saying something I couldn't make happen. I meant it when I said it. Being together in that home helped both of us. Whatever's happened since might not be our fault, but it's certainly what we have to take responsibility for. Remember what you used to say? If you let someone get away with something once, you can blame them. Let them do it twice and it's your fault.'

'You're not getting away with it twice, Lottie.'

A shard of fear drove itself into Frankie's stomach. 'That gallery isn't for Henry. Untie him and let him go. Then take me outside and throw me over the railings. As you say, I deserve it.'

'You do,' said Little Girl, 'but that's not what's going to happen.' She leered into Frankie's face. 'You're going to watch me jump over the side.'

Little Girl watched the shock register on Frankie's face before she had time to hide it. A small smile played across her lips.

Frankie flashed a look at Oliver, who seemed unconcerned with his mother's announcement that she was about to meet her fate. 'And what does that achieve?'

'My son has rung for the police. The real police. They'll find my body down there near that dreadful little car I gave you. And at the top of the lighthouse, they'll find you and your meddlesome little son. It might all be a little too Scooby Doo for my taste, but I'm sure we can rely on the plodding minds of the British police to reach the logical conclusion that you're responsible. You'll go away for a long time. Not only does that mean that you'll get to be the apple of some bad-ass kitty-kitty's eye, but you'll be separated from your kids. You won't be able to mother them. You'll have failed at the one thing you thought you were any good at.' She laughed, a high cold cackle that pierced the stormy air. 'You should be very careful choosing your friends. One day, they may choose you.'

Frankie watched as Little Girl, face tortured in mirth, fell to her knees.

Before anyone realised what was happening, something rushed through the air and pulled Oliver Ashley to the floor. Frankie stumbled backwards as Little Girl scrambled across the floor and backed against the glass wall.

Jonny's arms flailed wildly as he punched at Oliver's face and shoulders. Struggling to remain astride him, he smashed Oliver's head onto the floor. Oliver kicked back hard, catching Jonny with his heavy police boot. The two of them rolled first one way then the other, heads banging onto the floor and punches flying through the air.

Little Girl stood waiting, a crooked smile of motherly admiration creeping across her face. Jonny tried to place his hands round Oliver's neck and push him away, but Oliver yanked his head forward and sank his teeth into the back of Jonny's hand.

Jonny pulled his hand away sharply, the pain making him open his fingers. Oliver grabbed the momentary advantage to punch Jonny's chest hard. Jonny fell backwards and Oliver scrambled away, reaching behind him. Jonny tried to struggle to his feet to kick Oliver but, as he crawled onto his hands and knees, Oliver's hidden hand shot into the sky holding something between his fingers. There was a dull grey flash of metal.

As Jonny finally stood up, the lamp handle came down smartly onto the back of his head and he crumpled to the floor. Oliver shuffled away and stood by the door, holding the handle. Jonny lay senseless.

Frankie screamed, 'Jonny, Jonny! No!'

Shannon heard her mother's cry and froze. She was working away at the rope round Henry's hands. Henry tugged at it; he was almost free, held now by only one knot. Hearing the scream, he looked at Shannon. Shannon thrust the rope into his hand and pushed him against the railings. 'Stay there. Don't let them see you're loose.' She slipped a little further along the balcony until she was out of sight of the doorway.

Henry watched the door open and Oliver burst out of the lamp room. He stopped to look at the small boy clutching the railings, rope entwined around his hands. Henry shook, half in fear and half in a dawning realisation. 'You hit me. You brought me here.'

Oliver took one last look at him and disappeared through the door at the top of the stairs.

Henry was about to call out to Shannon when the door of the lantern room burst open a second time. Cora stepped out, followed by his mother. It was hard to work out what was happening. As Cora passed him and stood next to the railings, Frankie stepped up to him and pulled him to her. Henry yanked on the last strand of rope and released himself.

Frankie held him to her for the briefest of moments, then pushed him towards the stairway door. 'Run. Go, Henry! Run!'

Cora started to climb the railing.

'Don't do this.' Frankie grabbed Cora's waistband and pulled.

Cora placed a hand on Frankie's chin and pushed back. 'Go away. Leave it.'

Frankie continued to pull. Cora grabbed her hair and yanked her head down, trying to smash Frankie's forehead onto the rail. For once, Frankie's extra weight stood her in good stead and she held firm. She pulled Cora back as hard as she could, trying to move them away from the railings.

'Let me have another chance,' yelled Frankie, the wind carrying her words up into the sky.

Cora dropped her hands. Leaning back against the railings, she smiled.

Shannon shot past Frankie so quickly that neither woman saw her coming. Placing her hands out in front of her, she pushed Cora hard in the chest. Cora teetered and lost her balance as Shannon pushed again.

Cora screamed and scrabbled for a place to grab hold of before tipping backwards and disappearing into the rain and darkness. Her falling cry, a curdled scream that could almost have been laughter, split the air.

Shannon fell back onto the floor, sobbing, as Frankie crawled to her and held her. Neither of them could speak or had breath for tears. Frankie helped her daughter clamber to her feet and together they peered over the side.

Way below, the body lay smashed onto the white gravel. A few paces away stood Oliver, screaming at his mother. Below them, Henry cowered in the doorway of the lighthouse. Sirens and flashing blue lights split the noise of the storm. Oliver looked up, turned then ran through the gate and across the field.

Two police cars turned off the road and on to the lighthouse drive, drawing to a halt a little way from the body. Several figures climbed out and stood looking at it. A policeman walked over to Henry before glancing up and seeing Frankie and Shannon.

'I did it, Mum. I made you safe.' Shannon was shaking from cold and adrenalin.

Frankie felt herself let go. Her body throbbed with relief and fear. She pulled Shannon to her. 'You did, my darling. You gave her what she wanted.'

There was no way of telling the time. No clock on the wall, and they had taken her watch and phone. It was the narrowest bed she had ever been in. Lying on it, she could touch both walls of the room with her hands. Cool, smooth walls. Unadorned. She could look up and see the stained grey ceiling where a murky glass sphere held the light. In one corner of the room, a small metal cupboard stood bolted to the wall. A tiny window with little light coming through was too high to see out of. Hard to tell if it was day or night. Had there been no day since they'd arrived at the lighthouse? The darkness brought in by the storm had lasted.

Shannon, Henry and Frankie had found themselves at the local police station. Jonny was in hospital; he'd needed some stitches in his head wound and would be staying in for observation. Then the police wanted to talk to him about a missing car.

The victim was referred to as 'Cora Walsh', though no one seemed to know why. It was the name they'd found on a driving licence in a bag in the Hyundai, and yet they still couldn't track her down on any records.

Oliver Ashley seemed to be equally transient. He was on record as a new constable at Langley Police Station, but no one had seen him for days. Phone numbers and his address had proved fruitless; this was a family skilled at eluding people.

The police interviewed Shannon and Henry. Afterwards, Henry was put into local authority care for the night. The children were told they would see their mother soon.

The following morning, Frankie sat in an interview room. It was a tasteless corporate grey cell with one single bulb in the ceiling and red plastic chairs on either side of the table. The detective was someone she'd never met before. A sharp-suited woman with hair piled high, she had the look of someone who'd woken up one day to find that youth had passed her by before she'd had any fun.

The woman placed a notepad and a pen in front of her. 'Tell me what happened. In your own words.'

'I'd like to speak to my kids.'

The detective pursed her lips in disapproval. 'I'm not sure that's going to be possible. John is in the hospital.'

'Jonny.'

'Jonny is in hospital. He's doing fine, but there's some talk of a stolen car. I suspect the least he's looking at is a suspended sentence.'

Frankie breathed long and deep to calm a rising sense of panic. 'And Shannon and Henry?'

'Henry has been taken into care in a local authority hostel. I stopped by this morning. He didn't tell me anything.'

Frankie smiled. 'And Shannon?'

'Shannon was detained here overnight.'

Frankie's brain stuttered for a moment. Words would not come.

'She told the interviewing officer that she was helping you. Said that's why she did it.'

Like mother, like daughter, thought Frankie. She smiled at the detective. 'Do you have any kids?'

The woman looked a little taken aback. She shook her head with a rueful smile. 'It didn't happen. I seem to spend most of my time looking after everybody else's children in here.'

'Look after mine, will you? Please make sure they're okay.'

The woman leant forward and put both hands on the table. 'I don't think we need to worry about that yet. I just need to know what happened. Just tell me the truth.' She made a note on her pad.

Frankie reached across and held her wrist to stop her writing more. 'It's important to me that they are okay. That's all that matters. That's why I'm here.'

The detective looked at her. 'So tell me what happened, Mrs Baxter.'

Frankie smiled at her. 'It was me. I pushed her.'

Acknowledgements

Any book always belongs to so many more people than the name on the cover and *The Hoax* is no exception.

I knew I wanted to write a book in 2020, but I didn't realise that a global pandemic would give me so much time in which to do it. In January, a chance reading of a newspaper article gave me the central premise; it was about a woman who was deceived by her friend and former bridesmaid into giving up her job to take up a fictional new appointment. Bizarre but interesting. I made notes and planned to kickstart the book at a writing retreat in France at Chez Castillon run by my wonderful friends Mike and Janie Wilson (if you have a book lurking inside you, check out www.chez-castillon.com).

Plans change, and the lockdown in March 2020 made me start writing. Daily walks through our local park started to infiltrate themselves into the plot and, though I was pretty sure that I didn't want to write about a world suffering from a pandemic, much of what happened during that period seeped into the work. I took a diploma in criminal psychology alongside writing the piece, and so many people's comments and ideas were added as extra seasoning.

A huge thanks to Catherine Cousins at 2QT Books for taking me on board and getting the book out into the world.

Thank you to her team, Charlotte Mouncey for her wonderful ideas on the cover, and the indefatigable Karen Holmes for her patience and insight, and for making me aware that I'm not the master of the comma and the pluperfect that I might think I am.

Thank you to all the people who gave me such positive feedback on my first book *The Punishment* which gave me the temerity to think I could write another one.

Thank you to the fabulous Jane Wenham Jones, who has become my unofficial mentor and is never frightened of being a little 'teachery' in her edit and her feedback. It's her brilliant eye that hopefully means this book makes sense.

Thanks to my friends who may find just a little soupcon of themselves lurking within these pages. And thanks to my partner Richard, whose support and inspiration makes everything possible.

Printed in Great Britain
by Amazon

59907885R00218